"I meant to be a good wife,"

she said, as if in a dream, "but I never was. I didn't know what he wanted."

Looking at Kirsty in the soft glow from the stove, her body stretched out on the oak settle, her curved mouth soft and gentle, her face haunted by melancholy reflection, Mike knew what her husband must have wanted. He wanted it himself.

The prize was this woman's passion. And the yearning for it was an invitation to madness....

Just how crazy had her husband become? Crazy enough to kill?

Dear Reader,

Welcome to Silhouette **Special Edition** . . . welcome to romance. Each month, Silhouette **Special Edition** publishes six novels with you in mind—stories of love and life, tales that you can identify with— romance with that little "something special" added in.

June has some wonderful stories in bloom for you. Don't miss *Silent Sam's Salvation*—the continuation of Myrna Temte's exciting *Cowboy Country* series. Sam Dawson might not possess the gift of gab, but Dani Smith quickly discovers that still waters run deep—and that she wants to dive right in! Don't miss this tender tale.

Rounding out this month are more stories by some of your favorite authors: Tracy Sinclair, Christine Flynn, Trisha Alexander (with her second book for Silhouette **Special Edition**—remember *Cinderella Girl*, SE #640?), Lucy Gordon and Emilie Richards.

In each Silhouette **Special Edition** novel, we're dedicated to bringing you the romances that you dream about—stories that will delight as well as bring a tear to the eye. And that's what Silhouette **Special Edition** is all about—special books by special authors for special readers!

I hope you enjoy this book and all of the stories to come!

Sincerely,

Tara Gavin
Senior Editor
Silhouette Books

LUCY GORDON
Outcast Woman

Silhouette Special Edition

Published by Silhouette Books New York

America's Publisher of Contemporary Romance

To Wendy Corsi Staub to whom I owe so much

SILHOUETTE BOOKS
300 East 42nd St., New York, N.Y. 10017

OUTCAST WOMAN

Copyright © 1992 by Lucy Gordon

ISBN: 0-373-09749-2

First Silhouette Books printing June 1992

All the characters in this book have no existence outside the
imagination of the author and have no relation whatsoever to
anyone bearing the same name or names. They are not even
distantly inspired by any individual known or unknown to the
author, and all incidents are pure invention.

®: Trademark used under license and registered in the United
States Patent and Trademark Office and in other countries.

Printed in the U.S.A.

Books by Lucy Gordon

Silhouette Special Edition

Legacy of Fire #148
Enchantment in Venice #185
Bought Woman #547
Outcast Woman #749

Silhouette Romance

The Carrister Pride #306
Island of Dreams #353
Virtue and Vice #390
Once Upon a Time #420
A Pearl Beyond Price #503
Golden Boy #524
A Night of Passion #596
A Woman of Spirit #611
A True Marriage #639
Song of the Lorelei #754

Silhouette Desire

Take All Myself #164
The Judgment of Paris #179
A Coldhearted Man #245
My Only Love, My Only Hate #317
A Fragile Beauty #333
Just Good Friends #363
Eagle's Prey #380
For Love Alone #416
Vengeance Is Mine #493
Convicted of Love #544
The Sicilian #627
On His Honor #669

LUCY GORDON

met her husband-to-be in Venice, fell in love the first evening and got engaged two days later. After seventeen years, they're still happily married and now live in England with their three dogs. For twelve years Lucy was a writer for an English women's magazine. She interviewed many of the world's most interesting men, including Warren Beatty, Richard Chamberlain, Roger Moore, Sir Alec Guinness and Sir John Gielgud.

In 1985 she won the *Romantic Times* Reviewers' Choice Award for Outstanding Series Romance Author. She has also won a Golden Leaf Award from the New Jersey Chapter of the RWA, was a finalist for the RWA Golden Medallion in 1988. In 1990 she won the Rita Award in the Best Traditional Romance category for *Song of the Lorelei*.

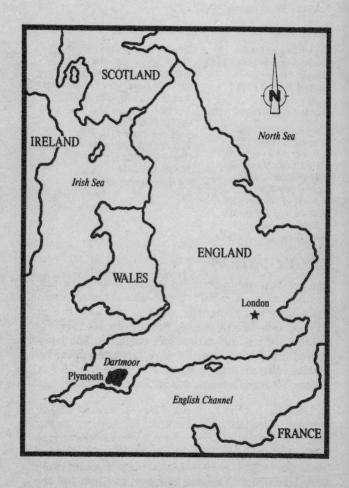

Prologue

The little crowd of black-clad mourners huddled around the open grave as the coffin bearing the young man was lowered into the frozen earth. The brass plate stated only the bald facts: that he had been called Peter Mullery and he had been eighteen when he died. It was left to his sobbing mother and set-faced brothers to remember that he had been a handsome boy with an infectious joy in life and that he had died because of a heartless woman.

The priest was intoning the last rites when he became aware of a changed quality in the atmosphere. Looking up, he saw that the mourners were no longer heeding him. Their gaze was fixed on a young woman who'd appeared at the entrance to the churchyard, her arms filled with evergreens. The bleak, white moors stretched away behind her, and the bitter wind lifted her long black hair. Apart from that soft disturbance she was motionless, watching the little crowd who stared back at her, and there was a tension in every line of her slim body that showed she was trying to summon up her courage.

At last she began to approach the grave. She held her head high, revealing a young face recently marked by anguish and horror yet still hauntingly beautiful. The silence of the mourners watching her had a fearful, menacing quality, yet her steps didn't falter. Perhaps her chin was lifted a little higher, as though she were fighting for the resolve to pay her final tribute in the midst of so much hate.

A murmur rose from the little crowd. Who would have thought that Kirsty Trennon would dare to show her face here? Even that sound stilled as she neared. Priest and mourners seemed paralyzed watching her, as though caught in a fearful dream.

She stopped at the open grave and looked down at the coffin from dark, brilliant eyes. Her lips moved soundlessly in the words "I'm sorry." Slowly she opened her arms and let the leaves fall.

The action shattered the spell that had seemed to bind everyone. Suddenly there was uproar. The dead boy's mother turned on her, screaming, "Murderess!"

One of the brothers snatched up a lump of earth and hurled it at her. "It's too late to be sorry," he shouted. "You'll not buy your forgiveness so cheap—now or ever. Get out, and don't show your face among decent people."

They were like animals now, turning on the intruder, ready to rend her apart. She fled blindly from the mob, tears streaming down her face. Stones struck her as she ran, and the hate-filled cry of "Murderess!" pursued her from the churchyard and out onto the bleak moors.

Chapter One

The wind was rising as Kirsty reached the farmhouse, and she turned in the doorway to take a last look at the moor, where the first snow of winter had already fallen. Beside her a large, shaggy dog shivered and hurried inside. The kitchen was blessedly warm after the freezing wind, but the silence of the house was like a chill.

She'd been alone in that silence for exactly a year. And on that thought the same weary treadmill started up in her mind: one year to the day since her husband had been arrested for the murder of Peter Mullery. One year since she'd been driven from Peter's funeral by his hostile family. Eleven months since her husband had died in prison, still protesting his innocence to a disbelieving world.

Tarn, the dog, wolfed down his supper and stretched out on the rag rug that covered the flagstones in front of the stove. Kirsty heated a tin of beans and ate them with bread. She lived off prepacked foods hastily thrown together, because the burden of doing all the work of Everdene Farm alone exhausted her and left no time for culinary skills.

It was a small farm, but still too large for one person. In her childhood there'd been four around the kitchen table, her fat cheerful grandmother and wiry grandfather, their son Will and little Kirsty herself. Will had been a handsome bull of a man who could have had almost any woman on Dartmoor for his second wife. But he'd buried his heart with his first, and his only love was the little daughter she'd left him. Kirsty had been her father's companion since she was three, and had one morning stumped out of the house after him, yelling, "I'm coming too, I am, *I am.*"

He'd laughed and swung her up on his shoulders, and after that she went everywhere with him. She had an instinctive affinity with everything about the farm; and beyond it, with the wild beauty of Dartmoor.

At first she thought all the world must be like this glorious wilderness with its expanse of moors, forests and bogs, its fierce, rocky tors and its mysterious, prehistoric stones. But Will had told her that Dartmoor was unique, a precious jewel set in the south of England, and they were specially privileged to live there.

The only part of the moor she didn't care for was the village of Princetown where the prison stood. Her first glimpse of it had made an indelible impression on her mind. The huge gray Victorian building with its five stories of tiny windows had filled her with horror for the men who were imprisoned behind granite walls, shut out from the natural beauty she lived with every day.

When she was fourteen her grandparents died. From then on she and her father shared the farm as equals. She could drive a tractor or help a calving cow as well as Will himself, and she took charge of the books, to his great relief. She was a natural farmer, he said, in everything but a tendency to be hasty.

"You jump into things without thinking," he told her once. "Your Ma was like that. She had a hot temper, too—got all fired up, spoke her mind—then found she'd spoken too quick—" he grinned "—just like you."

He said all this in the tone of doting affection that he always used, even when he was criticizing Kirsty. They were a mutually adoring team, and the next few years were unalloyed happiness.

And then Will had died suddenly in a tractor accident, and she was alone at eighteen. It had been the week before harvest, and she was in despair until the Trennon cousins, Jack and Caleb, came seeking work.

They were from the traveling people—Gypsies who roamed the country but considered Dartmoor their home and always returned for the harvest. She hired them gratefully. Caleb was the younger and taller of the two, a good looking charmer with a ready laugh. Jack was the quiet one, a burly man, broad of back and slow of tongue. He got through twice as much work as Caleb and could continue for hours without tiring or saying more than two words.

It was a bumper harvest, and the three of them worked from dawn till dusk gathering in the fruits that Everdene Farm offered so generously. Kirsty had never loved her home so much, and her thoughts went often to Will, in a silent promise to treasure the precious gift he'd left her.

Then she had a fall and broke her ankle. Jack carried her home in his trunklike arms. She thought of those arms working tirelessly and was frantic to think of how soon the farm would lose him.

When Caleb departed Jack remained, promising to stay until she was mobile. A few days later he returned from Ollershaw, the nearby village, and said with forced casualness, "Folks are starting to talk—you and me being alone here. Reckon we gotta do something."

"What can we do?"

"Either I gotta leave—or we get wed," he said with a shrug that was too consciously indifferent to be convincing.

She made a swift decision. Later she suffered agonies of guilt for what seemed a monstrous piece of calculation, but she did herself an injustice. There was little calculation, only a blind rush to safety. "I don't want you to leave, Jack," she said. "But can we . . . do you think we can make it work?"

He shrugged again. "Why not? Nice little farm. It needs me. And I need it. No more wandering for me."

It was the longest and most eloquent speech she'd ever heard from him, and it filled her with relief. He was marrying her for security, so it wasn't so bad that she didn't love him. It was a respectable bargain, the kind many women in her position had struck. "Let's do it then," she said, and he grunted agreement.

It didn't trouble her then that she was condemning herself to a loveless marriage, for she knew nothing of love. She was used to the local swains who tried their luck, entranced by her long black hair and dark eyes and the implicit promise of her curved mouth. She'd brushed them aside, going blithely on her way, with neither her heart nor her senses roused. Jack's kiss was awkward but not unpleasant, and the power of her gratitude felt like a kind of love. They were married a month later.

If she'd been fanciful she might have thought that somewhere Will was shaking his head and muttering, "Too hasty," but she wasn't fanciful, and so she never heard the warning.

In the years to come she had cause to wish she'd heard it. Her life with Jack was more or less contented, but as time went on his quiet manner shaded into surliness, and when he found his voice it was often to speak to her sharply. Gradually Kirsty understood that he wanted more from her than the security he'd claimed. He felt something that she didn't understand, never having felt it herself, but she knew that it made a mockery of her calm fondness for him. She could give him affection but not passion, and the knowledge was like a shadow between them.

Kirsty promised herself that she would make it up to him with children, but five years passed with no sign of a baby. To her dismay Everdene didn't prosper. Jack wanted a say in the running of the farm, but nature had created him a laborer, not a decision maker. He made unlucky deals, overruled her wishes and spent money on poor animals who didn't survive. Kirsty could have wept. Instead she resisted him whenever possible, which led to bitter quarrels.

And then Peter Mullery returned from university for the Christmas vacation. He was eighteen, slim, handsome and mercurial. He called at Everdene, seeking casual work. Normally there would have been none at that time of the year, but Jack had just spent their last penny buying pigs that would be delivered the following week. There was nowhere for them to live but an old barn that needed a lot of work. So Kirsty hired Peter with relief.

Jack had grunted with displeasure. "Caleb will be here soon. We don't need anybody else."

"Caleb might not show up for ages. You know how unreliable he can be. And those pigs are arriving next week."

"That's right, throw it up to me," Jack shouted. "Them's good pigs."

"So they may be, but this is hardly the time of year to—" she checked herself. "I merely meant that we need some help. You said so yourself."

"I meant someone who's used to hard work, not a boy who wastes his life on books."

"What's wrong with books? I sometimes wish I had time to read more."

He flung her an angry look and strode from the room, as he always did when he didn't know what to say.

Caleb took another week to show up, and by that time Peter was settled in. He worked hard, even coming to Kirsty to ask her for extra jobs, but he always lingered to chat. She enjoyed talking to him, for he was a poet, who showed her glimpses of new worlds. One day he told her she was beautiful, and she laughed disparagingly. "Not me," she insisted. "I'm tall and thin and my face is too long."

"You are willowy and slender, and you have the face of an El Greco Madonna," he said simply.

Her puzzlement must have showed, for the next day he brought her a book of El Greco reproductions. She looked at the pictures of Spanish women with their deep-set, heavy-lidded eyes and realized that her own looks were similar. But she missed the true likeness, which lay in the sensual mouths of these women contrasting with their aesthetic faces.

"Haven't you two got anything else to do?"

They looked up at the surly voice and saw Jack glaring at them. "It's lunchtime," Kirsty said soothing him, "and Peter was just showing me a book."

"Lunchtime's over, and we haven't got time for rubbishy books."

She was too angry to consider that Jack, whose formal education had been almost nil, might simply have felt left out. That night she tackled him for his rudeness and they quarreled. "I won't have him mooning over you," Jack shouted.

"He doesn't," she said indignantly.

"He does," Caleb put in, grinning. "I've seen him watching you when you weren't looking, and I know what he's thinking..." His voice trailed away as Jack turned on him, his eyes filled with murderous fury.

"You shut your filthy mouth," he raged, "or I'll shut it for you."

The next day Peter didn't appear, and Jack said, "I fired him, and I told him what I'd do if I caught him hanging around my wife again."

"Peter doesn't mean anything to me," she said firmly, "and you know that."

"Do I? You've got a secret place inside your head where I'm not allowed. How do I know what goes on in there?"

For three days there was no sign of Peter. Then one afternoon he appeared in the barn. "I thought you'd send me a message," he said reproachfully. "I've been waiting."

She couldn't bear his reproach. It was too much like Jack's. Was she always to be plagued by men wanting something she couldn't give? she thought wildly.

"I should have sent your book back. I'm sorry," she said, willfully misunderstanding him.

"Damn the book! It's you I want, Kirsty. I love you. Tell me you love me. I must hear you say it."

"Peter, please go away. I don't love you. I can't." She burst out in sudden despair. *"I can't love anyone."*

"I don't believe you. You were made for love. I can't sleep for thinking of you. Kirsty... Kirsty... my darling..."

He was struggling with her, snatching a kiss from her reluctant lips. Her flesh was cold and unresponsive, and she was suddenly angry with him as if he'd forced her to confront a secret deformity. She writhed in his arms, crying out a protest, and suddenly she felt him snatched away.

She steadied herself against the wall and saw Jack, his face dark with fury, drag Peter out of the barn and throw him to the ground. "Don't ever come here again," he shouted. "If I ever see you near my wife *I'll kill you.*"

Caleb was there in the confusion, seizing hold of Jack, his sharp eyes looking from Kirsty to Peter. Jack shook himself free and stared at Kirsty with something close to hate.

At this point she always tried to halt the flood of memories, but they were remorseless, forcing her to relive the terrible events that followed. There was the picture of herself sitting alone that evening waiting for Jack to return from the pub in the village, then Caleb's arrival, his worried enquiry about Jack. "I hoped he'd be home by now... Peter was there... there was a bit of a fight. Peter left but Jack went after him. I tried to follow them but I'd had a wee bit much to drink and I lost them..."

Jack hadn't returned all night, and in the morning Peter had been found lying face down in a stream in a small ravine. He was dead.

Jack was charged with his murder. He'd protested his innocence wildly, swearing that he'd only followed Peter a little way, then turned aside and spent the night walking the moor. But nobody believed him except Kirsty and Caleb. Many of the villagers had been in the pub, had heard the wild accusations Jack had thrown at the boy and seen his hate and violence. Peter had been a favorite with everyone. His neighbors condemned the man they saw as his murderer and turned their scorn on the woman whose mysterious beauty had caused the tragedy. Suddenly Kirsty found herself without friends.

She'd clung to the hope that the trial would reveal Jack's innocence. But there never was a trial. After three weeks on remand in jail, Jack had suffered a massive heart attack. In his last moments he'd lain with his hand in Kirsty's, whispering hoarsely, "I didn't do it... didn't... innocent... say you... believe..."

And she'd whispered frantically, "Yes, I believe you." And because she was torn with pity for him she added the words, "My dear."

She'd repeated again and again that she believed him, but he seemed to have gone beyond her and kept repeating, "Didn't... do it..." until at last he slipped away.

Only Caleb had stood beside her at the funeral. He'd stayed long enough to help with the spring lambing, but then he'd gone and she'd had to shoulder the burden of the farm alone. When summer came there was no word from him, and she was forced to hire casual help. She got the men no one else wanted, and they only just coped with a poor harvest.

She dreaded going into Ollershaw. Her female neighbors seemed to regard her as a witch, staring at her, then looking hastily away. Some of the men gave her hot-eyed stares that stripped her naked, and made excuses to talk to her alone. She hated the sight of their wet lips dripping with innuendos, hinting that a woman like her must be desperate for a man by now. A few of them made their way hopefully out to Everdene after dark, refusing to be discouraged and only backing off when they found themselves looking down the barrels of a shotgun.

Kirsty wondered bitterly why they'd been so quick to think the worst of her, but she couldn't see herself through their eyes and didn't know of the air of sexual mystery and magnetism that clung to her like musky perfume. It was more than mere beauty. It was an intimation of a suppressed volcano liable to erupt at any moment. She had no idea that every man who saw her thought that this was a woman a man might well kill to possess, or that every woman saw the thought in the eyes of her menfolk, and feared.

She began buying things in bulk so that she needn't make the trip to town so often. A month could pass without her talking to another human soul, and now this suited her. Whatever strange curse she carried could be decently hidden away from the world where it would do no further harm.

As her funds ran low she delayed paying the telephone bill until the company disconnected her. She finally paid, but the telephone had never been restored. She told herself she couldn't afford the reconnection charge, but the truth was she preferred it this way. Step by step she was retreating into a dark and dangerous place within herself.

By day she worked the farm dressed in boots and shapeless masculine garments, her hair scraped back under an old woolen hat, as though by concealing her femininity she could deny its power. At night she lay staring into the darkness, tormented by her guilt. She hadn't betrayed her husband, but she'd married him without love and destroyed him.

She still had all Jack's possessions. His clothing hung, neatly laundered and pressed, in the wardrobe of her grandparents' room. To dispose of it would feel like disposing of him, and her guilt wouldn't let her do that.

She stirred now, realizing that the evening had slipped away while she brooded, and it was time for bed. She climbed the stairs, Tarn at her heels. From her bedroom window she took a last look out at the snow. From this vantage point she knew she was facing in the direction of Princetown Gaol, although it was far out of sight, fifteen miles away across the moor. She shuddered, picturing the ugly granite prison. There had been an escape a few days ago, and the police had called briefly to ask if she'd seen any strangers. The man had probably been caught by now. Or perhaps he'd given himself up, defeated by the inhospitable moor in winter. Or he might have wandered until exhaustion and cold made him lie down where the snow would enfold him like a deadly blanket, and they would find his body with the next thaw. She closed the curtains.

She was awakened by the sound of the dog growling. She lay still, listening, but could hear nothing. Suddenly Tarn leapt off the bed and ran out of the room. Kirsty threw on her dressing gown and hurried down to where he was scratching at the front door. She took her shotgun and a torch from a nook by the door and stepped outside.

Snow had been falling hard while she slept, and through the darkness she could just make out that everything was covered in a thick white blanket. To her human ear the silence was unbroken, but Tarn made straight for the barn. Kirsty opened the door and moved quietly inside, letting the torch play slowly over the straw, but she could see nothing out of the ordinary.

Suddenly she heard a man's harsh breathing somewhere close by. It had a strange timber, but she couldn't stop to analyze that. She set the torch on a ledge, raised her shotgun and called, "Come out slowly. I've got a gun."

She heard hay rustling. Then the shadowy form of a man detached itself from the darkness of the bay. He was very tall, with harsh features and close-cropped hair. The crude glare from the torch struck his face from below, creating monstrous shadows that gave him a satanic look. Even in this poor light Kirsty could recognize the prison uniform. But she wasn't afraid. She felt only a kind of rage that he'd dared to intrude on her solitude.

The man made a movement toward her. His eyes were livid. "Stay there," Kirsty ordered firmly, raising the gun.

But he seemed not to see it. He made another swaying movement, reached out a hand, then pitched forward onto the ground at her feet.

Kirsty dropped to her knees and rolled him over onto his back. His clothes were cold and soaking, but his skin burned her fingers. His eyes were open, but he didn't react to the sight of her. His gaze flickered wildly around, never resting, as if in some vain search, and his breathing came in ugly gasps. Explanations could wait. First she must get him inside. "Try to sit up," she told him, placing her hands beneath his shoulders.

With his help she managed to haul him into a sitting position, but the effort left him more breathless than ever. "Put your arms around my neck so that I can lift you," she commanded.

He seemed to come out of his feverish dream. "Why?" he gasped.

"I've got to get you into the house."

He made a vague effort to push her away, groaning, "No—don't tell—anyone—"

"There's nobody here but me," she said. "Now, put your arms around my neck."

Her decisive tone seemed to influence him, for he obeyed. She clasped her hands behind his back and heaved. He was a big man and heavy, but she was strong. She managed to get him to his feet, and together they stumbled out of the barn and across the yard.

In the kitchen she helped him to a chair, banked up the stove, then sped upstairs to collect some blankets and a thick dressing gown that had been Jack's. She stripped him to the skin, noticing how the prison uniform hung on him as though he'd lost weight in his time inside. She had no awareness of him as a man. He was a problem to be solved, a sick creature to be kept alive until she could think what to do next.

When she'd got him into the dressing gown, she hauled the massive sofa out of the next room and into the kitchen. It would serve as his bed, and the kitchen was the warmest room in the house. She set some milk to heat on the stove while she laid out the blankets. When it was hot, she laced it liberally with whiskey and sugar and held it to his lips. "Drink this," she said firmly.

He obeyed without protest, and when he had finished, his head fell against her shoulder. She managed to drag him the short distance to the sofa. As she tucked blankets around him she felt him shivering violently, but his skin was still hot and dry. She was getting worried. If only the phone was working so that she could call an ambulance. But it would be morning before she could do anything. She built up the stove with logs, driving the temperature up until it reached the point where she could switch on the house's primitive central heating system.

For the next few hours she stayed beside him, fueling the stove when necessary, at other times studying him, trying to recall what she'd heard of him on the news. The only thing that came to mind was that he'd resisted arrest violently. The broad shoulders and large, powerful hands looked capable of violence, even now when he was so thin. He had three days' growth of beard, but beneath it she could see that he was in his late thirties, with a lean face, high cheekbones and a stubborn jaw. His hair was cut very short, and his skin had a pallor against which the blue-black stubble showed like a bruise.

His brows were almost straight, making a dramatic line over his eyes. His mouth surprised her. It was full and wide and made a strange contrast with the gaunt harshness of his other features. His lips moved constantly, muttering feverish words that she couldn't make out. Mostly his eyes were closed, but now and then they opened briefly. He would stare at her, without seeming to see her, then close them again.

He was in hell. He'd lived there for months and discovered that hell had many forms: betrayal, humiliated pride, rage and despair. The worst, by a long way, was betrayal. He'd ridden a switchback of disbelief, stunned realization, hope, frustration and fear.

Now hell had a new form, more like the traditional pictures of his childhood. He was sinking into a furnace. Someone was stoking the blaze about him, pouring liquid fire down his throat until he was overwhelmed by the heat. But instead of pain he felt only a desire to yield to the power that had taken hold of him. He'd been cold—so terribly cold—and afraid. But here there was only warmth and safety and blissful, dangerous contentment.

Opening his eyes by a fraction he saw an angel. She had a beautiful, enigmatic face, such as men saw only in their dreams, and her hands touched him as softly as a whisper. But what he noticed most was that terrible fires burned in her eyes, as though she too were in hell, the place where fallen angels were banished.

Kirsty slipped quickly out to the little shed where she kept her store of wood and hurried back, her arms filled with logs. It took three trips to refill the stove and leave a pile ready for use, and by that time he was restless again. She sat on the edge of the sofa and touched his face gently, hoping to soothe him. At once he turned his head so that his lips brushed her palm.

Kirsty snatched her hand back in alarm. Her palm burned where he'd touched it, and she could still feel the sudden electric shock that had streaked along her nerves. Strangest of all, she was sure she'd heard him murmur the words "Fallen angel."

"I'm going crazy," she told herself. "I've been alone so long I'm imagining things." She looked closely at the man's sleeping form. He was totally still, and there was no trace of either the words or the movement that had so disturbed her.

But suddenly he screamed, *"No!"* and started up into a sitting position, his whole body tense and rigid. Kirsty grabbed him as he tried to throw back the blankets. "No!" he yelled, fighting her. "No, damn you! *No.*"

His weakness had been replaced by feverish energy. His eyes were open and their wild, staring look told her he wasn't seeing her, but someone else, someone who filled him with hate. It was like fighting a madman and it took all her strength to hold him down while he raved and lashed at her.

"Get away from me," he shouted. *"Don't touch me..."*

She didn't notice his free hand until it struck her a stinging blow across the face, sending her sprawling onto the floor. But the fit passed as suddenly as it had started, and when she got to her feet, she found him lying back on the sofa, motionless, staring unseeingly into space. She hurried to wrap him up again, and he let her do as she liked, without protest.

She was seriously worried now. If she couldn't get him some help soon he might die here in her kitchen, and the thought appalled her. *No more deaths,* she begged inwardly. *Please, no more deaths.*

"You've got to stay alive," she muttered, barely knowing she was saying the words aloud. "You've *got* to."

He turned his eyes on her. His madness had gone and he seemed to see her properly for the first time. "Why?" he asked in a hoarse whisper. "So that you can send me back there?"

"Please understand," she said wildly. "I can't help you. You need a doctor or you could die."

A fit of violent shivering came over him. He clung to her until it passed, his fingers digging into her arms. When it was over he was exhausted, but his burning eyes still held hers. "Let me...die, then," he gasped. "I'd rather die than...be shut in. You can't...understand...."

She thought of Jack, whose heart had broken behind bolts and bars, and suddenly there was a lump in her throat that made it painful to speak. She nodded. "I do understand. More than you can know."

"Then don't...tell anyone. Give me a chance. If I can get away—" his breathing became more labored "—get away...prove...what really happened...innocent... prove...innocent..."

She stared at him, feeling the hair rise on the back of her neck. "You say...you're innocent?"

He misunderstood her tone and made a feeble attempt at a cynical smile. "Oh yes, that's what...they all say...isn't it?" The smile faded and a terrible intensity possessed him. "But it's true. I didn't do it. I swear I didn't. *Help me.*"

"Oh, God," she whispered, "what am I going to do?"

His eyes became glazed and she could see he was sinking back into delirium. He began repeating the word *innocent* again and again like a hypnotic prayer, and every time he said it her torment increased. If there was any chance that it was true, how could she send him back to that place?

At last he calmed down and lay sleeping. Kirsty slid to the floor and sat close to the stove. She needed the heat because of the terrible shivering that suddenly possessed her. But the shivering wouldn't stop, and she realized that no heat could warm her now. For a year she'd coped with her memories by deadening them, but this stranger who'd come mysteriously out of the storm had brought them all to agonizing life. For a moment she hated him. If only the phone was working so that she might call someone and have him taken away, and then she could retreat once more into her safe numbness. But then she realized it was already too late for that. He was here, and for good or ill she must see it through to the end—whatever the end might be—or have her peace destroyed forever.

"Right," she muttered, getting to her feet. "If it's got to be done, let's do it properly."

There was still plenty of whiskey. Jack had bought the bottle just before his arrest, and she had never touched it. She heated up some more milk, added plenty of sugar and a liberal dose of the spirit. It took coaxing and determination to awaken him and get it down his throat, but she succeeded. He fell back into a troubled sleep, and she let him stay that way for an hour before repeating the process. He was as much starving as sick, and she had to revive his energy somehow before he could manage a square meal.

The night seemed to last forever. She stayed by him, making him drink whenever she could. Sometimes he lay quietly, at others the delirium would return and he would toss about, trying to throw back the covers and crying out that he was innocent. Every time she heard the word, Kirsty felt the hairs stand up on the back of her neck. The room was full of ghosts, and she wanted to protect him and be rid of him simultaneously.

"Hush," she said frantically. "Don't say that."

His eyes were open again but she didn't know if he could see her. "Must say it...don't you understand? Someone's got to believe me. I didn't do it—say you...believe me...."

And suddenly she was back in the prison hospital, knowing what she must do to bring peace to a tormented man. Slowly she took his hand between both of hers.

"Yes, my dear," she said. "I believe you."

Chapter Two

He awoke to find himself in an unfamiliar room. It was almost in darkness, with light coming from just one small table lamp. The fire that had consumed him was gone, leaving him light-headed, with an eerie sensation of floating weightlessly and understanding everything. He knew, for instance, that the woman sitting on the floor beside him was lost in an inner world of her own, and that it was a bitter, lonely world, where she brooded silently over some terrible secret. And suddenly he recognized her. "Fallen angel!" he murmured.

She looked up sharply and he saw the quick anger in the most wonderful pair of dark eyes he'd ever seen. "Why did you come here disturbing me?" she asked abruptly.

"I only meant to hide in your barn for a few hours." His gaze fell on the phone and he groaned in despair. "I suppose you've called them and they'll be here soon."

"The phone doesn't work. No one's coming." She rose to her knees and studied him anxiously. "Your fever seems to have broken, thank goodness." She touched his face, then felt the dressing gown and gave a sharp exclamation. "You're soaking. I'll get you some dry things."

She vanished, and at once he thrust aside the blankets. His eyes were fixed on the phone. She might have been lying. He set his feet to the floor and tried to rise, feeling as if weights were pulling him back. He managed to stand, and stayed for a moment, fighting the dizziness, then put one foot in front of the other, clutching furniture as he inched toward the telephone with painful slowness.

"What do you think you're doing?"

He turned and saw her standing there indignantly, a pile of clothes in her arms. She tossed them aside and hurried across the floor, but he held out a hand to fend her off. "Keep back," he said breathlessly. "I want to know if you're telling the truth."

Sweat stood out on his brow with the sheer effort of standing upright. The phone seemed a million miles away. She forestalled him, darting past his hand to lift the receiver and hold it out so that he could hear the silence. The relief was so great that he swayed and had to clutch her. She supported him back to the sofa, saying, "You've been here five hours. If I'd called they'd have been here by now."

"Five hours?" It felt like a few minutes.

"Get out of this dressing gown before you catch pneumonia."

She removed it with brisk movements and began to towel him dry. For the first time he realized that all his clothes were gone. He was embarrassed by his nakedness before a stranger, but this decisive young woman didn't seem to notice. She produced a pair of dry flannel pajamas, helped him into them and made him sit in the chair while she put fresh blankets on the sofa. "Lie down," she said when she'd finished, and he, who'd sworn never to obey another order once he got out of prison, meekly did as she said.

But when his head had stopped swimming his suspicion returned. "So you haven't called anyone—because you can't. But now it's nearly day..."

"I could lock you in and run for help," she agreed. "Do you think I will?"

He tried desperately to read her face, but it was in shadow. "I don't know," he said at last despairingly.

"I don't know, either."

The abruptness of her speech struck his ear oddly. She seemed to find words with an effort, like someone who spoke little and had to remind herself how. At that moment a fragment of memory drifted back to him. "You told me," he said slowly, "that you believed me innocent."

He had a feeling that she'd gathered herself together, actually growing smaller. He could just make out that her eyes had become remote, almost angry. "Did I?" she asked without warmth.

"You must know you did." His eyes grew puzzled as another bit of memory slotted into place. "And you called me 'my—'"

"All right, perhaps I said it," she agreed quickly. "I don't really remember."

"I think you do. But you regret it now, don't you?" He sensed her withdrawing farther from him as he pressed her. The birth and death of hope in the same moment sent a stab of pain through him, and his voice rose in anger. "You only said it to keep me quiet."

"No, I—" she broke off sharply as though every word was dangerous. She was backing away until she almost vanished into the shadows, and the very air seemed jagged with her tension.

"Did you mean it?" he demanded harshly.

Her voice reached him, haggard, desperate, the voice of a woman at the end of her tether. "*I don't know.* I don't know what I believe. I don't know what I'm going to do. You're right not to trust me."

He tried to suppress the anguish of disappointment with cynicism. "I haven't trusted anyone for the past year," he observed.

After a pause she said shortly, "Neither have I."

He felt awkward, knowing his words had struck a nerve, but not understanding why. "Where am I?" he asked to break the silence.

"Still on Dartmoor. This is Everdene Farm, about fifteen miles south of Princetown. My name's Kirsty."

"Mine's Mike Stallard. Does that mean anything to you?"

"You're the man who escaped from the prison three days ago. I knew that as soon as I saw you."

"And it doesn't trouble you?"

"I'm not afraid of you, if that's what you mean."

"Considering you've got a gun and I'm as weak as a kitten, that's hardly surprising," he said wryly.

But even as he said it he knew he did her an injustice. She had a strange, elusive detachment that contrasted oddly with her earthy surroundings. Her marvelous eyes were distant even when they looked at him, as though she lived partly in another world, where she'd gone beyond fear.

She heated some soup and brought it to the sofa. "This will make you stronger," she said, "and you'll feel better after another sleep."

"I can't sleep if I don't know what's going to happen."

"I won't give you away... yet. We'll talk first. That's a promise. Take this."

He obeyed her and fell asleep again almost at once. When he awoke it was light. He felt better than he had for days. The sound of footsteps coming from the next room made him tense with dread, but it was only her. She didn't notice he was awake, and he watched her through half-closed eyes. She was his only hope, and it was vital to size her up, but he found his mind dwelt more on the lanky grace of her tall frame, incongruously covered by old jeans and boots. He thought of women he'd known who spent fortunes on couture without achieving a fraction of her instinctive elegance. But that had been another existence.

Then she turned her head, and for the first time he saw her face in daylight, with nothing to hide the ugly bruise on one side of her mouth.

Kirsty looked up quickly as she heard Mike suck in his breath in a sharp hiss. "What is it?" she asked.

"Come here," he said urgently, and when she approached he reached up to take her shoulders, staring at her. "Who did that?"

"Did what?"

He touched the bruise gently, trying not to hurt her. Even so he felt a tremor go through her and she pulled away sharply. "That," he said. "And don't tell me you walked into a door. Someone hit you across the face, and he hit hard."

Incredibly a glimmer of humor lit her eyes. "As a matter of fact," she said, "it was you."

"What are you talking about?"

"You were delirious and flailing your arms about. I tried to make you stay on the sofa and you socked me so hard I went flying."

He groaned. "I was dreaming—or hallucinating. They came to arrest me and I fought them off. That must be when I hit you. I'm sorry."

She shrugged. "Forget it. It was obvious you didn't know what you were doing."

"It really happened that way. I fought them as hard as I could. I *had* to because I was innocent and I needed to be free to prove it. But no one would listen. That was the worst," he added, remembering grimly, "that no one would listen."

"I know," she said softly.

He looked at her. "How do you know?"

For a brief moment her guard had slipped, but his question made her flinch away and become wary again. "Never mind," she said shortly. "Tell me what happened to you."

"A lot of money vanished from my company," Mike said. "When I discovered the loss I confronted my junior partner, Hugh Severham, about it. He tried to blind me with computer language. The joke is that it was because of his genius with computers that I wanted him in the firm. The next thing I knew he'd tapped a few keys and suddenly all the evidence pointed to me."

Mike paused as if he needed his courage for what came next. "I was late spotting the danger because my mind was on my coming marriage." He gave a short, harsh laugh. "I remember telling Lois that we'd have to postpone the honeymoon until I'd sorted things out, but

I never realized—'' He stooped and took a shuddering breath. ''I went to the church and waited for her. The music started . . . she was coming down the aisle . . . the most beautiful woman in the world. I was so proud when she stood beside me. . . .''

His brow was damp. Kirsty could see the effort it cost him to go on, but she couldn't make herself stop him. Her whole being was tense, listening. ''The priest said, 'If any of ye know cause or just impediment why this man and this woman may not lawfully be joined together, ye are to declare it.' And the next moment a man called out from the back of the church, 'The wedding must stop. The groom is under arrest.' ''

''Oh no,'' Kirsty breathed.

''They arrested me in front of a churchful of fascinated spectators. Hugh was there, grinning like a cat that had swallowed the cream. I fought them. I had to stay free to prove my innocence, but it was no use. . . .''

He'd risen on one elbow but now he fell back, exhausted with the effort. ''I landed a few punches, but there were so many of them, I hadn't a hope. All I achieved was a reputation for violence, which made the police oppose bail on the grounds that I might 'intimidate witnesses.' ''

''I thought it was only people charged with murder who were refused bail,'' Kirsty said quietly.

If he noticed a sudden strangeness in her tone he gave no sign of it. ''I wasn't exactly refused,'' he said bitterly, ''but the figure was set at a sum I couldn't raise. People I'd thought I could rely on suddenly vanished, or maybe Hugh got to them. Lois did her best to find the money, but she had nothing of her own, only the jewelry I'd given her. It wasn't enough.''

"I was tried and sentenced to ten years. The judge made it clear that the sentence was set high because I hadn't 'cooperated with the police'—in other words, told them how to get the money back. The idea is that I'll eventually crack and tell them in order to get parole. But I *can't* tell them. I don't know. *Ten years.*" He groaned. "I had to escape…you don't know…there's no way to describe it…bolts and bars…the sound of metal doors slamming…."

"Yes," she whispered with a shudder, wishing he'd stop.

He seemed not to have heard her. He went on. "The claustrophobia…the lack of privacy…and the despair at the years that face you…hopelessness—"

"That's enough," she shouted, jumping up and backing away from him. Seeing him stare, she recovered herself hastily. "I can imagine why you had to escape. But what can you do now?"

"I have one chance. It's a man called Con Dawlish. He's a computer freak with a genius for hacking into places where he's no business to be. If he could get into the firm's mainframe he might just be able to backtrack on all the transactions and show what Hugh did and how."

"How do you know he didn't help your partner frame you?" Kirsty asked.

"Because Con is the most shiningly innocent man I've ever met. He never steals or does any harm once he's into a system, just leaves a cheeky message to say the security needs improving. All he cares about is the challenge."

"Then why didn't he come to your help at the time?"

"My lawyer tried to contact him, but apparently he was seriously ill and being cared for by a sister, who blocked all messages. But recently I heard that he was up and about again. His name is well-known in the prison. Some of the inmates got there through copying his methods without his morals. If I could find him now I know he'd help me. But I have to move fast. He's elderly and frail. I don't know how much time there is. You *must* help me, Kirsty. Don't send me back. Help me get away from here.''

In his agitation he'd seized her hands in both of his and was holding them hard. His eyes were fixed on her face with a terrible intensity that wouldn't let her go. Kirsty felt herself being drawn into a hypnotic spell that made her heart beat faster and a lump come to her throat. She tried to speak, but her mouth was suddenly dry. And besides, what was there to say? For a moment she'd been on the verge of telling this stranger that she would do whatever he wanted without question, but that was mad. How did she know he was telling the truth?

Without warning he loosened his grip, looking down at her left hand, which still bore the wedding ring Jack had put there. Through the contact of their flesh she felt the hope drain out of him, leaving anguished defeat behind, and the sensation caused her exquisite pain. ''I should have realized,'' Mike said dully. ''When will he be back?''

''My husband is dead. There's nobody here but me, and nobody comes here if they can help it.''

He raised his eyes to her in an agony of pleading.

''It wouldn't work,'' she said desperately.

''Why? Because you're a solid, upright citizen who thinks once a man's accused he must be guilty? No smoke without fire, is that it?''

She flinched at the hated phrase that had dogged her after the double tragedy, and burst into harsh, angry

laughter that made him stare. "No," she said scathingly, "I'm not a solid upright citizen. I'm a witch, a bad
woman, little better than a murderess. Anyone around
here would tell you that. I know how easily solid, upright citizens can be wrong."

"Then we have that in common," he said slowly,
watching her pale face.

"Yes, we have that in common.

"Help me, Kirsty."

She looked into his eyes, dark in his livid face, and saw
in them a reflection of her own hell. She had no more
will to fight him. What was going to happen had always
been inevitable. "Yes," she said slowly. "I'll help you."

Kirsty slipped out of the house to retrieve her gun
from the barn, and at once she saw danger. Mercifully,
the heaviest snow had fallen after Mike's arrival, covering his tracks across the moor. But within the yard,
plain for all to see, were the two sets of prints they'd left
when she'd helped him into the house. Outside the snow
was fresh and unmarked, indicating that no one had
passed this way to see the incriminating signs. They
would probably be left alone for days, but she was taking no chances. Seizing the spade, she shoveled vigor-
ously until there was a clear path across the yard, and all
footprints had vanished.

She supposed she was breaking the law, helping a
convicted criminal to escape, but that knowledge was
slightly unreal to her. The reality was that this man was
like herself, an outcast. The world had unjustly blamed
and rejected them both, driving them to survive in any
way they could. Probably, she thought, this was why she
felt drawn to him. They shared a secret no one else could
understand.

The project wouldn't really be dangerous. The snow and her isolation would keep them safe from curious strangers. She was well stocked with food and could soon build up his strength. When the snow eased and he was ready to go, she could guide him off the moor in darkness.

When she'd finished shoveling, she took her gun from the barn and returned to the house. Mike was sitting on the edge of the sofa, warily eyeing Tarn, who seemed undecided about him and alternately growled and sniffed at him. "He's confused by Jack's clothes," Kirsty explained.

"Was Jack your husband?"

"Yes."

"You're young to be a widow. What happened to him?"

"You can't stay down here, it's too dangerous. I'll fix a bed upstairs," she said quickly, and disappeared before he could answer.

She made up the big brass bed where her grandparents had slept and went to fetch him. She found him halfway up the stairs, taking it slowly and breathing hard, and helped him the rest of the way. As he got into bed he said, "You told me nobody ever comes here, but you must have some employees."

"Nobody," she said shortly.

"You mean you work the farm alone?"

"That's right."

"But how can you?"

"I can because I have to. I might ask how you escaped from Princetown Gaol. Nobody ever gets away from there."

Their eyes met. He nodded. "I had to. So I did."

"I'll help you, Mike, but we don't ask each other questions."

His lips twisted in a wry smile. "That's the code of the convict. Are you on the run, too, Kirsty?"

"Perhaps. In my way. But you don't ask. Ever."

"All right. Understood."

She left the room and went downstairs to fix breakfast. A trip to the hen coup produced five large brown eggs, which she scrambled for the two of them. She took his portion up and watched him tuck into it. "I must get to work," she said. "I'll lock the doors. If you hear anyone outside, stay here and don't move. They can't get in. Don't be tempted to put any lights on."

Before leaving the house, she stripped the sofa of blankets and pushed it into the back room. Then she cleared some books off the top of an old oak chest, shoved in his prison uniform and replaced the books. If anyone looked in from outside there was nothing unusual to alert them. After piling some logs into the stove, she left to take care of her animals.

The closest to hand were the pigs, who waddled eagerly toward her. She fed them but didn't linger to scratch them fondly as she normally did. Next came her small flock of black-faced sheep who lived on the tor that rose behind the house. For them she loaded the wagon with feed, attached it to the tractor and headed out into the snow, which was beginning to fall again.

By the time she reached them it was coming down hard, settling on their thick coats as they stood in stolid endurance. They had been Will's pride and joy, and it was their fine wool that helped the farm break even. She hauled the heavy feed from the wagon and tipped it into the huge trough in the center of the field. There was enough there for several days if she was prevented from getting to them. But she couldn't go home yet. She had other friends who depended on her in the winter.

After another mile she saw them, sturdy little Dartmoor ponies, waiting at the place where she always dropped their hay. They gathered around her, whinnying as she came to a halt and began hauling down the bales of hay. They were small, thickset animals, some almost as broad as they were tall, with short legs and blunt heads. Even in her present crisis Kirsty stayed a moment to run her hands lovingly over a rough coat or accept a nuzzled greeting. She had adored the ponies ever since she'd first ridden one as a child, and in her worst moments of feeling an outcast had often come seeking them, knowing that in this company, at least, she would always be welcome and never harshly judged.

At last she tore herself away and drove the tractor home, feeling wet, cold and weary. Although it was only afternoon the light was fading fast, but to her relief there were no lights on in the house. A quick sprint up the stairs revealed Mike lying asleep. He stirred and kicked away the blankets, and she tucked them firmly about him again. As she hurried down she knew a sensation of something like triumph. They'd won the first round.

In the kitchen she got out the prison uniform and began cutting the legs into small pieces which she tossed into the stove, thanking her luck that the material had dried out.

As she neared the pockets she slipped her hand inside to make an automatic check, not really expecting to find anything. But her fingers closed over some small pieces of thin card. She pulled them out and found that they fitted together to make a snapshot of a woman.

She was beautiful, with perfect, regular features and a swirling mass of shining blond hair. Her makeup was elaborate and her eyes laughed at the camera, while her lips seemed to twitch provocatively.

Kirsty stared at her, realizing that this glamorous creature must be Mike's fiancée, Lois. There was something unreal about her, as though she belonged in a television commercial for shampoo. Yet Mike had known her, loved her, wanted to marry her. In his torment he'd tried to kill her memory, but he'd failed. He'd kept the torn pieces because she still lived in his heart. For the first time Kirsty sensed something alien about him.

When she'd finished destroying the suit, she took the picture upstairs. As soon as she reached the landing she heard sounds coming from Mike's room. Alarmed, she hurried inside and found him tossing about on the bed. His eyes were closed, and he muttered constantly, words she couldn't make out, and when she touched him she found his fever had returned. She thought with dread of what could happen if he was allowed to throw off his blankets as he was trying to. She managed to calm him and tuck him in, but when she returned ten minutes later to check, she found them tossed on the floor. "Mike," she said, trying to shake him awake, "Mike. You mustn't do this."

"Sorry," he whispered. "Stupid of me . . ."

"What was stupid?"

"Felt better . . . wanted a wash . . . bathroom . . ."

"You idiot," she said furiously. "Now you've caught cold again."

"Sorry." He drifted off.

The next few hours were a nightmare, with Mike needing to be constantly watched as he threw the bedclothes off at every opportunity. Kirsty managed to get to the kitchen long enough to fix herself a hasty snack, but she hurried upstairs with it and ate it in snatched mouthfuls between restraining him. As the afternoon wore into evening, and then into night, his fever deepened, and she became afraid.

"Mike, *please,*" she cried, trying to get through to him through the fog of delirium. He was looking at her through half-open eyes, and she couldn't tell if he was aware of her or not. In a desperate attempt to reach him, she assumed a half-humorous rallying tone that she was far from feeling. "You can't die on me now. How would I explain it? Have you thought of that? No, of course you haven't."

Her unsentimental tone roused him to mutter, "S'easy. Put me back in the barn. Say...found me there."

"In my husband's pajamas?" she demanded scathingly.

"Uniform...change..."

"I've destroyed your uniform. If you die now, I'm in big trouble."

After a long pause he said indistinctly, "A'right. F'you...angel..."

It seemed to have worked because he grew calmer and lay still, although his breathing was labored. Kirsty slipped away to her own room long enough to put on her pajamas and dressing gown and hurried back.

To her relief she found that he'd quietened and now lay still. She settled herself in a chair by the bed, prepared to wait out the night.

She awoke with a start, realizing that she'd nodded off into a doze made restless by the uncomfortable chair. She twisted, but the hard wood seemed to have bruised her all over. The empty space beside Mike looked inviting, and as he still seemed quiet she climbed onto the bed, lying outside the blankets.

At once she could feel him trembling. She leaned over and touched him gently. "Mike?"

He was shaking with ague, his eyes open and staring. "Cold," he muttered, "cold . . ."

His skin was hot but he didn't seem to feel it. Whereas before he'd tried to throw off the clothes, now he huddled them around him, moaning, "cold . . . cold . . ." through chattering teeth.

She fetched more blankets, piling them onto him, then getting into the bed so that she could hold him better. She had instinctively kept on the dressing gown but after a few minutes the heat of the blankets forced her to abandon it. She could feel the length of his hard body close to hers, but the first shyness soon vanished as she realized he was unaware of her. She held him more tightly, trying to soothe him, and soon she felt him relax. She lay still, arms aching, staring into the darkness, wondering what she was going to do. Her head warned her to seek help before it was too late, but her heart understood the anguish that made him prefer death to imprisonment. She was still worrying at the problem when exhaustion claimed her.

But even in sleep there was no rest. She was in one of those strange dreams where the dreamer knew she was dreaming. The four pieces of the picture seemed to come together, and Lois stepped out, cool, beautiful and frighteningly sophisticated beside the farm woman. Kirsty didn't know why she should find Lois frightening, but it was so. Lois's hands were smooth, white and elegant, while her own work-roughened hands seemed to grow to monstrous size. They were so big that she couldn't see Mike. But she heard his cry of *"Lois,"* and the gladness in his voice made her struggle to awaken so that she didn't have to listen anymore.

It seemed hard to awaken. She couldn't escape the sound of him calling for Lois over and over. Then she realized she was awake after all, and Mike was lying with his head on her shoulder, murmuring in a voice full of longing.

"Mike," she said urgently, trying to shake him awake. *"Mike..."*

"Lois..." he whispered, and there was a timbre in his voice that seemed to go through her. She'd never heard a man speak a woman's name in that tone. She began to shake him again, but stopped as she realized, with intense relief, that his flesh felt cool. The crisis had passed, and the best thing for him was to sleep in peace.

She began to edge slowly backward across the bed, meaning to slide out gradually. But he held her. "Don't go," he murmured. "Stay here with me...I want you..."

You want Lois, she thought grimly, and I'm leaving. She tried again to move but this time his arm tightened strongly across her body, his grip surprisingly powerful after his recent weakness. She was reluctant to awaken him, but she would have to risk it. She twisted in his arms, trying to push him back, but suddenly she felt his hand on her bare flesh, sending unfamiliar tremors through her body. She stiffened with shock.

Looking down she saw that the buttons on her pajama jacket had come open during the night. His hand was on her waist, but starting to drift upward toward her exposed breasts, and as the long fingers trailed across her skin she felt electric shocks shiver through her so powerfully that the breath seemed to drain from her lungs. As he reached the swell of her breast and enclosed it in his palm she let out a shuddering gasp.

She was swept by sensations so new, so violent and all-encompassing that it was like being robbed of herself.

Nothing in her whole life had felt like the touch of this man's hand. There was a power and yet a sweetness to it, a promise of infinite joy in some world still unknown to her.

But it wasn't her in his arms, she reminded herself wildly. His embrace was for Lois. She had stolen it and must find the strength to renounce it. She tried to struggle, but somehow his face was above hers and his lips were on hers, and she was sinking, drowning, melting into ecstasy. Her heart was pounding in her breast. She didn't ever want this to stop. For the first time in her life she was experiencing passion, and everything that had seemed vital a moment ago faded to nothing beside the overwhelming discovery.

Hardly knowing what she was doing, she began to kiss him back, her lips making soft, urgent movements that she hadn't realized they knew. It was a wanton kiss, the kiss of a woman who was trying to entice a man further. She, who had never touched a man with desire before, instinctively knew just the moment to part her lips invitingly, offering the dark warmth to his invasion. The feel of his tongue inside her was another revelation, sending rivers of delight flowing through her being, causing a throb of anticipation deep within her that made her press her body urgently against his.

And then it was all over. It stopped as suddenly as it had begun. His hands fell from her, and his whole body rolled away. Not once had he opened his eyes.

Kirsty lay, frozen with shock, for a full five minutes before she could force life into her limbs. She had to get out of this room before Mike awoke, saw her and perhaps realized, what had happened. She felt suddenly scalded with shame. She was shaking all over, but she didn't stop moving until she was in her own room.

There she dropped onto the bed, dazed and torn between two opposing instincts. Her body still held the memory of his lips and his hands, the feel of his flesh against hers. She was burning with unfamiliar sensations. A door had been opened by a fraction, and through the crack she'd had her first glimpse of the beauty from which she'd always been excluded. The glory of it had made her gasp and reach out eager hands to push the door open wide, only to find it slammed shut again.

He wasn't hers. She had deceived herself and him, but at some point in his fevered dreaming he'd stopped being deceived, recognized her for an impostor and turned away from her in disgust. She was a thief, a cheat, a wanton. Her neighbors had known that all along. They could see the flaw in her to which she herself had been blind. But she saw it now and shuddered at its ugliness.

After a long time she rose and began to pull on her work clothes. She moved slowly, like a woman stunned. Finally she scraped back her hair into a knot and rammed the woolen hat down hard over her head, so that not a single stray lock of hair escaped. Then she forced herself to go down and start the day's work.

Chapter Three

The brass spokes of the bedstead were the first thing Mike saw, and for a moment he thought he was back at home. Strange how he still thought of his parents' house as home, although he hadn't been there for more than ten years. Nor had it felt like a home to him when he'd lived there. He'd been an alien, a cuckoo in the cozy nest with its unchanging rhythms and its assumptions that were never questioned.

But *he'd* questioned them. He'd broken every taboo in sight, and his parents had been shocked. His father seemed to be there now, looking at him, shaking his head in mystification at this son who harbored dreams of grandeur. "You'll come to a bad end, son, always thinking about money. Money's not the most important thing in the world."

"It is if you haven't got any," he heard himself answering bitterly. He had a sharp tongue to go with his sharp brain, and rows with his parents always ended with him saying something thoughtless that hurt them. He hated the stricken look that would dawn in their eyes, hated himself for causing it, hated himself more for not knowing how to say sorry, for not being the son they would have liked, hated them for being disappointed. In the confusion of pain and self-reproach the world didn't seem big enough to contain his conflicting feelings, and he would set his chin and glare, so that they shouldn't know he was hurt, too. That had been important to a young man.

In his mind, his mother intervened, saying quietly, "Don't blame your father. He's always done his best for you."

"I'm not blaming him, Ma. It's this place and everything about it I loathe."

She stared, bewildered. "But we have a good life here."

A good life: his father had gone into the mine because in the little northern town of Valeby there was nothing else to do. He'd hacked coal in the days when miners were paid chicken feed and accepted it because that was how the world was. It had broken his health and left them to live off an inadequate pension in a small, rented house. A good life!

Their only child had been born when they were both forty and deeply set in their ways. They couldn't cope with his youthful rebellion, and he was maddened by their cheerful acceptance of poverty and the way they were tossed about by the decisions of other people.

He was intelligent and shrewd, but did badly at school because academic subjects bored him, except for figures, which he could juggle in his head. He left at the first possible moment and went to work on a building site. Tall and strong for his age, he set himself to master every skill in turn. He was much in demand, and the money was good.

At nineteen he'd fallen for the local beauty, cutting out the opposition with ease and carrying her off. He dazzled her with his looks and strength, and he assumed that the affair must end in marriage. In that sense he was still the child of his conventional background. He'd even bought one of the tiny houses he was helping to build. But the beauty backed off at the prospect of domesticity and was last seen in the passenger seat of a Mercedes owned by the local rich playboy.

The boss offered to buy back the house "for the same sum you paid for it. And that's generous of me, lad, because they're not selling well."

But it was a lie. Mike knew the last ones were selling at three times the price of the first. The country was on the verge of a housing boom, with prices doubling and tripling overnight. He couldn't look that far ahead, but his nose told him to hold on to the house.

That nose was a valuable ally both then and in the years ahead. It sensed the perfect moment to sell and how to invest the three-hundred-per-cent profit in more houses. He grew adept in making quick killings. When he had enough he went to the bank and persuaded them to set him up as a builder. He worked on his own sites, doing everything his men did and doing it better. In five years he was a millionaire, but he tripled that in three more years and went on to diversify. He set up New World Properties, bought historical buildings and converted them into luxury hotels. Sometimes the local conservationists protested at the wreck of their heritage, but there were ways of persuading planning departments to ignore them.

His parents had watched his progress aghast. That had puzzled him. They should have been proud of his success instead of being almost ashamed of him.

"These are homes, son," his mother had said once, "homes for people. You keep talking about units of accommodation."

His mother's distress, in particular, baffled and annoyed him—not hurt him—he was quick to reassure himself of that. But it was exasperating that she simply didn't realize what he'd achieved. Gradually he'd stopped going home.

Now he was the one with the flashy car, complete with telephone and portable computer. With his mathematical brain he was at ease with computers, but he lacked the subtle genius of the true expert. No matter. He'd learned that he could buy anything he wanted, so he bought Hugh Severham. Or so he'd thought.

He'd learned also that a rich man didn't have to marry a woman he wanted, and it was simpler not to. Lois had been different: simply the most beautiful, sophisticated, elusive woman he'd ever known. She'd been a prize, sought after by many men, and as with the earlier beauty he simply cut out the others and claimed her.

Lois had been born to money and had grown up among men with smooth hands and smoother voices. Mike mentally stigmatized them as a load of nancy boys. He knew he was known among her society friends as a rough diamond, a man whose silk suits couldn't mask his blunt ways. But he didn't want to mask them. Bluntness cut through a lot of hassle and time wasting. He'd offered her the biggest diamond she'd ever seen and asked, "Yes or no?" She'd said yes at once. In his pleasure at success he'd forgiven his parents for disappointing him, and made a triumphant visit home to introduce his new fiancée.

But it had fallen flat. The old people were polite but he could tell they didn't like Lois. The sense of strain was almost tangible, and everyone had been glad when the visit ended. Mike had left Valeby in a silent rage, swearing never to return. He'd invited them to his wedding, overriding their gentle reluctance, insisting on sending a car and putting them up at the best hotel in London. So they'd been there when his wedding had ended in humiliation.

The last time he'd seen them had been at his trial; his mother in tears, his father set-faced. They'd looked at him and he'd known what they were thinking: that he'd always been destined for a bad end. The pain of that knowledge had been so shattering that it was only by hardening his heart to flint that he'd been able to deny it. He'd refused to let them visit him in jail, telling himself that Dartmoor was too far for them. The truth was he couldn't have borne it.

Lois had visited him a couple of times, then he'd told her to stay away. Despite her pretty protestations it was clear she thought him guilty. A couple of months later one of the guards had shown him the paper with the news of her wedding to Hugh Severham. He'd cursed her, but then thought drearily, what was the use? What had he expected her to do?

In the past he'd derided the sentimentality of those who resisted his efforts to erase green fields with bricks and concrete. But in prison he'd longed for the sight of natural surroundings instead of iron bars and granite. The old lags told him that there was no escape from Princetown. "If the screws and the dogs don't get you, the moor will,'' they said. He hadn't believed them. Until he'd tried it.

He'd thought of the moor as his friend, hiding him from pursuit. But it had been a pitiless enemy, seeking his life and almost winning.

She had saved him. In his sleepy state she had no name, but was simply the eternal ''she,'' giver of life, bringer of light and warmth. He'd sensed her close to him in the night, driving out the bitter dreams of Lois, enfolding him with comfort. He'd felt the beauty and sweetness of her body next to his: the everlasting woman, lavishing her bounty on him, until the pictures in his head faded to nothing and his sleep became calm and untroubled.

Then his mind cleared and he remembered that her name was Kirsty, and she was a real person. The events of last night came back. She'd tended his fever and stayed with him, even slept beside him to keep him safe. He felt awkward to think how he'd dreamed of her, how real the touch of her naked flesh had felt against his hands. Luckily she need never know, unless . . .

Embarrassment swept him at the thought that it might not have been a dream, that he'd abused her hospitality by forcing caresses on her. Perhaps she'd endured them out of pity for his sickness.

She would be coming in soon and he would see the truth in her face. The next moment he heard her footstep outside the door.

The sight of Kirsty confirmed his worst fears. She looked as if she'd been through some harrowing ordeal that had drained her of strength. Her glorious long black hair was out of sight, hidden beneath a woolen hat that enclosed every lock with forbidding thoroughness. She couldn't have warned him off more clearly, and his

shame grew as he thought he saw accusation in her eyes.
He wanted to run to the ends of the earth, but he could
only lie there while his benefactress stood, pale and
withdrawn, at the end of the bed, obviously preferring
to keep a distance between them. He'd have liked to beg
her forgiveness, but he knew he must follow her lead in
pretending nothing had happened.

"I'm sorry I was stupid enough to get cold again," he
said quietly. "I have no right to cause you so much
trouble." Tentatively he held out a hand to her. "Kirsty, *thank you* sounds so inadequate for all you're doing...."

"Then don't bother saying it," she said brusquely. He
dropped his hand, feeling as though she'd slapped him.

"I've destroyed your uniform," she went on. "I found
this in the pocket." She held out the pieces of the picture and he took it. "I suppose that's Lois?"

"Yes, but—"

"Then it's clear to me what I must do. I should have
thought of it sooner. Give me her phone number and I'll
go into the village and call her. She's the right person to
help you now."

She was anxious to get rid of him quickly, he thought.
"I'm afraid that's no use," he said. "I'd be the last person she wants to hear from. She's Mrs. Hugh Severham
now."

Her face seemed to change as though a ripple passed
across the surface of water, but her expression remained unreadable. He noticed her hands clenching
nervously on the brass knobs at the end of the bed.
"Hugh?" she echoed. "You mean she married your
crooked partner?"

"That's right."

"And that's why you tore her picture up—because you hate her?"

Suddenly he understood what she was afraid of. She thought if he'd turned against Lois he would be making more advances to her. He hastened to reassure her. "I thought I did, but then I got to thinking and realized I couldn't really blame her. Ten years is a long time." He was talking urgently, trying to clear away any mutual awkwardness.

She gave a thin smile. "So for you, Lois is still—?"

"I remember her as a lovely lady, and I don't hate her," he said quickly.

"You'd better look after the picture. I'll get your breakfast."

She departed quickly, leaving him with a feeling of relief. He'd done his best to put her mind at rest.

Mike slept and ate his way through the next three days. Kirsty came to his room only when necessary, and then she wouldn't approach him if she could avoid it. He hated lying there, feeling useless, but he obeyed her orders, feeling it was the least he could do.

One morning he awoke feeling well again. Pulling a curtain quietly aside he saw that a gray misty dawn was creeping over the moor. He could hear the creak of a bucket, followed by the murmur of her voice and some clucking that meant she was feeding the hens.

He went into the bathroom and splashed water onto his face. He was longing for a bath, but hadn't dared try it before in case his weakness returned and he needed her help to get out. Now, still leaving the lights out for safety, he ran the water. It felt blissfully good as he sank into it.

By the time he returned to his room Kirsty was there. "I had a bath," he explained. "I thought I'd get up today. Is there something else I could wear?"

"You'll find my husband's clothes in the wardrobe," she said and left the room.

Inside the wardrobe were a couple of cheap suits, one looking as if it might have been kept for "best," and several pairs of trousers that appeared shabby but recently cleaned. The shirts were the same. He appeared downstairs a few minutes later, wearing a nondescript sweater and corduroy trousers. "I resisted the temptation to shave," he said, feeling his chin that now had a week's growth of black beard.

"Good. Let's hope your hair grows soon," she said, not taking her attention from the stove.

"I hope it isn't too painful for you, seeing me in these clothes," he said. "He obviously hasn't been dead very long."

"My husband has been dead for a year."

He gasped. A year, and she still had all his clothes and small possessions. What sort of man had he been to keep his wife's devotion for so long?

"Now that I'm up, I'd like to help around this place until I go," he said as she brought the eggs to the table.

"You can't leave the house yet. It's too cold and you might be seen."

"Then I'll cook. I'll do the housework. My mother taught me to cook and clean. She said I'd need it in case no woman was daft enough to marry me."

"Fine. If you can do the chores I'll have more time for the farm."

"Was your husband any good at housework?" he ventured.

"He was neat. He'd grown up in a small caravan. Apart from that he didn't understand about housework."

"A caravan?"

"He was a Gypsy."

"Then—this wasn't his farm?"

"No, it was mine—if that's important."

Her tone was a clear discouragement, but he pressed on. "I'm not trying to pry—just to be friendly, and understand you."

"You don't need to understand me," she said quietly. "I told you—no questions."

Soon afterward she got ready to go out to work. "Is there much for you to do at this time of year?" Mike asked.

"I have the sheep to see to. And the ponies must be fed."

"Why, if they're wild? Isn't that a waste of good animal feed?"

"They may seem wild but they all belong to someone. In spring the farmers round them up and sell the best. They're usually quite small and placid, and they make ideal first mounts for young children."

He frowned. "But if they're running free, how do you make sure you only feed your own and not someone else's?"

"You don't. You can't. I don't care about that as long as they don't go hungry. Nor do the other farmers."

"But isn't it very uneconomic?"

"Yes, very." She added pointedly, "About as uneconomic as feeding stray creatures I find in the barn."

"Touché. Don't get mad at me. I was only thinking of your interests."

"You're a town man," Kirsty said, as if she were describing an alien from another planet.

"Meaning I don't understand country ways?"

"Meaning you don't understand *Dartmoor* ways." She put on her coat. "I'll be in at lunchtime. See what you can do with beans on toast."

From the window Mike watched her in the yard, pitchforking the hay onto the rear of the tractor. She managed the weight with ease and grace, and he became fascinated by the twisting movements of her slender frame as she dipped and tossed, dipped and tossed. Even in such a mundane activity it seemed she was incapable of being awkward or clumsy.

Then she turned and saw him watching her, and the look she gave him contained so much accusation that he drew back quickly, feeling as if he'd been caught spying on her nakedness.

A little while later she drove out of the yard and vanished from sight into the whiteness of the moor. He shivered, remembering his days lost in that freezing wilderness. It seemed impossible that he would ever see her again. But at lunchtime she returned, cheerful.

In a very short time the incredible became the mundane. Mike repaid his hostess in the only way open to him—by trying to make her life easier, with varying degrees of success. He wasn't the cook he fancied himself, but as long as he kept his dishes simple Kirsty managed to eat them. It was when he became adventurous that things fell apart. His attempt at goulash was fit only for Tarn. The dog fell on it with joy, and thereafter pestered every night for further treats. He plainly preferred Mike's failed experiments to Kirsty's carefully measured and healthy offerings.

When she wasn't there he warded off boredom by becoming an efficient housekeeper. He had a neat mind, which was offended by Kirsty's slapdash domestic arrangements, and within a few days she was complaining that she could never find anything because he was forever putting things away. But she admitted that the house had never looked so tidy.

Encouraged, he began a massive spring cleaning. Since he never did anything by halves he became lost in his work and was only just finishing when he heard her returning after a day's work. He opened the nearest drawer and pushed the contents aside to make room for some odds and ends. But the movement disclosed two pieces of paper lying at the bottom. One of them was a marriage certificate between Jack Trennon and Kirsty Wade.

Kirsty had never told him her surname. Now he felt there was something familiar about it, but the memory remained elusive. The other paper was Jack Trennon's death certificate. Mike glanced at it, meaning to put it away, but the words *Princetown Gaol* caught his eye. Stunned, he read the rest.

Jack Trennon had died of a heart attack in Princetown Gaol a year ago. Suddenly Mike remembered hearing about a prisoner who'd died just before he himself had arrived, a man who'd murdered his wife's lover. They'd said the wife was a slut who had every man in the district lusting for her and knew it...and enjoyed it. One of the other prisoners came from the locality and had seen her. "Ripe and ready for it," had been his coarse description. The consensus was that the husband had done the murder, but the guilty one had been the woman who drove him to it. And now, with a groan, Mike recalled the man's name: Jack Trennon.

The discovery that his savior was the same woman whose adultery had brought tragedy on two men made him want to bellow a protest to the heavens. But the next moment his mind cleared and Kirsty's face came before him, defensive and unhappy, but not backing away from the risk of saving him. He thought of her lonely life, the way she'd come out to the barn that first night with a gun, her only protection. She didn't fit the picture. She must be the same woman, but something was all wrong.

"How dare you."

Kirsty's furious voice broke into his reverie and in the next moment she'd snatched the paper from his hand and confronted him, eyes blazing. "How dare you pry into my private affairs," she raged.

"I wasn't. I found it by accident."

"You were studying it," she accused.

"Only because I recognized the name of the jail."

"And now you know more than you've any right to."

"Does it matter?" he prevaricated. "I'm hardly likely to care that he was a convict—"

"He wasn't a convict," she flashed. "He was never convicted of anything. He was never even tried. A trial would have found him not guilty."

Mike cursed himself, realizing that there were gaps in his knowledge. "I'm sorry. The story I heard was pretty confused, and I dare say most of it was wrong. Let's forget it."

But she seized his wrist, gripping him so tight that she hurt him. *"The story you heard,"* she echoed, wild-eyed. "What did you hear?"

"Nothing—I don't remember. It was a long time ago."

"What did you hear?" she asked through gritted teeth. "Or needn't I ask?"

"I expect they got most of it wrong," he said desperately, knowing he was making it worse with every word. "Prisoners gossip because there isn't much else to do. Details get magnified."

"And I'll bet I got magnified into a cheap slut, didn't I?" she demanded. "A woman who slept around and drove her husband to commit murder. That's what they said of me, isn't it? *Isn't it?*"

Dumbly he nodded his head. He would have liked the ground to open and swallow him up. Kirsty was looking at him as if he'd struck her. He could still see faint traces of the real blow he'd given her the first night, and he knew that what he'd done now was a thousand times worse.

Kirsty felt as if the world had spun violently on its axis, shaking her off into a void. This man was beholden to her, at her mercy. His opinion of her as a woman shouldn't matter. But it did. The thought that he'd heard every filthy slander about her was unendurable. With shaking hands she took Jack's death certificate from him. "If you're well enough to pry into my affairs, you're well enough to leave," she said in a dead voice. "I want you to go at once."

"Now? In broad daylight?"

"I want you out of my house." She pulled open a drawer, snatched out some money and thrust it at him. He backed sharply away.

"You can't think I'd really take that?" he demanded.

"You have to. If you get caught in my husband's clothes I'm in trouble, too. Take it and get as far away as you can. Do me that favor."

Very pale, he took the money. They both knew he had no alternative. Watching his face, Kirsty knew a bitter satisfaction. Let him know what shame felt like. Then he'd feel what he'd done to her. "There's a heavy coat hanging upstairs," she said. "Take it."

His mouth tightened but he turned away without a word. Kirsty watched him go upstairs, feeling as though she were dying. But she wouldn't flinch from this. She told herself that the past year had hardened her to flint, and she was glad of it. She made her way slowly to the door.

Then her eyes widened with horror as she saw two policemen approaching the entrance to the yard. Any second now Mike would be coming downstairs. There was no time to think. She grabbed her shotgun and raced out into the yard, yelling at the top of her voice, *"Clear off out of it."* The policemen stiffened, but Kirsty checked herself sharply and lowered the gun, saying, "Oh, it's you. Sorry. I thought it was someone after my hens. I've had that much trouble . . ."

The younger of the two men looked sternly puritanical, with a cold stare that made shivers of apprehension go through Kirsty. The older one, whose manner was more genial, was called Barker, and she'd seen him around before. Barker greeted her politely and introduced his colleague as Constable Stourbridge. "We've had no luck with this escaped convict," he explained, "so the force has called in some help." Kirsty had the impression he wasn't pleased about it.

"Why come and ask me?" she demanded belligerently. "It's obvious what's happened to that feller, isn't it?"

"What do you mean by that remark?" Stourbridge asked coldly. He had a town accent that Kirsty instinctively disliked. She knew his kind. He would expect a country bumpkin, so she would give him one.

"Well, he's dead, isn't he?" she demanded, broadening her speech. "Been out there a week. You'll find the body when the snow clears in spring. It's my hens I'm worried about. Two of them gone missing."

"Do you have a permit for that thing?" Stourbridge interrupted, eyeing the shotgun.

"'Course I do. And my Dad before me. And his before him. And—"

"Kirsty's family has farmed this land for years," Barker put in quickly. "The gun permits have always been in order."

"Nevertheless I should like to see—"

"What are you gonna do about my hens?" Kirsty shouted.

Unwisely Stourbridge allowed himself to be provoked to retort, "They've probably been taken by a fox and it's nothing to do with..."

"Ah, but who says it were a fox? Who says it ain't a hen thief? Tell me that."

"Have you heard any disturbances?"

"Course I have. Four nights ago. Clucking summat dreadful. But nowt to see when I get out there. 'Cept a few feathers lyin' around."

"It could be our man," Stourbridge mused. "Four nights ago."

"What would he want with my hens?" Kirsty demanded. "Can't cook 'em, can he?"

"Were there any tracks in the snow?" Stourbridge asked intently.

"How could there be? Snow's a mess since I took the tractor up to feed my stock."

"Then you've no idea what direction the culprit may have taken?"

"I never saw no culprit," Kirsty responded with heavy sarcasm. "Just a hole where two hens should have been, and I'm telling you—"

"That'll do," Stourbridge snapped. "You should have reported this at the time."

"What? 'Cause a couple of hens went missing?" Kirsty queried, gazing at him stupidly. "If every time—"

"Quite," Barker interrupted hastily. It was plain that nightmare visions of paperwork about missing fowls were dancing before him. "If it was Stallard he'll be far away by now, but my guess is that it was foxes." He began to urge a reluctant Stourbridge toward their car.

"Wait," Kirsty yelled after them.

Stourbridge looked back eagerly. "Yes?"

"If you see a couple of hens..."

Barker got his colleague into the car practically by force and drove off hurriedly. Kirsty watched until they were out of sight before doubling up over the gun, a prey to the first attack of hysteria in her entire life. Her heart was pounding with fright, and the laughter that bubbled up inside her was like screaming. Mike found her like that a moment later.

"Kirsty...are you all right?" he asked anxiously, leaning down to take hold of her.

She straightened up, choking with mirth. "His face...did you see his face...?"

"No, but I heard everything. You were wonderful. I thought it was all up with us."

"So did I—but when I said about the hens..." She collapsed against him, shaking with laughter.

"Let's get inside quickly." He steered her into the house and shut the door firmly behind them. "All right, let it out," he said, putting his arms about her and steadying her against his chest while she shook with sobs of laughter. "You've put up with more than any woman should be asked to take." Now that his own apprehension was passing he managed a grin. "I guess it was pretty funny at that."

"I was so afraid you'd appear..." she gasped. "All I could think of was to yell 'Clear off,' and hope you'd understand."

"I did. I just froze where I was. You were terrific the way you tackled them."

"They think I'm mad," she said, "or stupid, or both." This seemed terribly funny and she went off again into gales of laughter. Mike looked at her with concern.

"Hey, come on," he said, hearing the hysterical edge. "Try to calm down now." He stroked her head, trying to soothe her, and his movements dislodged the hat. He pulled it off, feeling her silky hair stream over his hands. The touch of his fingers seemed to get through to her, for she looked up into his face. She was still shaking uncontrollably, but although the sounds coming from her mouth sounded like laughter, tears were pouring down her cheeks.

"It's all right," Mike said softly, taking her face between his hands. "It's over now. You were wonderful, the way you thought fast and didn't lose your nerve. You kept me safe again."

"Yes," she whispered, "safe... safe..."

He couldn't bear the distress in her wild eyes. With no thought but to calm and comfort her he bent his head and laid his mouth gently over hers.

He heard her give a gasp, and drew back to look down at her. The hysteria had gone and now her face showed plainly the strain of her ordeal. Her body was trembling against his, and suddenly all his good resolutions drained

away and desire leapt up to take their place. "Kirsty,"
he muttered in a voice that was suddenly thick and
husky. *"Kirsty..."*

He thought she whispered yes, but he couldn't be sure
because his mouth was over hers again, tasting the tears
on her lips. A surge of protectiveness mingled with his
passion. She'd endured so much for him, and he had so
little to offer back, only the warmth of his arms and the
homage of his lips.

She was quite still as he explored her mouth. But it
wasn't a passive stillness. Rather it was as if she was
yielding to his kiss with silent wonder, letting him carry
her along.

Kirsty scarcely knew what was happening to her. She'd
been racked by pain, then by fear, and somehow her
courage had endured. But now the danger was tempo-
rarily over she had neither strength nor energy left. She
was shocked at how close she'd come to abandoning
Mike to his fate. All she wanted now was the reassur-
ance of his arms about her, the warmth of his body
against hers, and the knowledge that he was still safe.
The touch of his lips sent scurries of delight through her.
"Mike..." she whispered, "I didn't mean it. Promise
you won't go. I don't want anything to happen to you."

"I ought to go. I'm only a danger to you."

For answer she clung to him, drawing his mouth down
to hers. It was true. He was a danger to her, but not the
kind he meant. The danger lay in the desires he could
kindle in her, desire that she feared because of the de-
struction she seemed to wreak on men. She knew she
should push him away, but the need to hold him was too
strong, driving out all other instincts. It was sweet to
caress his mouth with her own and feel his lips move in
answer. It was sweeter still to feel his tongue seeking en-

try, exploring her, inflaming her with erotic sensations that burst upon her as a wondrous revelation.

She thought of the other night when he had touched her naked skin, and longed for him to do the same now. She wanted to touch him in return, exploring the wonder of a man's body when it was vibrant with desire for her.

But a change was coming over him. She was aware of a tremor that racked his frame, and then she felt herself being gently but firmly pushed backward. He was breathing hard and his hands clenched and unclenched convulsively on her shoulders. "Dear God, what am I doing?" he said harshly. "I'm sorry, Kirsty. I'm behaving unforgivably, but I never meant to insult you, I swear it."

"Insult—?"

"All those stories about you. I told you I didn't believe them, and here I am acting as if they were true, as if you were any man's for the taking and I had only to—" he wrenched himself away from her. "Try to believe that I'm ashamed of myself. After all you've done for me I should have had the decency to show you more respect—"

"Respect," she whispered, in a daze. The last thing she wanted from him was cold respect. She wanted him to strip her naked, carry her to bed and claim her willing body again and again. He'd roused passion in her, and only he could teach her how to rejoice in it. Instead he proposed to drive that passion back into its lonely lair, crushing and stunting it with respect.

"Mike—please—" she began, but he stopped her.

"You don't need to say it. I insulted you once today without meaning to, but I'm not going to do it again. I want us to forget that this ever happened. Please Kirsty, do you think you can bring yourself to forget?''

It was on the tip of her tongue to tell him everything that was in her heart, but she forced herself not to. What good would it do when she knew the real reason for his sudden self-control? Not respect for her, but memories of Lois and perhaps hopes for a future with her. She took a step back from Mike and surveyed him with her head up.

''Of course,'' she said bleakly. ''I've forgotten already. You're quite right. It's better this way.''

Chapter Four

As the snow melted the day drew nearer when Mike would be well enough to leave. It was nearly two weeks since his arrival, and their luck had held. There had been no more calls from the police or anyone else.

The lower part of his face was now covered with stubble that matched the inky blackness of his hair and turned his eyes an astonishing blue. As they sat together in the evenings, Kirsty had to struggle not to look at him, but when she thought he wouldn't notice, her gaze would always creep in his direction. There was a kind of bitter pleasure to be found in contemplating the sensual lines of his lips, his shapely hands and hard, lean body that filled out and grew stronger every day.

Through him she had discovered desire, and now, through him, she was discovering frustration. These days he never deviated from his resolve to treat her with respect, never touched her if he could help it. But he couldn't prevent the sound of his deep voice from thrilling through her, or her flesh aching for the lack of him.

She wondered if this was what it meant to be in love, but she felt something vital was missing. Love implied a tenderness of the heart such as had softened Will's voice whenever he spoke of Kirsty's dead mother. The bond she'd felt with Mike from the first wasn't tenderness, but a kinship of suffering. They were both outcasts, neither of them bound by loyalty to a society that had condemned them. No, she assured herself, she wasn't in love with him. Her body had been overcome with inexplicable madness. When he was gone she would return to her calm self. And so the sooner he left, the better.

Then he would address some commonplace remark to her, and the sound of his voice saying her name would make her heart thump. And she would wonder how a woman could ever recover from madness like this.

"I'm going to Ollershaw," she said to him one morning. "The local paper comes out today, and we can find out what they're saying about you. Then I think you should leave tonight. The snow could start again at any moment."

Ollershaw was little more than a hamlet, with no more than fifty dwellings. It had one church, one pub and one shop, called Fowler's, which sold a little of everything and doubled as a post office. Kirsty traveled in the cab of the tractor, which she parked on a patch of common land just outside Ollershaw, and headed for Fowler's.

She was dismayed to see Terry Fowler behind the counter. He was nineteen, a spotty, slack-mouthed youth who always tried to keep her talking while he eyed her with prurient curiosity. "I'll take my mail," she said, pointing to the pigeon hole where she could see one letter. "And I'll have the local paper."

"T'ain't ready yet," he observed.

"It's Thursday. It should have arrived."

"Oh yeah. S'arrived. But we ain't undone them yet. Do that s'afternoon."

"I can't come all the way back this afternoon," she protested.

"No need. I'll bring it out to your place." His moist pale eyes lingered over her, and she flinched.

"Please don't bother," she said crisply.

"No bother. Must be lonely out there." His mouth twisted into an awful parody of a suggestive smile. "Specs you'd like the company."

Kirsty was used to the implication that she was desperate for a man, but now it disgusted her even more than usual. She glared at Terry, but what saved her was the arrival of Mrs. Fowler, oozing frosty respectability. "Something wrong?" she demanded.

"Terry was just telling me the local paper wasn't ready," Kirsty informed her. "He kindly offered to bring it out to my home."

As she had expected, this produced results. "Get it now," Mrs. Fowler snapped at her son, moving so that she was between them.

At another time Kirsty might have derived grim amusement from the idea that she threatened the virtue of such an unappealing specimen. Today she just wanted to get home quickly. She turned away, opening her letter for the sake of something to do, although she'd recognized the logo on the envelope and knew what the contents would be. She glanced over them with distaste.

"Weather's been bad," Mrs. Fowler observed.

"Very nasty," Kirsty agreed.

"Must be hard out there alone."

"I manage, thank you."

"But how much longer? My brother would make you a fair offer for the place."

"I've already turned him down."

"Folks is asking how long you can keep going with everyone against you. You'll sell in the end."

Kirsty's eyes glinted. "Well perhaps I will, Mrs. Fowler. But it won't be to any of the folk around here who've persecuted me. I can get a better price anyday from these people." She showed the letter.

"'F. Colley & Son,'" Mrs. Fowler read. "Who might they be?"

"Property developers. They want to buy Everdene and turn it into a hotel and 'Dartmoor Theme Park,' Nice, eh?" she added as she saw Mrs. Fowler swelling like a turkey.

"You wouldn't. You was born and bred in these parts. You wouldn't do that to the place."

"Wouldn't I? Don't ask me to be neighborly. Who's been neighborly to me? Spread the word. If I get any more hassle I'll sell out to Colley and leave the rest of you to cope with whoever moves in." She was bluffing. She would die before she sold Everdene, but the bluff might buy her a little peace.

"What's more," she went on, "the next time your son fancies himself as Casanova, tell him I—" her voice faded as something caught her eye. She reached down, pulled out a national paper from the rack and studied the name that seemed to leap out at her. Her heart began to thump with dismay.

"Here's the local," Terry said, returning.

Kirsty took it from him quickly, paid for both papers and dashed out of the shop, leaving mother and son staring at each other. She ran all the way to the tractor and got home as fast as she could.

"What's wrong?" Mike demanded as soon as he saw her face.

"What was the name of that computer expert you were counting on?"

"Con Dawlish. Why?"

"Is that him?" She showed him the paper, the front page bearing a picture of a man with a gentle face and a shock of white hair. He was in a wheelchair, being pushed along a corridor by a woman in nurse's uniform. The article read:

Con Dawlish, the computer whiz whose mischievous exploits have delighted the public while being less delightful to the force of law and order, on his way to the States for a critical heart operation. It is rumored that an international financier, grateful for Mr. Dawlish's exposure of flaws in his system, is picking up the tab.

"No," shouted Mike, hurling the paper across the room. "No."

"Mike, please," Kirsty begged. "I know it looks bad but—"

"Bad? Con was my one hope, and he's gone." Mike slammed both fists down on the dresser, slammed them again and again in helpless, frustrated rage. But he stopped and sat down wearily on the sofa, looking as if there was no strength left in him anymore.

"He'll be back when he's better," Kirsty argued. "It's just a question of time."

He groaned in despair. "How much time do I have? Even if Con recovers, it could be months. And if he doesn't . . ." He dropped his head into his hands.

She sank onto her knees beside him, enfolding him in her arms. "Mike...Mike..." she didn't know what else to say. He was deep in an agony that she couldn't reach although her whole soul reached out to him. This was what it felt like to love someone, to feel his pain as acutely as her own, to know that nothing in the world mattered except making things right for him. But she couldn't tell him of the feelings that overflowed her heart, so she only whispered his name over and over, her cheek resting against his tousled dark hair.

"I'm finished," he whispered. "I've no hope left now."

"That's not true," she said quickly. "You've got me, Mike. And as long as you've got me, you've got hope."

"I can't run you into any more danger by staying here. I must go."

"No," she cried fiercely. "That would be like giving up, and I won't let you do that. We're going to find a way, even if you have to hide here for months. They're not going to get you, I promise."

He looked at her as if seeing a revelation. "Where do you get your courage from, Kirsty? I thought I had plenty, but you put me to shame."

"It doesn't need courage, it just needs common sense," she said in a rallying tone. "This is the perfect hiding place, and as winter gets worse you'll be even safer. They probably think you're dead by now. Don't you see? We have everything going for us."

He managed a faint smile. "Everything going for us. Only you could have said that in the face of disaster."

"Disaster is a banned word from now on," she said. "So is *defeat, losing, finished* and anything else that means the same."

"Kirsty, it's easy for me to take risks. I have nothing to lose, but you—"

"I have nothing to lose, either," she said simply.

"That's not true and we both know it."

If only she could tell him how completely it *was* true; true in a way that hadn't been so ten minutes earlier. As she knelt beside him, trying to shoulder his burdens, she'd discovered the vital missing "something" that was love. The passionate identification with a man, the certainty that if things could be made to go well for him, nothing could be wrong in all the world. That was love. And so was the discovery that she would endure any suffering if only he need not suffer.

"You have a lot to lose," Mike was saying, "including your freedom if you're caught sheltering me. And if you went to prison you'd lose Everdene. *Think* what you're doing, Kirsty."

Her freedom, her beloved farm. Once they'd been important. Now only he was important. "I have thought," she said. "It's too late to turn back now."

"Then, if you're prepared to do this for me, what can I say but a humble thank you?" He cupped her raised face gently between his palms. Kirsty held her breath at the sweetness of that touch, feeling her heart thumping madly. Surely he could see her newly awakened love glowing in her eyes, telling him more than words could ever do? She felt joy grow within her as he leaned down and touched her lips with his own. "Kirsty," he said softly.

"Yes ... yes ..."

"There's something I want to tell you, and you must listen carefully because it's very important. If we're to live under the same roof for a while there must be no secrets or hidden feelings."

She nodded, unable to speak. In a few moments she would be in his arms, giving back passion for passion, discovering the glory of love. "Tell me," she begged.

"It's just this—I want you to know that I'll never abuse your hospitality. I kissed you just now because it was the only way I could think of to show my gratitude and admiration. But that's the last time, I promise. We'll be brother and sister, and I swear I'll never lay a finger on you."

Disappointment was like a blow over the heart. Brother and sister. That was *his* wish, but he was projecting it onto her. His eyes were warm and kind, but she could see in them no trace of the feeling that suffused her.

"You do trust me to keep my distance, don't you?" he asked anxiously. "Say you do, or I can't stay."

"Yes, Mike, I trust you. Brother and sister. That's the way it will be." She got to her feet, moving like an automaton. To have her love rejected within a few minutes of its birth was a pain she would grow used to, but just now she needed time alone. She hurried out of the room.

Next day Mike surprised her by getting downstairs ahead of her. "Tea," he said, pressing a mug onto her.

She accepted it gratefully, but said, "What are you doing up? It's barely six o'clock."

"If you can get up at this unearthly hour, so can I. If I'm to stay we must work out a way I can help you."

"But you already do."

"I mean more than housework and cooking. I mean—" Mike floundered as his ignorance of farm work caught up with him "—pigs . . . and hens . . . and things," he finished lamely. "All right, laugh." For

Kirsty was chuckling delightedly into her tea. "But you keep a lot of animals close to the house. I can feed them."

"And clean them out?" she asked innocently.

"Whatever is necessary," he said manfully. "I found a jacket with a hood upstairs. If I wear that and stay in the area of the yard it's safe enough."

She thought hard. "All right," she said at last, "but it'll be much harder than you think."

He looked offended. "I'm used to manual work."

"I thought you were a businessman."

"That was lately. Look," he showed her his hands. "They're builder's hands. That's how I started. Just show me the work."

"Fine. I'll be down in a moment."

When she was dressed, she led him out of the front door, did a sharp left turn and straight in by another door. "This is a traditional Dartmoor longhouse," she explained. "Humans one side, animals the other. There used to be a connecting door but my grandfather bricked it up, so now we go around the long way. I don't actually keep animals in here anymore, but I use it to store feed."

He helped her load some into a wheelbarrow and trundled it across the yard to the barn where the pigs lived. He couldn't help sniffing the air as they went in, and Kirsty immediately said, "Put aside your prejudices about pigs. They're actually very clean animals. They have mud baths in summer simply to keep cool. It's just like you having that shower."

"I'll take your word for it."

She laughed. "That's Etta, that's Cora, that's Hanna."

"You give them *names?*"

"You have a name, don't you?"

"But I'm an individual."

"So are they. They're as different as people. Hanna's the greedy one, Cora's the maternal one, her litters are always twice as big as the others, and Etta is the affectionate one. Aren't you, my pet?" As if in answer one of the huge pink animals had advanced to have her head rubbed. "She loves this," Kirsty said, obliging. "But don't worry. You won't have to do it. Just feed her."

He watched her running her hand over the massive head as if petting a dog. She was completely unself-conscious, and her face was alight with tender affection. This was a new Kirsty, he realized. There seemed to be dozens of them.

"If they're individuals to you, how do you ever manage to eat them or sell them?"

"I don't. I just sell the piglets. They farrow twice a year."

"If they're individuals, how come you don't house them better?" Mike asked, regarding the sty with a builder's eye.

"It was built in rather a hurry and never properly finished," Kirsty said in a strained voice.

"By your husband?"

"No, by..." she stopped abruptly. "You're quite right. It needs rebuilding before I call the boar walker again."

"I take it that the boar walker—" Mike stopped delicately.

"Brings the boar," Kirsty explained. "Without a boar there'd be no piglets and no need for a farrowing sty."

"It's a whole new language to me." He sighed. "The only word I understood was *build*. I'll start today."

"You?"

"Well, I'm a builder. I ought to be able to manage a sty."

"Make sure you put a low rail around the sides. It gives the piglets somewhere to escape when Mum rolls over, otherwise they get flattened."

He applied himself to the problem, producing a series of designs that made Kirsty chuckle. "When I was putting up houses I always started off with a proper plan," he pointed out. "Are Etta, Cora and Hanna entitled to any less?"

"Certainly not," she agreed at once.

Mike went to work with a will, and within a short time the pigs were housed in deluxe accommodation. There was a deep satisfaction in working with his hands again, and an even deeper satisfaction in doing something for Kirsty.

He wondered about the little slip she'd made and the way she'd caught herself up. He hoped she would let her guard slip again, because he wanted to understand her. Her magical sensuality and beauty, so determinedly hidden away from men's eyes, her defiance of a hostile world and her air of being complete in herself—these things made her more intriguing than any woman he had ever known. For all her strength and self-sufficiency, she aroused in him a powerful urge to take care of her. He couldn't voice it, for fear of a rebuff, but he tried to show it by quietly doing everything she asked of him. In a short time there wasn't a wall to be repaired, a gate that didn't shut or a window that needed fixing anywhere on the place. But though he waited hopefully, she kept a strict guard on her tongue, and he began to think he would never be allowed to glimpse her private thoughts again.

He spent a day lying low in his room while the boar walker came and went. Almost at once the weather closed in again. Kirsty worked tirelessly outdoors while he fretted at his inability to lighten her heaviest loads. As Christmas approached the days grew ever shorter until it was dark at four in the afternoon. Mike nailed blankets over the lower windows and worked by the light of a small reading lamp, so that he could have a hot supper ready the instant she returned.

On Christmas Eve she warned him she would be later than usual. "I have to take something to the ponies, and I'm going to church on my way home."

"Don't go," he said protectively. "I hate to think of your neighbors being unkind to you."

She smiled. "Don't worry. It's the season of good will."

As soon as she'd gone he got to work on the surprise he'd been planning for some days. When evening came he listened anxiously for the sound of the tractor, and when he heard it he went to open the front door and welcome her in. "Was it all right?"

"Fine. Nobody disturbed me," she said cheerfully, and he understood at once that she'd sat alone and ignored in the church. He felt a kind of rage for her, but Kirsty's face was calm and content, as though she were at peace with herself. It was a kind of peace he had never known.

"Come inside," he said, drawing her into the warm.

As soon as she entered the kitchen she grew still, looking about her in wonder. After a long moment her silence began to worry him. "Is it all right? I found the decorations at the bottom of the wardrobe. You never said anything about them, so I wasn't sure—"

"They haven't been used since my father died," she said, gazing in rapture at the paper chains that hung from the ceiling. "I made that one when I was a little girl. I thought it had fallen to bits."

"I found some glue and mended it." He regarded her tenderly as she went around the room touching things gently, and something in the childlike wonder in her face gave him a pain in his heart. She had so little, and even that little was threatened by his presence, yet she had shared with him unstintingly.

"My grandfather created that glittery thing," she told him, pointing high. "I was five years old and I thought it was magic. He held me up to look at it—we had such Christmases in those days—such Christmases—" Suddenly she couldn't speak anymore.

"Come and get warm." He rubbed her hands between his.

Kirsty let herself be ministered to, carried away with delight and the warmth and care with which he surrounded her. How different, she thought, from her last Christmas, her first as an outcast. For a brief moment she thought how delightful it would be if she could keep Mike hiding here forever, but the next moment she castigated herself for being selfish.

When they were sitting on opposite sides of the stove, with Tarn curled up on her feet, Mike said tentatively, "Didn't you ever put decorations up when your husband was alive?"

"He thought it was a waste of time," Kirsty said. "What Christmas meant to him was meeting his mates in the pub. Once, when we'd been married about four years, I reminded him that Christmas was supposed to be for families. And he said—he said, 'Well, where's our family, then?' He wanted children, and he blamed me for being barren. Perhaps he was right."

"Who says you're barren?" he demanded indignantly.

"There's more than one way of being barren, Mike. I gave him nothing in my heart, and he knew that."

She was saying more than she'd meant to say, but the warmth from the stove and the sweetness of being cared for relaxed her and smoothed the rough edges of her consciousness away. As if in a dream she went on, "I meant to be a good wife, but I never was one. I didn't know what he really wanted, so how could I give it to him?"

Looking at her in the soft glow from the stove, her body stretched out on the oak settle, her curved mouth soft and gentle, her face lit by melancholy reflection, Mike knew what Jack must have wanted, because he wanted it himself. The prize was this woman's passion, but neither of them had known how to kindle it, and the yearning was an invitation to madness. Just how crazy had Jack Trennon become. Enough to kill?

"What happened, Kirsty?" he asked gently.

She turned drowsy eyes on him. "Is it so important? Very well, then. I'll tell you. Peter Mullery happened. I didn't understand him, either. He talked poetry and a lot of nonsense to me, but I thought he was fooling. I didn't know the difference, you see—" She broke off and stared at the bars of the fire.

"And then?" He was almost holding his breath.

"Jack misunderstood. I told him nothing had happened, that Peter didn't mean anything to me, but he didn't believe me. They had a fight in the pub, and Jack followed him out onto the moors. He didn't come home all night, and the next morning Peter was found dead.

Jack swore he hadn't done it, but nobody believed him, except me and Caleb.''

"Who's Caleb?"

"Jack's cousin. He's a kind of brother to me, and I don't know what I'd have done without him.''

"Then where's he been all this time?"

"He's one of the traveling people. Jack was, too, but he was ready to settle down. Caleb will never settle down. I understand why he had to go, but it left me with no one to talk to. I've come to feel that in a sort of way I may have been guilty. If it weren't for me, Jack and Peter wouldn't have been fighting...''

"But if you don't think Jack killed him ...?"

"I don't—at least ... I don't know..." Kirsty twisted her hands as she tried to voice the terrible thought, "I didn't think so at the time, but someone must have done it, and Jack had a cruel temper. I don't believe he meant to kill Peter, but if they were fighting he may have done it by accident ... how will I ever know?''

Mike shook his head helplessly, unable to answer it. It seemed to her unanswerable.

"If only he'd trusted me," she said in a whisper. "I'd never looked at another man, and Jack knew it. He should have trusted me.''

"Some people find it hard to trust," he said. "It has nothing to do with the other person. It's just a kind of caution about the whole world.''

"Perhaps I'm too trusting," she reflected with a melancholy smile. "I trusted you when a sensible woman wouldn't have.''

"I'm glad you're not a sensible woman.''

She sighed. "But it wasn't just Jack. The others, too, our neighbors, people I'd thought were my friends. They all turned against me, and I don't know why.''

She said the last words like a forlorn child, and Mike felt a painful stirring of his heart. He didn't know how to answer. He couldn't say to this unhappy woman that she carried a quality about her that would always inspire fear and distrust in some, and obsession and desire in others. He understood it all too well. But that was a subject that couldn't be touched on between them, and especially tonight, when she'd opened her heart to him, offering him her own trust, which he would die for rather than betray.

While he was pondering these thoughts, a sound made him look quickly across to her. He smiled as he saw that she'd solved his problem by falling asleep.

He touched her gently and drew her to her feet. Arms entwined they climbed the stairs, and at the door to her room he kissed her cheek and said good-night. He felt as if he'd been through a wringer.

That night he slept with the curtains open and was wakened by the moonlight on his face. Getting up he looked out on the pitiless landscape and shuddered, thinking of what his fate might have been in that frozen waste. But for her.

He reached into the wardrobe and took out the gift he had made for her. It was a workbox, created from leftover bits of wood, planed and polished to beauty. He'd made it in secret, working on it when she was gone and hiding it when she returned. Now he thought of another way to surprise her.

He made his way quietly down the corridor and stopped outside her room, frowning as he listened. From inside was coming the sound of jerky little cries. Mike hesitated a long time. If she was having a bad dream he knew he should go away and respect her privacy, but he also knew he couldn't leave her in distress. At last he opened the bedroom door.

Kirsty was lying on her back, her eyes closed. The sounds that broke from her throat were like nothing he'd ever heard before, but they made him think of an animal in a trap. He laid the box on her bedside table and sat on the bed, taking her shoulders in his hands. "Kirsty," he said, shaking her gently, "Kirsty..."

Either his touch or his voice seemed to calm her, for the terrible cries ceased and she lay still, but without waking. In the moonlight he could just see a faint glisten of moisture on her face, and when he touched her cheek he found it damp. He cursed himself for resurrecting her nightmare.

She turned suddenly. The pajama jacket, too large for her slim frame, slithered away, leaving one white, beautiful shoulder exposed. Mike drew the jacket across to protect her from the cold, and his fingers brushed her skin. It was like silk, and suddenly he was swept by a surge of desire so powerful that he had to hold himself tense against it. For a moment he couldn't breathe with the violence of his longing to draw the material back and lay his lips against that perfect skin. He knew he mustn't yield to temptation while she was vulnerable, must go away right now. But he had no energy to leave. It took all his strength simply to sit there and fight for self-control.

And he only half managed it. He could control his hands but not his thoughts, which stripped away her clothes to reveal the long, beautiful frame that haunted his dreams. Nor could he control his loins, which ached with the need to possess her. His mind might shout frantically of honor and gratitude, but his manhood was oblivious to them. It was hard and urgent, knowing only that this woman was desirable, and in her sweet flesh lay its true home.

For a long moment the battle raged back and forth, while Kirsty lay, unaware, in his hands. He moved his fingers softly against her skin. It was dangerous but he couldn't help himself. It would be more dangerous still to bend and touch her lips with his own, and yet . . .

At the last moment there came into his mind, like a restraining hand, the memory of her saying, "I trusted you when a sensible woman wouldn't have."

He was breaking that trust right now, and if she awoke and discovered him it would devastate her. Another betrayal would be more than she could take. Cold fear ran through his body, driving out passion. He released her and drew back. His brow was damp with strain.

He rose from the bed, moving slowly not to awaken her, and backed until he could open the door. She stirred in her sleep, snuggling further down in the bed, with the covers hunched about her ears. She was sleeping peacefully now, her nightmare gone.

Mike stood for a moment in the doorway, watching her tenderly. "Good night Kirsty," he whispered. "Merry Christmas."

Chapter Five

The iron hardness of winter gave way to early spring. Rain fell in a deluge, swelling every stream on Dartmoor and turning the land to mud.

Despite the tough conditions, Kirsty knew a kind of happiness. She might not have Mike the way she wanted him, but he was there with her every day. She kept his Christmas gift constantly by her bed, so that it was the first thing she saw when she awoke.

She scoured the papers for news of Con Dawlish, and at last she was rewarded by some pictures of him relaxing in the home of his millionaire benefactor, on the way to recovery. Pleasure and pain warred in her. She was glad that Mike still had hope, but the day when he would leave her seemed to threaten. She didn't want him to leave, ever.

The pigs were in farrow and flourishing. Kirsty checked them last thing in the afternoon before returning to the warmth of the house and the cup of tea Mike would have waiting for her. She would sit down and he would haul her boots off, ordering her to stay there and do nothing. This had become their routine, and there was a settled cosiness about it that was balm to her spirit.

She was thinking of all this with happy anticipation as she scratched Etta's back one afternoon. "You're a beauty, aren't you?" she murmured, and Etta grunted.

She heard a step behind her and half turned, thinking Mike had followed her into the barn. Then she felt a hand come around her waist—another hand twisted her shoulders, and a well-remembered voice with a laugh in it said, "She's not the only one who's beautiful." Before she had time to think a man's arms were holding her close.

After the first moment's shock she reacted quickly, seizing his shoulders and holding him away. "*Caleb*. What are you doing here?"

"Now there's a fine greeting," he exclaimed, while his merry eyes mocked her. "Don't I always come to see you?"

Out of the corner of her eye she could see Mike in the yard. She twisted around sharply, forcing Caleb to turn his back to the barn door. "Not at this time of the year. You're either too early or too late." She hugged him tightly, thus giving herself the chance to see the yard over his shoulder. Mike had gone. Her racing thoughts followed him inside, saw him hurrying around the kitchen, clearing away anything that might have revealed a second presence.

"That's more like a welcome," Caleb said, returning her hug. "Your heart's going like a racing pigeon's, darlin'. Is that all for me?"

In fact her heart was thumping with apprehension. This was a disaster. Somehow she must keep Caleb outside long enough to give Mike time. She pulled back to look into his face, but kept hold of him, to say, "It's more like annoyance that you didn't come before—like last summer, when I really needed help."

"Ah, yes. I meant to come, but circumstances over which I had no control...a little local difficulty...you know. Unfortunately the magistrate knew my face and it added three months to the sentence."

"You've been in jail?" she asked, aghast.

"Sure. It runs in the family, darlin'."

"That's not funny," she snapped, pulling away from him.

"No it isn't. I'm sorry. I just didn't want you to take my little misadventure too seriously. I don't."

She realized he was speaking the truth. What had been a tragedy to Jack and Mike was just one of the ups and downs of life to Caleb. "Would it be rude to ask what you did?" she asked.

"Why do you take it for granted that I did anything?" he grumbled.

"Because I know you, Caleb. You're a rogue."

He grinned, accepting the description as a compliment. "I'm a man who likes to live by my wits. The trouble is, they sometimes let me down. They did this time. I acted as middle man in a little deal." His voice became plaintive. "How was I to know the stuff was hot?"

"How long did you get?"

"Eighteen months, but I only served half. They let me off the rest for good behavior."

She'd recovered enough to smile and say, "Good behavior? You?"

"I'd have been back for the harvest if I could have made it. But I'm here now, at your command. How about a drink for a thirsty man?"

"Later. Let me show you what's been happening on the farm first," she said, taking his hand and brooking no refusal.

She got him well clear of the house and managed to keep him away for fifteen minutes before he said, "If I don't get that drink soon, I'll expire from thirst."

To her relief there was nothing in the kitchen to give Mike away. She thought of him in the room overhead and prayed harder than she'd ever prayed in her life before.

Caleb ate the meal she set in front of him, barely looking at it. His glance rarely left Kirsty. "I don't like your hair scragged back under that cap," he complained.

"It's convenient," she said repressively. "And that's all that matters."

"Come now, you're too young to be talking like that. It's all in the past."

"It'll never be in the past for me, Caleb. Everyone around here thinks the worst of me."

Caleb's strong, comforting hand was over hers. "You'd think they'd find something else to gossip about by now, wouldn't you?" he asked.

She squeezed his hand, warmed as always by his kindly support. Caleb studied her face. "You've changed a lot."

"It's not surprising, is it?"

"No, but—" he suddenly reached out and swept off her woolen hat, releasing the glorious black hair to tumble around her shoulders. "That's better. Now you look more like the Kirsty I used to know."

She was barely aware of what he was saying. Something had alerted her. It might have been a sound or a movement, but she was suddenly sure that Mike was standing on the landing above. "You'd better go if you're to be in time to get a room in the pub," she said in a strained voice.

Caleb was stroking her hair. "Now why should I want a room in the pub when I can stay here like I always used to?" he asked coaxingly. "Come on now, darlin', Caleb's here to take care of you."

She ducked away from his hand. "When you stayed here before, Jack was alive."

"And now Jack's been dead a year. Aren't you finding life a little—shall we say, lonely? A year's a long time for a woman like you to be without a man."

"A woman like me!" she echoed. "Are you going to be like the rest, Caleb, and put me in a pigeon hole labeled 'Bad Woman'?"

"Hush now," he said, laughing. "I only meant that you've been a widow too long. After all, when a woman gets used to—well, I don't suppose Jack was any great shakes in the hay, but still—"

He pulled her against him and laid his lips on hers. Everything in her protested but she controlled the temptation to thrust him violently away. Caleb's temper was unpredictable and she didn't dare risk this escalating into a scene. She resisted him passively, refusing to respond and holding herself still in his arms. When she did put her hands up it was to ease him away from her. "Let me go, Caleb," she told him firmly, but still trying to keep the mood light.

"You don't say that as if you mean it," he laughed.

"Don't force me to show you how much I mean it," she said, her eyes narrowing.

"I think I might just take that chance."

His hand was cupping the back of her head, making it impossible for her to pull back as he lowered his mouth to hers again.

And then, just in time, a shadow darkened the doorway, and a young woman's voice said sharply, "So there you are."

Sighing, Caleb released Kirsty and turned to the newcomer. "I told you to wait for me in the village," he said in a voice that had a slight edge. "Kirsty, this is Jenna. She's a friend of mine."

The two women greeted each other, with relief on Kirsty's side and sullen reserve on Jenna's. She was about nineteen, dressed in shabby shirt and jeans that showed off her voluptuous figure, and her attitude to Caleb was proprietary. "I got bored waiting," she said, moving closer to him and regarding Kirsty with suspicion.

"No need to wait any longer," Kirsty said quickly. "Caleb was just leaving."

He allowed himself to be drawn away by the young woman, his amiable air seemingly unaltered. But Kirsty had glimpsed a new side of Caleb that disturbed her. She was used to thinking of him as a friend, feckless and a little unscrupulous, but basically kind and brotherly. But today she'd seen in his eyes the frank, ugly lust she hated in other men. Caleb would have gone as far as she'd let him, despite the fact that he was probably living with Jenna.

Kirsty followed them out into the yard and stood watching as they left, determined to stop him coming back. She felt strung out and ready to snap to the slightest thing. Caleb's unwanted touch had made her sharply aware of Mike, who never touched her if he could possibly help it. All the weeks she'd spent yearning for his caresses, wanting him in her heart and her loins, all these had rushed on her suddenly in an ache of deprivation and pain.

She hurried back to the house and looked up the stairs to where she was sure Mike had been standing, but there was no sign of him. "Mike," she called.

Receiving no answer she went to his room and found him standing by the window in the semidarkness, watching Caleb and Jenna vanishing into the distance. He turned and she saw that his face was dark with fury. "Why didn't you push him away?" he demanded coldly.

"What?"

"You heard me. Why didn't you push him away, Kirsty?"

"I told him to get off me—"

"Did you?" he asked coldly. "I saw the two of you muttering together but you were very careful to keep your voices down, and he didn't look like a man being rejected. He was finding something very funny."

"Caleb finds everything funny. It's his way."

A contemptuous look came over Mike's face. "And I dare say you know a lot about his ways, don't you Kirsty?"

"If that means what I think it means—"

"You can bet it does," he said grimly.

"Then I think you must have gone out of your mind." Tension made her temper rise swiftly. "Who the hell do you think you are to interrogate and insult me?"

"Insult?" He gave a crack of mirthless laughter. "That's rich. That's the biggest joke of all time, and it's on me. When I think how afraid I've been of insulting you, how I've trodden on eggshells to keep my feelings to myself, because I was trying to show how much I respected you, then I know what a fool I've been. *He's* allowed to paw you just as he pleases—''

"That's not true," Kirsty said indignantly.

"Don't make me laugh. All you had to do was kick him on the shins. Or you could have slapped his face or—''

"And have the whole thing flare up into a big scene that I couldn't have controlled," she said sarcastically. "I was trying to defuse the situation."

"Then you've got a helluva funny way of going about it. You can't 'defuse the situation' with a lout like that." Mike ran a hand through his hair, trying to calm down. He knew he was behaving irrationally, but he was helpless in the grip of the most powerful jealousy he'd ever known. With a colossal effort he brought himself under control, but Kirsty promptly inflamed the situation again by defending the man.

"Caleb isn't a lout," she said firmly. "He's been a good friend to me and I don't turn against my friends just because they make a mistake."

"What a fine sentiment! But I know what would have happened if I'd made the same 'mistake.' You never let the barriers down an inch for me."

"You never wanted them let down."

"Correction. I never *asked* for them to be let down, because I put a brake on myself for your sake. But if you didn't know that I've spent the last two months in torment from wanting you, thinking of you, dreaming of you, losing sleep over you and not being able to have you, then you need your eyes tested."

Mike was breathing hard, and his eyes flashed with some powerful emotion she'd never seen in him before. Kirsty stared at him as she realized what he'd just said. Soon there might be joy, but for the moment the irresistible current of Mike's fury swept her along too fast for thought. "But perhaps you enjoyed keeping me at arm's length, knowing that I was on hot coals for you, Kirsty," he went on grimly. "Perhaps you're really the tease they called you—" But instantly her face told him he'd gone too far and he backed off, saying hastily, "You didn't hear that. I never said it—"

"You'd better not have said it," she blazed. "Who are you to judge me? What do you know about me? Nothing, or you couldn't talk like such a fool. I'm not going to let you use me as a substitute for Lois—"

"What the devil has Lois got to do with this?" he yelled. "Can't you stick to the point for one minute?"

"Lois *is* the point. She's always been the one you wanted. Did you think you were going to make love to me and think of her?"

Mike breathed hard. "Lois and I are finished," he said with exaggerated patience. "She happens to be Hugh Severham's wife. That's it as far as I'm concerned."

"Oh, no it isn't."

"Meaning I'm a liar?"

"Meaning you should be more careful what you say in your sleep."

"How would you know what I say when I'm asleep? You're never there. You've insisted on keeping your virtuous distance down the hall—"

"*I've* insisted—?"

"And I, fool that I am, have respected that. We haven't spent one night together."

"What a convenient memory!" she scoffed. "I'm not talking about the last couple of months. I'm talking about the first couple of nights, when I'd hauled you, looking like a drowned rat, out of the barn. I got in with you to keep you safe, and I heard *all* about Lois.''

Mike stared at her. "And you believed—what did you believe? I can't follow the workings of your mind."

"It's simple enough. I don't like being a substitute for another woman. It was Lois you put your arms around that night and Lois that you—well, never mind."

"But I do mind," he said, his eyes kindling. As she tried to turn away he took hold of her. "What did I do?"

"If you don't remember, it doesn't matter," she said furiously.

"You're unbelievable. All this time you've kept me at arm's length—"

"*I've* kept *you*—?" Kirsty eyed him grimly, furious at this injustice. "You're the one who said 'brother and sister.' Or is that another thing you don't remember?"

"No, I'm not like you, remembering only what suits me," he snapped. "But it was brother and sister because that's what *you* wanted."

"The hell I did!"

"The hell you didn't!"

"Don't tell me what I want," she yelled. "I know what I want. I want you. I always have, but you're too dim-witted to see it."

Mike tore his hair. "Woman, may you be forgiven for a wicked distortion of the truth! So *I'm* dim-witted? What about you? How come you didn't know I'm burning up for you?"

"I don't believe you," she said breathlessly.

"Well I'm tired of arguing about it," he growled and pulled her into his arms.

The moment she felt him holding her all Kirsty's tension vanished. She'd wanted his lips so desperately, and now here they were, crushing hers with a fierce passion that called all her own desire up in response. She'd dreamed of this kiss through lonely, troubled nights, and now it was no mere dream, but a burning reality, and she surrendered to it with joy.

His mouth was hard and purposeful on hers, and now it was herself he was kissing, herself he wanted. Her lips answered his in the silent, untranslatable language of passion, telling him unspoken secrets, learning lessons too subtle to be put into words.

His tongue was inside her, exploring, inviting, possessing, making electricity streak through her body. She was coming to vibrant, erotic, alarming life, invaded by sensations more powerful than any she had known before. She'd thought she'd discovered passion that first night he'd embraced her. Now she knew that was just the pale shadow. Passion was this forest fire that swept through her, destroying her old self, creating a new one with only one thought and one will—to unite with him.

"Do you believe me now?" he growled against her mouth.

"Yes...yes..." she whispered mindlessly. "I've been such a fool. I thought..."

"It doesn't matter what either of us thought," he said huskily. "Nothing matters now."

"No," she agreed ecstatically. "Nothing but this."

As he kissed her he was pulling her shirt out of her slacks, sliding his hands beneath to find the bare skin. She heard his grunt of satisfaction as he discovered that she didn't wear a bra and he was free to cup her breast in his hand. The moment his fingers touched her nipple she nearly went out of her mind with pleasure. Her hands, which were working on his shirt, faltered as sensation rippled through her, making her shake with its force.

She didn't know exactly when he'd pulled her down to the bed, but she was there, and so was he, lying beside her, crushing her against his bare chest where the hair grew thickly, then immediately releasing her to finish taking her clothes off. She helped him feverishly. She wanted to be naked for him and with him. Only then could they forget the barriers that the world had heaped up between them and be only man and woman together. She sighed with delight as he ran his hands over her long limbs, narrow waist and rounded breasts.

"I always knew you were beautiful," he murmured, "but you were so determined to hide yourself from me..."

"I thought you didn't really want me..." she whispered.

"Well, now you know better." He covered her mouth on the last word and everything was lost in their kiss. His mouth was hard and purposeful on hers, coaxing and commanding her to open to him, which she did willingly. Everything about her was his, including the secrets that his tongue teased out, making her gasp as he explored her swiftly, then slowly. She'd never been kissed like this before, by a man who knew how to turn a kiss into a work of erotic art. She would have wanted it to go on forever, but for the tempting anticipation of deeper sensual delights still to come.

He was teaching her about those delights now, sliding his hand down between her thighs and caressing her gently in a way that sent her wild. His fingertips discovered the place that was hot and moist, throbbing with urgency. She gasped with the craving to have him inside her, and at last he moved between her legs which were parted for him, and entered her with one swift movement. Her gasp became a groan as the pleasure of feeling him within her became almost agonizing. She had dreamed of their passion, but her dreams had never even been close to the reality.

"Did I hurt you?" he asked anxiously.

"No—no—I want to feel more—*please* Mike—"

She wasn't quite sure what she was pleading for, but he seemed to know, because he began to thrust with a slow, powerful rhythm. With every thrust she felt the pleasure driven deeper into the heart of her, until it pervaded her loins and spread out from there, streaming to every part of her body, so that her toes curled and her fingers dug into his back. He had made her body completely, overwhelmingly his, and now it had its own will, doing things she'd never dreamed of, making love to him with abandon, giving and taking, responding, initiating, drowning in total sensual fulfillment.

Now she was free to give to him from the bounty with which nature had endowed her. The years of chilly seclusion fell away from her flesh as if they had never been. The body that no other man had ever been able to bring to life was aflame for this one man. This was the indescribable secret from which she'd been shut out, the power that made fools of men and women, but made them gods, too. She might pay all her life for this moment, but the sacrifice would be worth it.

She drove her hips forward to meet him, eagerly seeking the sensation of his power deep in her loins. He began to move faster. Their need was too urgent for subtlety. Later there might be time for tenderness and love. Now there was only a voracious animal demand that had to be satisfied before the rest of the world fell into place. Kirsty's hips began to move faster in rhythm with his. There was something waiting for her, something that dwarfed even the joy that had gone before, and she was impatient to discover it.

The next moment it claimed her, catching her up in a whirlwind and spinning her over the edge into the abyss, where she was buffeted to and fro. With every passing second the pleasure grew more intense until the whole universe seemed to explode. She was a microcosm, a speck, thrown against a screen of blinding radiance, to live a moment with brilliant intensity, and then to die as the screen shattered into a million pieces.

Her heart was thundering. She was gasping with shock, but Mike's arms were strong about her and his eyes smiled into hers, although he looked a little anxious. "Are you all right?" he asked.

She nodded, beyond speech, and clung to him until she felt herself grow calmer. "I never knew," she whispered. "I feel as if I'd spent all my life on a tightrope over a chasm, and never knew. *Mike...*"

He held her, kissing her soothingly until he felt the tension leave her body. At last she ceased to cling to him and fell back on the bed, feeling deliciously relaxed. "What were we really fighting about?" she murmured.

He grinned. "I guess we both know the answer to that one."

Laughing, she went back into his arms, reveling in the pleasure of sharing a lover's joke. At some indefinable point in their shouting match they'd both understood why it was happening and how it was bound to end. Through the mish-mash of pride, frustration, jealousy and passion each had picked up the signals of the other's thwarted desire.

"Have you really wanted me all this time?" she mused.

"Every minute."

"I wanted you so much, but it was all Lois with you."

"Hush. That's over. I told you."

"But that night—"

"I was delirious. I knew it was you when I awoke the next day, and I was so embarrassed in case you were angry."

"All this time I've wanted you, Mike."

"If I'd known that, nothing could have kept me away from you. But I felt I owed you a duty to keep my distance."

She made a face. "Duty. Horrid word. It causes so many misunderstandings." She ended in a gasp, for Mike was trailing his finger tips across one rosy nipple that had peaked in expectation. "Oh Mike, don't let's talk."

"Right," he agreed. "We'll have all the time we want for talking later. I want to know everything about you— but that can wait."

He closed his mouth over hers and began to love her again. Kirsty expected a repeat of the previous experience, but it was more than that, for now she was a new person. She had gone through a door from which there could be no turning back. The love of the heart had become the love of the body, and although a beginner she was an eager learner. Even her instincts had learned, so that she knew what Mike wanted from her and offered it up gladly.

He loved her now with tantalizing slowness, drawing out each sensation until it yielded up every last drop of pleasure. Kirsty arched and threw back her head as his lips enclosed each nipple in turn, teasing it with his tongue and sending forks of delight shimmering through her. The gentle scratching of his beard on her skin added to the teasing delight, and between her legs the soft, hot throbbing had begun again. She wanted him shamelessly, but now she could restrain herself enough to wait a little, so she lay there, content to revel in what he was doing to her senses, running her fingers through his thick, black hair.

When he'd finished she let her hands explore further, enjoying the feel of hard muscles beneath his skin. He'd been so weak when he first came to her, but now he was as strong as nature had meant him to be, and for tonight that strength was hers. She traced the long line of his back and narrow hips leading to neat, firm buttocks and long thighs. He grinned at the expression of naive wonder on her face. At this moment Jack's name couldn't be mentioned between them, but he knew enough to guess that her husband had never inspired her to wondrous discovery. It was as though she was making love for the first time.

At last she could no longer be restrained, and she lay back, pulling him over in a way that mixed pleading with insistence and which made him raise his eyebrows at how far she'd traveled in a short time. He complied, sliding between her parted legs and entering her slowly, letting her savor the sweet moment to the full. Despite their recent loving his power was undiminished. His loins seemed made of steel, thrusting hard into her, taking her into a new world where everything familiar had vanished. Here there was no fear or danger, but only timeless joy. At last the raw, basic sensuality that lay at the heart of her being had found its release. A sudden wildness possessed her. It sprang from the wildness of nature, whose child she was, and it was rooted in the earth that was her true home. A cry broke from her as she abandoned herself to the lusty pleasures of erotic love, arching against Mike, enfolding him with her legs, drawing him deeply into her. She took him by surprise, breaking the control of his movements, and before he knew it he was being drawn toward a climax of her instigation. He tried to hold back, to take command, but she wouldn't allow it, and the next moment his cry mingled with hers as they came together.

As he regained his composure he surveyed her with a touch of indignation. But her eyes were closed and her mouth was curved in a blissful smile. After a moment he grinned and kissed her. He didn't mind their bed being a battle ground as long as he won sometimes.

Kirsty surfaced slowly through a haze of joyous unreality. The world, which had spun madly, shooting off bright colors into outer space, had settled back into normality, but now normality was different. Where there had been ugliness, now there was beauty, where there was bleak loneliness, now there was safety and contentment.

"Why are you smiling?" Mike asked.

"Was I? I didn't know. I was just feeling happy. I want to go to sleep in your arms and sleep for a long time."

"We will. But first . . ."

"Yes," she said so eagerly that he laughed as he reached for her.

Kirsty raised her face for his kiss, feeling the sweet warmth begin to creep over her again. But this time it was spoilt by something on the edge of her consciousness, that disturbed her and wouldn't go away.

"It's only Tarn making a fuss in the yard," Mike said, trying to draw her attention back to himself. "He's probably found a rat."

"No, that's not his ratting sound," she said, sitting up, now fully alert. "There's somebody out there."

"You're imagining things. Come here."

"No, he was like that the night you came. I have to go and check." Reluctantly withdrawing from his embrace she got out of bed and pulled on a dressing gown.

"I don't like you going out there alone," Mike said.

She smiled at him fondly. "Are you afraid I might find a bad character in the barn?"

"Take the gun."

Time had drifted by while she was in Mike's arms, and now it was night. Collecting a torch and the shotgun, Kirsty made her way quietly across the yard into the barn and looked in, flashing the torch around. What she discovered made her sigh with exasperation and dismay. There, sitting on the hay, a tipsy grin on his face, was Caleb. "What are you doing here?" she demanded.

He got unsteadily to his feet. "Jenna's a very jealous woman, and she quite misunderstood that little incident this afternoon. We had a row and she threw me out. I needed somewhere to sleep." He gave her a sly look. "I hope you appreciate my tact in settling for the barn instead of coming to the house, where I gather I'd have been in the way."

"What do you mean?" she asked sharply.

"Oh, come on, darlin'. I know you're not alone. I'm a man of the world."

She pretended not to have heard this. She had to get Caleb away from here before he turned difficult. She went and hauled him to his feet. "I think you should get back to Jenna," she said. "She'll forgive you."

He sighed mournfully. "But I don't want Jenna. I want you, and she knows it. She won't forgive me for that."

"Caleb, listen." She shook him by the shoulders. "There are enough stories about me. Don't make it worse for me by letting people see you here. Please go now."

He didn't seem to hear. He was talking in a tipsy sing-song. "You couldn't blame poor Jack for being posses-sive. He saw the way men looked at you, and he knew what they wanted—what we all wanted—flies around a honey pot—"

He flopped against her so suddenly that she missed her footing and fell on her back into the hay. He landed on top of her and lay there, still muttering tipsily while she tried to get him off. But he was dead weight on top of her and she couldn't escape.

But then, all in a moment, Caleb vanished. Powerful hands seized him from above and shook him like a rat. It seemed to sober him because he wriggled free and managed to swing a punch. It sent Mike staggering back, but he recovered and launched himself at Caleb. The two men went crashing to the floor, kicking and punching, while Kirsty watched in dread as the nightmare repeated itself. Mike's face was distorted by hate. Something in-side her screamed. She'd seen that wild look on a man's face before, and it was she who'd put it there.

Mike got to his feet, dragging Caleb with him, hold-ing him up while he aimed again. "Stop it," she cried. "For God's sake, let him go."

"Not till I've taught him a lesson," Mike said be-tween gritted teeth. He landed the punch and it slammed Caleb back against the wall. His eyes were closed and his head lolled.

"You've killed him," Kirsty whispered. "Oh no—please—"

"I ought to have killed him for daring to touch you," he growled. "But stop worrying. He'll wake up." He re-leased Caleb, who crumpled into the straw.

He spoke reassuringly, but in truth he was shaken by himself. For a few moments his thoughts had been murderous. Looking in her face he saw that she understood everything in his mind and was appalled by it.

"Mike, you've got to get out of here before he wakes. Go *now,* while it's dark."

"I can't leave you with him—"

"You haven't got any choice. If you stay here we're both finished."

It went against the grain to leave her, but he knew she was right. He let her pull him back to the house, but he was in turmoil. He wanted to stay, but he was torn by a contrary impulse to escape, not from his pursuers, but from her. She could make him forget the things that were important to him: clearing his name, regaining his power and his wealth. And she roused in him a possessiveness that scared him with its force.

Kirsty ran upstairs and began to throw clothes into a bag with a feverish haste that revealed to Mike how badly she wanted him gone. When she pressed money into his hand he took it reluctantly, but knowing he must. "I'll send this back as soon as it's safe to write," he promised.

"No," she insisted frantically. "Don't write. Don't contact me. Please Mike, go quickly." She thrust a hastily scribbled map into his hand. "Luckily there's a moon to show you across the moor. Follow this line and you'll reach the road in an hour. It will take you to Plymouth, where you can get a train."

"I'll be back, Kirsty. When I've cleared myself I'll come back."

But the memory of his eyes, lit by savage jealousy, swept over her, making the horror live again. "No!" she cried in anguish. "Don't *ever* come back here."

"Kirsty..."

"Don't come back," she pleaded. "I'll be all right. Go away. Forget about me, *please.*"

He had no time to argue. Caleb might come round at any moment. She hurried across the yard with him as far as the exit to the moor.

"Kirsty..." he said once more, touching her face.

But she backed away as if his touch was poison. The woman who had melted in his arms was gone, leaving this stranger who only wanted to be rid of him. Mike dropped his hand. "Thank you for everything," he said, feeling how inadequate the words were. "Goodbye."

"Goodbye. Go now. Hurry."

She watched him for as long as she could see him, only turning away when he neared a scattering of trees and disappeared in shadow. Her heart was thumping painfully. At this moment dread was stronger than any other feeling. When Mike was lost from sight she slipped back to the barn where Caleb still lay. To her relief he was breathing strongly, and as she watched he turned over and settled himself more comfortably in the straw. She left him and returned to the house.

He was still there next morning when she went out to feed the pigs. The clanking of the bucket awoke him. "Heaven preserve us, the head I've got on me," Caleb groaned.

Kirsty braced herself to act her part. "I don't know what you were drinking last night, but it was powerful stuff," she observed cheerfully.

"But it wasn't just the booze," he said, struggling to his feet. "You've got a boyfriend, haven't you? An evil man with a punch like the devil."

She managed to chuckle naturally. "Actually he wasn't my boyfriend, just a drifter I hired for a day. He

thought you were attacking me and came to my rescue.
I explained to him that we were old friends who'd just
had a little misunderstanding. Go into the kitchen. I'll
get you some breakfast."

"Is he there?" Caleb asked warily feeling his chin.

"No, he's gone. You're quite safe."

When she joined him he was already cooking breakfast. He poured her a cup of strong tea, just the way he
knew she liked it. As she sipped it he said penitently,
"When I've had a drop, I say things I don't mean. And
do them, too, sometimes. But you won't be holding my
weakness against me, will you?"

"As long as it doesn't happen again. Like I said, we're
old friends, Caleb, and I'd like us to stay that way. But
only friends."

"You told me once I was like a brother to you," he
reminded her. "I should have respected that instead of
spoiling it."

"It's not spoiled," she said warmly. "I haven't forgotten how kind you've always been to me. Go on being
my brother."

He squeezed her hand. "Then as a concerned brother
I'll ask what the devil you mean by hiring drifters you
know nothing about? There's an escaped convict on the
loose. How can you be sure it wasn't him?"

Kirsty's heart was hammering but she shrugged care-
lessly. "After all this time? He'll have left Dartmoor ages
ago, if he's still alive."

"You're probably right. But don't hire men you don't
know. Let me work for you. You'll be needing help with
the ploughing soon." When she looked doubtful he said,
"Word of honor, there'll be no more trouble. Jenna
needs a job, too, and she's good with sheep. If you take
her on she'll keep an eye on me."

After a moment Kirsty nodded. Her heart wanted to acquit Caleb. He'd been her only friend when she needed him, and now he was her only friend again. "All right, I'll hire both of you."

Just before he left she said casually, "Do me a favor, Caleb. My name is black enough without—"

He winked. "Your secret is safe with me, darlin'."

For the rest of that day she went about with a deceptive appearance of calm. The violent events of the night and the need to allay Caleb's suspicions had kept her at a pitch of tension that allowed no room for other feelings. But as night fell and she sensed the emptiness of the house a wave of grief washed over her. Her joy had been so fleeting, snatched away while she was still lost in the wonder of it. For a few hours she'd come alive in Mike's arms, and now he was gone, and she might never see him again.

Suddenly she had no endurance left to fight off despair. She leaned heavily against the wall and there broke from her a cry of pure anguish, a primeval wail that went on and on in an unbroken lament. A passerby, hearing that sound drifting across the darkened moor, would have known it for what it was: a desolate creature keening for its lost mate.

Chapter Six

"For the last time, Kirsty, will you be sensible?"

Kirsty glanced at Caleb's frustrated face as she put her boots on. "I wish it *was* for the last time," she said. "When will you give up trying to wear me down?"

"Wear you down, you stubborn woman! As well try to wear down granite!"

"Don't waste your time, then."

"But you need the money," he almost shouted.

"I don't need it enough to kill my friends."

"Friends! They're ponies, for heaven's sake!"

"To me they're friends. I'll sell some of them for riding, but I'm not selling any to the slaughterhouse and that's final."

They were in the farmhouse kitchen, getting ready to go out for the annual roundup of ponies. Some were sold as mounts, but many were sent for slaughter to be turned into dog meat. This was something Kirsty had never done, and she wasn't going to do it now, although her overdraft at the bank worried her more with every passing day.

Jenna leaned against the wall, watching the other two with bright, malicious eyes. She was as frank in her suspicious dislike of Kirsty as she was in her infatuation with Caleb, and Kirsty knew the sight of them squabbling cheered her up.

Two months had passed since the night Mike had vanished into the darkness. During that time Kirsty had heard nothing. No suspicious policemen had come knocking at her door; Mike had never been recaptured, nor had he contacted her.

She'd meant it when she'd told him not to write, but soon afterward she'd convinced herself that a letter would arrive for her. It would say something innocuous like, "Arrived safely, everything's fine, your affectionate cousin." It would be signed with a name that started with *M*, any name except Mike. She would know what to think, but no one else would be any the wiser. But weeks turned to months and no letter arrived. He might have vanished off the face of the earth.

She had driven him away, fearful of another tragedy, but time had dimmed that fear. Now she longed for him with all her heart and soul, but mostly with her body. Her passion had been slaked only briefly. Deprived of him it flared up again, flaming more fiercely for having savored what it now lacked. Night after night she lay awake, tortured by the need of this one man and the fulfillment only he could give.

By day she was gripped by a feeling of malaise that wouldn't free her. It was spring, one of the busiest times of the year for a farmer, but she could no longer move with her old lightness of step, and everything was an effort. Today she would gladly have let Caleb get on with rounding up the horses without her, but for the suspicion that he would sell some to the meat packers if she weren't there to stop him.

It was a bright, pleasant day. The snow had gone, and although it was still cold the fresh moorland flowers were beginning to show their heads. Most of the farmers she knew were out today. Some of them nodded briefly to her, but didn't exchange friendly chat as they would once have done.

Jenna was naturally gifted with the ponies. She rounded up several that would make excellent mounts. Caleb seemed to have vanished in the melee of pounding hooves and noise.

"Is that one yours?" Jenna demanded, indicating a gray, larger than the others.

"Yes, he's mine."

"Good saddle horse. Decent price. Let's go for him."

The horse stood quietly while Jenna slipped a halter on his head, but as soon as Kirsty mounted him he began to object. She held on, hoping he'd calm soon, as the sweet-tempered animals usually did. But he made a fight of it, and she began to fear she wouldn't hold him. A sensation of nausea was creeping over her and she felt faint. Suddenly the sky whirled over her head, and the ground came up to meet her. The last thing she knew were two arms breaking her fall.

She came round to find herself lying on the ground in the shade of some trees, with Jenna fanning her. The other woman's expression startled Kirsty. It was pure, concentrated hatred. "So the truth has caught up with you at last," Jenna spat out.

"What are you talking about?" Kirsty demanded weakly.

"Don't play the innocent with me," Jenna snapped. "Everyone knows what you are, and they'll know it even more now. Whore! Tramp!"

"How dare you talk to me like that!" Kirsty struggled to get up, but her head was still swimming. Caleb had reappeared from somewhere, and now he came over, but before he could speak Jenna turned on him, flashing out words in a language Kirsty recognized as Romany, although she couldn't follow it. She could tell that Caleb was indignant at what Jenna was saying. He seemed to be attempting a denial or explanation, but Jenna cut him short with a kick on the shins before storming off.

"What was that about?" Kirsty asked.

"There's no reasoning with Jenna," Caleb complained. "She's convinced herself that I'm the father."

"The *what?*"

"The father—of your baby. You shouldn't be rounding up ponies in your condition. I could have managed."

"Caleb, wait," Kirsty begged. "You've got it all wrong. I'm not pregnant."

"Aren't you? Jenna's convinced that you are, and she blames me." He grimaced and rubbed his shin. "Do me a favor, and tell her who the father really is before she cripples me."

"Oh, no," Kirsty gasped. "It's not possible."

"Do you mean that literally?" Caleb asked.

That checked her. She met his gaze and found he was looking at her with eyes grown suddenly shrewd. "I just don't believe it," she said firmly.

"But suppose it *is* true. You're in a financial mess as it is. It's going to be worse with a baby."

"There's no baby," she said desperately.

"Of course there isn't. But just in case, why don't you have a look at the little beauties I've got here?" He helped her to her feet and showed her where he'd tethered six small shaggy animals. "They're all a bit long in the tooth so you won't be losing much," he said coaxingly. "And you can get a good price."

She thought of how bad things were at the bank and how much worse they could get. Six animals sold to the slaughterhouse would tide her over for a while. All she had to do was turn her head away and not look at them.

A soft whinnying broke into her thoughts. She tried to tell herself that she didn't recognize the sound, that one pony was just like another. But it was no use. She knew every one of them. In the dark days when she'd climbed the hills in search of creatures who didn't shun her, they'd come to her trustingly. Now they stood in patient silence while she decided their fate.

Quietly she took out her knife, sliced through the ropes that held them and watched as they galloped away. "I know," she said in answer to Caleb's groan. "I'm crazy. Let's leave it at that."

"Hey, Kirsty," called one of the passing men, "you must have a rich boyfriend if you can afford to do that." A general laugh went up.

Kirsty ignored them and went back to work, thankful that the day was nearly over. She worked mechanically for the hour that was left, aware of many eyes on her. The rumor that she was pregnant would be all over the moor by tonight. But it couldn't be true. She was barren. Five years with Jack had surely proved it.

But her heart knew differently. Five years with a husband she didn't love, or one night with a man who'd taught her the meaning of passion. There was no comparison. In Mike's arms she'd come home, and the flowering he'd caused in her emotions and senses was reflected in the physical flowering inside her.

He was gone and she might never see him again, but suddenly she was swept with an onrush of glorious happiness such as she'd never known before. She was a woman of the earth, born and reared close to the land and the rhythms of nature. And now she was a part of those rhythms, caught up in a glorious cycle of fertility and renewal.

If only she could tell him about his baby and see the joy dawn in his eyes, have him enfold her and their child in his arms in the gesture of loving protection that men had used since time began. She had never felt her loneliness as intensely as now.

She wondered how she could ever have missed the signs of pregnancy. Although it was still early, her face was already slightly fuller, and she was normally so slim that the least change showed at once. Her mind magnified the slight increase to huge proportions. She was convinced that everyone must see the difference. In this she was wrong, but it was true that her pregnancy was known. Jenna had seen to that. The sidelong glances of curiosity and contempt Kirsty was used to happened more often now.

About a month after the roundup, she made one of her rare trips to the village and went into Fowler's to collect her mail. There were two customers ahead of her, and while waiting her turn she glanced idly over the headlines of the national papers. Suddenly she stiffened and the blood began to pulse in her veins. Her hand was shaking as she reached out to lift one of the papers.

There was Mike looking back at her from the front page, but it was Mike as she had never seen him before. His beard was gone, but the face revealed wasn't the haggard desperate face she'd first seen. This was a confident smiling man. The caption was An Injustice Put Right.

Dazed, she read the story. Mike had managed to contact Con Dawlish, who'd returned to England, fully recovered, and the old man had performed miracles of computer hacking. He'd discovered not only Hugh Severham's methods, but the details of his Swiss bank accounts, in which reposed the missing money. Armed with these Mike's lawyer had gone to the police, and Hugh Severham was now under arrest.

Mike was a free man. He stood in the center of the picture, flanked by Con on one side and Lois on the other. She was holding on to Mike's arm and gazing up at him adoringly.

"I married on the rebound," the reporter quoted her saying, "but my heart always belonged to Mike."

When she reached home, Kirsty settled down to read the paper more thoroughly. There was a feature inside, giving the full history of the fraud that had stripped thirty million pounds from the coffers of New World Properties. When Kirsty read that sum she gasped. *Thirty million.* Mike had said only that a large sum of money had been stolen, and she'd thought of perhaps a hundred thousand, which would have been a vast sum to her. But to him, evidently, it would have been peanuts.

Now she saw how naive she'd been. Mike operated in a different world from her. She thought of the scarecrow she'd saved from death and tried to connect him with this sophisticated man in the picture, with his expensive, tailored suit. Everything about him exuded money and success. She told herself how glad she was that things had worked out well for him, but there was an ache in her heart. Once there might have been a hope that he could win his freedom, and she could go to him joyfully and show him his child. But now she knew that she could never seek out this rich man. She studied Lois's face, and the way her manicured hands clung to Mike's sleeve, and shut the paper abruptly.

In the days that followed she was filled with tension. Surely Mike would contact her, to thank her and ask how she was. But days turned into a week, then two weeks, then three, and there was no word from him. She refused to give up hope. Next time there would a letter waiting for her. But there never was. Mrs. Fowler looked at her with curiosity and amusement, her eyes pausing on Kirsty's thickening waist just long enough to say that she understood this sudden need for a letter.

Kirsty came out of the store one morning to find a small crowd waiting on the pavement, their faces covered in cynical smiles. She took a deep breath, raised her head and tried to walk on, but she found her way barred by a heavy young man with a red face. She recognized Abe Mullery, Peter's older brother. "Well—" he sneered "—has he written yet, whoever he is? Or don't you know his name?"

"Get out of my way," she said steadily.

"I'll move when I'm ready. First I want an answer. You ain't heard from him, have you?"

Kirsty looked at him in silence, her heart thumping. Abe pressed nearer, crowding her up against the wall. "You won't hear, neither. A man wants only one thing from your sort of woman, and he's had it. That's obvious, ain't it?" He put his hand on her stomach.

"Don't touch me," Kirsty shouted, fearful for her baby.

"Don't touch me," Abe mocked. "That's not what you usually say to a man. It's not what you said to my brother when you led him on like a whore and killed him."

"That's enough," came a crisp voice behind Abe. Everybody looked, to find Abe's mother, who stood there with sixteen-year-old David, her youngest son and her favorite since Peter had died. "Get off her before I thump you and make your head spin," she ordered Abe.

She was half his size, but he obeyed at once. "Just a bit of fun, Ma," he explained. "Teach her a lesson."

"I said that's enough," Mrs. Mullery snapped. "She's pregnant. You ought to know better." But her eyes on Kirsty were cold and unrelenting. Her hate was undiminished, although some primitive instinct made her defend their common womanhood. "Best if you don't come here more than you have to," she said harshly. "He ain't gonna write, whoever he is. Why don't you sell up and get out? Go and live somewhere where they don't know your shame."

"I'm staying in my home," Kirsty said in a shaking voice, "and none of you are going to drive me out. *I've done nothing wrong.*"

A burst of ribald laughter greeted this. Then they began to leave, indifferent now the entertainment was over. Young David Mullery seemed transfixed, staring at Kirsty, until his mother put her arm protectively around his shoulders and urged him away as if getting him out of range of an evil spell.

Kirsty got home somehow and lay awake that night wondering how long she could survive like this. Her enemies were right. Mike had taken all he wanted and forgotten her. Gradually she began to retreat back into the dark, dangerous isolation from which he'd briefly rescued her.

For two weeks it rained steadily. When it finally stopped, the ground had turned to mud. Jenna called one morning to collect Tarn to help her move the sheep to better pasture. "Don't bother returning him," Kirsty said. "I'll be out with the tractor this afternoon and I'll come for him myself."

It was the busiest time of the year, the time when the fields must be ploughed and sown. She set Caleb to do some urgent repairs in a barn roof and tackled the ploughing herself. After several hours of it she was worn out, and a kind of terror gripped her when she realized how quickly she was tiring these days.

Wearily she made her way to the uplands where her flock now grazed. The sun had managed to come out, and she found them contentedly drying themselves and nibbling the grass. Some ponies wandered down from the higher ground. There was enough food for them now and they had no need of help, but they came just the same, and she fondled their rough coats lovingly, accepting their nuzzled greetings. At last she mounted the tractor, signaled for Tarn to jump up and headed for home.

With a mile still to go she came upon a curious sight. A car was pulled up at the side of the road, its wheels bogged down in mud. Kirsty had seen muddied cars in these parts before, but never one like this. It was a gleaming monster, built on sleek lines, with this year's number plate: the car of a rich man.

She climbed down from the cab. Tarn followed and dashed off in search of rabbits while Kirsty studied the car more closely, wondering where the driver was. Probably gone on to find help, she thought. Looking up, she saw a man coming toward her. He was about a hundred yards away, too far to see clearly. But something about his walk was familiar, something about the set of his head on his shoulders, something her heart would never forget until the day she died. She found she was having trouble breathing. And then, in a blinding, unbelievable moment, she knew.

It seemed to take an age for him to cover the distance between them, and by that time she'd got herself under control. Joy that he hadn't forgotten her warred with dismay. The trappings of wealth turned him into a stranger; worse than a stranger, an alien. His first words confirmed it.

"I've been meaning to write to you." He shrugged awkwardly. "But it was hard to know what to say."

And you were too busy, she thought.

"Did you hear what happened?" he asked.

"Yes, it was in the paper. I'm very happy for you."

"I'd have come before, only—"

"There's no need to explain," she said politely. "I'm sure you've had a lot on your mind."

He wanted to say that *she* had been on his mind, but this aloof, courteous stranger gave him no opening. She was different, he thought. Her face had subtly altered, as though a new light lay on her features. And she seemed to hold herself differently, although her heavy raincoat made it hard to tell. He remembered their last meeting, and her passionate plea that he should go away forever and never return. "My car got stuck in the mud," he said, struggling for words. "I was looking for a farmer to give me a tow, but all I could see is moorland going on forever, so I came back."

She indicated the tractor. "I can give you a tow."

He got the ropes from the trunk and she helped him fix them. In ten minutes the car was out of the ditch and they were surveying the damage to the front wheel.

"That needs work before I can drive it," Mike said. "Is there a good garage near here?"

"Yes. I'll take you."

"No need. I'll call them."

He reached into the car and casually produced a portable telephone, made a call to get the number and within a few moments was talking to the garage. His voice had a brisk authority that underlined the change in him more effectively than money. "I'm sure you're busy but I need a quick job," he said impatiently. "Naturally I'll pay extra. Tomorrow morning then. Be at Everdene Farm at nine o'clock sharp."

"What?" Kirsty said sharply.

Mike had hung up. "You don't mind, do you?"

"It's a bit late to ask me that."

"But it's only common sense for me to be there. Why should you make difficulties about it?"

"I just think you're very rude to tell them first and ask me afterward."

"What possible difference can it make?" he demanded, raising his voice slightly.

"I think good manners do make a difference," she said, raising hers further.

He gritted his teeth. "Kirsty, I have just driven four hundred miles. I'm tired, I've gotten lost, I nearly overturned in a ditch, and the last thing I'm in the mood for is a lecture about manners."

"I can't help that. I don't like the way you walk in as though you owned me—as though you owned Everdene—" She broke off, struggling for something to accuse him of. She knew she was overreacting ridiculously, but disappointment had destroyed her sense of proportion. Their reunion should have been wonderful, not this irritable encounter.

Before either of them could say another word a cascade of yelps broke over them. Tarn, tired of rabbits, had returned and, recognizing the benefactor who'd brightened his life with culinary treats, launched himself onto Mike, barking with joy. Mike didn't even notice the wreck of his suit. He felt only an overwhelming relief that here at least was a welcome.

"I'm sorry," Kirsty said frostily, eyeing the damage.

"Well, at least now you've got to invite me home." He took a bag from the car trunk and climbed up into the cab beside her. Tarn squeezed in between them, distributing mud everywhere.

They drove home, towing the car behind them. Mike felt sore at heart. He'd looked forward to this day, but everything had gone wrong. She wasn't glad to see him. When she'd told him to stay away she'd meant it. He thought of the letters he'd written to her, all of which had been torn up in frustration because there were no words for the elusive feeling that drew him to her. In the months apart he'd gone crazy wondering if she was all right, if she still thought of him. He'd pictured her face when they met again. And when the moment came she'd looked at him with an aloofness that chilled his heart.

As he entered the farmhouse a delicious smell assailed his nostrils. "Stew," Kirsty said briefly, throwing off her raincoat and going to the stove. "It's been simmering all day so it should be ready. I expect you want to change your clothes?" Receiving no reply, she turned to find him staring at her, a thunderstruck expression on his face. She realized that her jacket must have concealed the slight swell of her pregnancy, but now there was no more concealment.

"Kirsty—" he hesitated "—am I imagining things?"

"No." She tried not to let her voice reveal her inner tension. The next few minutes would be so important. "I'm going to have a child."

"My child." It was a statement, not a question. "My God, I'm a fool! It never crossed my mind. All this time I was hoping I hadn't left you in any trouble, but I meant trouble with the law. I never dreamed of this." He passed a hand over his eyes. "I should have realized—"

She shrugged. "It doesn't matter."

"Does anyone else know?"

She turned blazing eyes on him. "I want this baby, Mike. I won't get rid of it."

"Did I ask you to?" he demanded.

"You were going to. If other people don't know, it'll be easier to deal with the problem quietly. That's your plan, isn't it?"

"Why must you always put the worst construction on everything I say?" he asked sharply. "Actually my plan is to marry you."

The cool announcement, without reference to her wishes, roused her ire. "Indeed? Suppose I have other plans?"

"Such as what?"

"Such as living my life without help or interference."

"You'll certainly live it without help as far as your neighbors are concerned," he observed grimly. "I only wondered if they knew, in case they were giving you a hard time. From your nasty temper I gather they are."

"Nothing I can't cope with, having coped with it before."

"Kirsty, please, can't we stop this? I didn't come here to fight you. I came to find out how you are."

"Which you could have done at any time over the last few weeks," she threw at him, relieved at last to voice her real grievance.

He gritted his teeth. "Haven't you had the wit to realize why I stayed quiet? By coming back, I've as good as told the world that you helped me. I didn't dare do that until I'd been officially promised that there'd be no charges over my escape. I heard that only yesterday evening. This morning I got into my car and drove without stopping to find you."

Her pulses leapt, but she said stubbornly, "You could have written."

"You told me not to, in no uncertain terms."

"You didn't have to take any notice," she said crossly.

Suddenly the annoyance died out of his face, and he gave a grin that made her heart turn over. "How familiar this is," he said. "We were always fighting when we didn't really want to."

A reluctant smile twitched the corners of her mouth. "You speak for yourself. I want to."

"All right," he said, drawing her into his arms. "We'll fight later."

His kiss was like a blessing, driving out all the strain and unhappiness. After so long it was good to feel his big, hard body against hers. All the churning contradictory thoughts that tormented her faded into nothing. Whatever else was between them, this one thing hadn't changed. His tongue could still ignite her desire.

"Mike," she whispered, "take me upstairs, quickly."

"Is it safe for you?"

"Of course. It's too soon to worry about that."

He took her hand and they ran upstairs together, heading instinctively for his old room. He undressed her with feverish hands, kissing her all the time. She was radiant under his caresses, the sadness of the past weeks forgotten as the ache left her heart, and her body remembered why it had been created. Their first loving had been a discovery. Now she found that her flesh had held the memory of his touch, ready to reawaken at any moment, making passion flare through her at lightning speed.

When they were naked they tumbled together onto the bed. She parted her legs for him at once and claimed him, as he claimed her. But though his need was overpowering she could sense him keeping a rein on it for her sake. His arms were strong about her, but the movement of his loins was slow and controlled as he entered her. She uttered a long, low cry of fulfillment and desire, clasping him tightly against her breast, while the feeling went deeper, deeper into her. "Yes...yes..." she gasped. "Oh, Mike, I've missed you—so much."

"I was always here," he murmured. "And you were always with me. You knew I'd come back if I could."

She tried to answer but sensations were sweeping her, driving out coherent thought. All the lonely, unsatisfied love that had tormented her since he left went into her embrace. Mike had become a different man in everything but this, and for now this was all she would allow herself to think of. He was hers again. His tender touch proclaimed it. So did the way he smiled down at her as they became one. The feel of him inside her was unbearably good, and his gentle care for her made it perfect.

As her excitement mounted she began to thrust against him, driving him on, inciting him to greater passion. He responded at once, matching himself to her rhythm. They had known each other so briefly as lovers, but already they were wise in each other. The total physical rapport, which had first tortured and then delighted them, now canceled the months apart, making each do instinctively what the other wanted. As their moment approached, Kirsty looked into the face of her lover, loving him, trusting him, giving herself to him totally, abandoned to joy. She had waited all her life for this, and it was worth the wait.

Afterward Mike ran his hand possessively over the slight swell of her stomach, and his face held a look of such disbelieving wonder that she wanted to weep. But instead she fell asleep in his arms with the ease of a contented child.

She awoke to find him sitting on the bed, gently shaking her. "I've brought madam a cup of tea," he said, lightly kissing her.

"Mmm, lovely." She looked out of the window to where the sun was shining. "What time is it?"

"Nearly nine."

"What? I should have been up ages ago."

"Stop worrying. I've done the chores. I thought I'd let you sleep."

"I can't remember when I last slept this late," she said wonderingly. She cocked a cheeky eyebrow at him. "Did you cook breakfast, as well?"

He laughed. "I'll do that next. I had to make some phone calls."

"But the phone isn't—oh yes, you've got a portable, haven't you?"

"Luckily, yes. I gather you still can't afford to have yours connected. I got a shock when I realized how bad things are, but don't worry. I'm here now, and everything's going to be all right."

She frowned. "What do you mean, you realized how bad things were?"

"Your books make very grim reading."

"You've been going through my books?"

"You left one of them open on the table downstairs. I checked the others to see if everything was that bad."

Kirsty's mellow mood vanished abruptly. "I didn't leave the others open on the table," she said.

"No, but I know where you keep them. It doesn't take much to see you're in a bad way. When your bank manager starts writing letters in that tone, things are on a downward spiral."

"You've read my private correspondence?" she demanded, aghast.

"A letter from a bank demanding immediate repayment of your overdraft is hardly personal. Anyway, I've told him he'd be wise to keep quiet for a while."

"You *told* him—?"

"His name was on the letterhead. I called the directory to find his home number, called him there and explained the situation."

"What situation?" Kirsty asked, a dangerous edge to her voice.

"That I'm taking care of things now and he'd get a check for the overdraft immediately. He let slip a couple of unguarded remarks which make me suspect he's hand in glove with one of the locals who's trying to buy you out, and that's why he's been putting so much pressure on you. That's only my gut instinct, but my instincts about money are usually right. He wasn't pleased when I told him that now you could afford to hang on for an offer of top price."

Kirsty pulled herself sharply up in the bed. "Did you," she said, speaking with difficulty, "have the unspeakable impertinence to say that I was going to sell Everdene?"

"Only when you get the best price for it."

"How *dare* you interfere in my affairs!"

"They're my affairs too now, surely?"

"Not until I say so, and that will be never if this is how you behave. No price will ever be enough for my home."

"It can hardly go on being your home once we're married—"

"Who says we'll ever be married?" she flashed.

His mouth hardened. "I don't know why you're being so unreasonable—all right, yes I do. I know I can be a little overbearing . . . perhaps more than a little . . ."

"Try 'like a bull at a gate,' " Kirsty said grimly.

"I appreciate that you're nostalgically attached to this farm, but it has very little economic value."

"You didn't take this lofty attitude when you came here for shelter," she retorted, stung.

"Kirsty, please believe me, I'm endlessly grateful, both to you and Everdene for saving me, and I'm here to show my gratitude. But my attachment is to you, not the place."

"If you understood the first thing about me you'd know that you can't make that distinction. Everdene, me, Dartmoor, it's all one."

"Now you're just being sentimental."

"Well, you thank your lucky stars that I *am* sentimental, because if I hadn't been you'd have been packed straight back off to jail," she cried hotly.

His mouth tightened. "I don't want to argue about that. I like seeing things done properly. That's my way. You can't have that baby in the back of beyond, where we might not be able to get you to the hospital if things should go wrong."

"It's been good enough for the women of my family for centuries, and it's good enough for me."

"Well, it's not good enough for me. My child is going to be born in civilized surroundings. I'm sorry if I expressed myself badly, but when you think about it I know you'll see I'm right."

Kirsty's head seethed with so many furious things to say that she couldn't get any of them out. While she was still trying to organize her thoughts there was a stream of yelps from Tarn, followed by a knock on the front door. Mike looked out of the window. "They've come to see to my car," he said. "We'll talk later." He patted her shoulder and walked out, leaving her in turmoil.

What she'd seen in the last few devastating minutes was Mike as he really was. The weeks of hiding, dependent on her, had distorted him, showing her only his gentler, more tolerant qualities. But now, with his money and authority restored, his natural self had reappeared. And she didn't much like him.

One of his expressions had struck an ominous chord—*"I don't want to argue about this,"* had reminded her of the times Jack had declared, *"I ain't got time to waste on words,"* when he'd known he was wrong but was determined to have his own way. She'd coped with Jack. But from Mike such bullying obstinacy would be a thousand times more painful, because, despite her dislike, she loved him.

Gradually her turmoil subsided, and resolution took its place. She knew that her father, who'd headed her off so many impulsive actions, would have warned against what she was about to do, telling her to think carefully first. But although her temper was up her mind was calm. The decision she'd made was best acted on quickly.

In the yard below Mike paid off the mechanic. As he turned back he was confronted by the incredible sight of

Kirsty carrying his suitcase toward the car. While he watched in astonishment she raised the lid of the trunk and put the case inside. "Hey, I'm not going yet awhile," he protested.

"Yes, you are, Mike," she said pleasantly. "It was nice of you to come, but you don't belong here now, any more than I belong anywhere else."

"Now look, I only want to do what's best for you and the baby. I may not have been very tactful but I'm certainly right."

She looked into his face and saw nothing in it that she recognized. How could she ever have thought she and this man could be united? "You may be right about money, Mike. I'm sure you know a lot about it. But you know nothing about anything else, including me. *Sell Everdene?* You couldn't have talked me into that if you'd tried for a thousand years. But you didn't even try. You just walked in, assumed you knew best and mounted a takeover."

"I've already apologized for being tactless."

"I don't mind your being tactless. It's your being so wrong that frightens me—wrong about everything that matters, about me, about the things I love."

"Getting up with the dawn to feed the animals," he flung at her with grim irony, "being cold and tired and poor—these are the things you love?"

"Seeing the dawn come up on the most beautiful place on earth," she countered. "Feeling my friends nuzzle me when I feed them, watching the earth grow fruitful under my hands—*these* are the things I love. And I'll teach my child to love them, too."

"If you're still here. How much chance is there of that without me?"

"A lot more than there is *with* you, apparently. I'll manage, Mike. I've fought off threats to Everdene before. At the moment the biggest threat is you. That's why you're leaving."

He ran a distracted hand through his hair. "I simply don't understand the way your mind works."

"I know. And you never will. Please go before you do me irreparable damage."

He became very pale. "And our child. Maybe I have a few things to teach him?"

"And maybe I don't want him to learn from you. I'll back my values against yours any day."

"Kirsty, if you send me away now, I won't come back," he warned.

She might have flinched. It was hard for him to tell. But there was no yielding in her eyes. "Goodbye, Mike."

His face hardened. "Right," he said grimly, "if that's the way you want it." He pulled open the car door and slammed it shut after him. "Goodbye, Kirsty." He started the engine and drove off without giving her another look.

Chapter Seven

When Mike had gone, the loneliness was more terrible than ever. Kirsty told herself that her pain was disappointment at the man Mike had turned out to be, and not heartbreak. They could never have been happy together. It was better to part now. But the pain wouldn't go away.

Over the next few days she found reasons to rue her hasty actions. Once Mike had pointed it out, it was obvious that the bank had offered a mortgage to a local farmer, who was badgering her to sell, and had been using her overdraft as a lever to get her out. She hadn't made the connection, but Mike had seen it at once. His business instincts might have saved Everdene if she hadn't driven him away. Then she reminded herself that he hadn't wanted to save it. He'd dismissed her beloved home as an encumbrance "of little economic value." And she hardened her heart.

When a letter from the bank arrived a few days later she braced herself for bad news. But the paper inside was an acknowledgment of a check that cleared her overdraft and left a thousand pounds to spare. There was nothing to indicate who had done this for her. But she knew.

There was no question of returning the money in a dramatic gesture of defiance. She couldn't afford to. Besides, this was a business transaction. He'd paid off his debts and would now forget her. She started to write a businesslike letter of thanks, tore it up, tried again on a warmer note, tore it up and abandoned the attempt. She began to think Mike had been right. There were no words in which they could write to each other. After dithering uncharacteristically for a week, she wrote him a chilly, formal acknowledgment and sent it to the bank with a covering note, asking them to forward it to Mike's bank.

Her relief at being solvent again was short-lived. One morning neither Caleb nor Jenna turned up for work. Investigation revealed that they had both left the district the evening before. Kirsty had always known Caleb was unreliable, but it was a shock to discover that he would leave her in the lurch without a word. She could only speculate that he was in trouble again and lying low until the dust settled, or Jenna had dragged him off to get him away from herself.

The feeling of malaise returned. It seemed that troubles continued to pile in on her while her energy was seeping away. With an effort she pulled herself together and contemplated the work ahead.

She returned home one evening to find her yard taken up by a gleaming Range Rover that looked as if it had been purchased yesterday. It was as right for rough terrain as the other car had been wrong; the vehicle of a man who'd come to stay. While she stood in breathless hope, Mike came out of the house and stood glaring at her. He didn't look as if this was a happy reunion. He looked furious.

He didn't want to come back here, she thought. But he came anyway. Why?

At last Mike pulled her note from his pocket. "How dare you write to me like this?" he demanded.

"What's wrong with it?" she said. "It's polite."

"Damn politeness! When were you and I ever polite?"

"Why are you here, Mike?"

"Because I'm crazy. Because I can't stay away. I don't know why." His voice grew desperate. "Kirsty, are you going to stop wasting time and kiss me, yes or no?"

"Yes," she said, putting out her arms to him.

They kissed and held each other tightly, but there was more relief than passion in the embrace. He didn't try to make love to her, but took her inside and helped her off with her outdoor clothes and made her sit by the stove, which he'd lit. "We can do all the talking later," he said.

Kirsty nodded agreement, put her feet up on the settle and let him care for her. It was bliss not to return to a cold, empty house. The details could wait. "Don't tell me you've cooked the supper?" she said, trying to introduce a lighter note. "Tarn will be pleased."

"Then he'll be disappointed, unless he likes Indian take-out."

"He likes anything. But he's never had Indian food. Neither have I."

"I bought some on the way. It's a passion of mine. I hope you take to it."

He produced a bottle of wine, served her a chicken curry with rice, and watched her face as she ate it. "It's good," she said, unable to keep the surprise out of her voice.

Mike grinned. "I do get it right sometimes," he observed.

A silence fell. Kirsty guessed that Mike felt as awkward as she did. They had reached a curious limbo, one in which they were bound by ties from the past and yet essentially strangers. Their skirmish had alarmed both of them, and now they were treading on eggshells. "Why didn't you let me know you were coming?" she asked cautiously.

"I was afraid you wouldn't let me in."

"How *did* you get in? I'm sure I locked the door."

"You did, but I learned how to pick a lock in jail. I made sure I was too firmly installed for you to throw me out now. In fact I—" he hesitated.

"What have you done that I'm not going to like?"

"Nothing—at least, nothing much. It's just that you're not using that back room, and I need an office while I'm here, so I—well—"

"You sort of took over," she said. Silently she registered the tell-tale phrase *while I'm here*. But she kept her own counsel. "That's all right. As you say, it wasn't being used. But how will your firm manage without you?"

"I've got a brilliant assistant who can keep things going as long as he can contact me here. Your telephone will have to be—that is—it would be helpful if—"

She smiled at his unpracticed attempts at tact. "I'll have the telephone reconnected," she promised. "I'm surprised you haven't got it fixed up already."

"Well, I did actually give the company a call on the car phone," he said, with such a nervous glance at her face that she burst out laughing. "They'll be here to-morrow," he finished. "And that's the last of my confessions."

Afterward they sat together in the glow of the stove. "Mad at me?" he asked.

She shook her head. "Glad to see you. I thought you'd never come back. That's what you said."

He shrugged. "I often say things hastily that I don't mean. But believing that, you let me go?"

"I had to, Mike. I am what I am, just as you are what you are, and neither of us can change."

He put a hand quickly in front of her mouth, silencing the dangerous thought before it could be spoken. He'd lied. He very rarely spoke hastily and always meant what he said. He'd fully meant never to come back. Let her stew in her own juice, he'd thought. He was better off away from her.

But he'd found he was never away from her. She haunted him like a living ghost until at last he'd given in and come back to her. Of course, it was only for a short time, while he talked her around. But he, not she, had been the one to yield, and for a man who prided himself that no one got the better of him—not protesters, not planning departments, not women—it was an unsettling experience.

He pushed the thought aside, preferring to concentrate on more pleasant things, and laid his hand gently on her stomach. "Everything all right?"

"Everything's fine."

"But no more work for you," he said in a decided tone.

"Are you going to feed the pigs?" she asked, cocking a humorous eyebrow at him.

"You'd like to see me, wouldn't you?"

"Wouldn't I just!" she exclaimed with relish, and they both laughed uneasily.

"Sorry to disappoint you, but there are pig men for that, shepherds for sheep and people to do the ploughing."

"The ploughing and sowing are just about finished."

"All right, I don't know a lot about farming, but I'm going to get people who do know."

"*I* know."

"But you're pregnant," he reminded her patiently.

"Well, pregnancy isn't some sort of disability—especially among farming people. Cows have calves, pigs have piglets and women have babies."

"Great. I'll buy you a new farrowing sty."

"It would probably suit me better than cotton wool. Mike, my mother was driving a tractor the day I was born."

"Before or after?" he asked ironically.

"Very funny. You know what I mean."

She was looking at him with an expression of quizzical hilarity that made him want to kiss her. He realized he'd never seen her look so lighthearted before. If only, he thought, he could get her away from here, to sensible surroundings, all their problems would disappear. Then a thought occurred to him, and his heart gave an uncomfortable lurch.

"What is it?" Kirsty asked, seeing his face grow blank and distant.

"Nothing," he said hastily. "That is—I suddenly thought of my mother."

"Something unhappy? Is she dead?"

"No, very much alive." He found it hard to say more, but Kirsty clearly expected it. "It's nothing important—what you were saying reminded me that she used to take in washing to make ends meet, and according to my father she insisted on finishing a load just before she had me.''

"A woman after my own heart.''

"No, you're not a bit alike,'' he said quietly.

"But still, I'd love to know her.''

"Maybe—later. Just now we have a lot to decide.''

Kirsty dropped the subject, but she was puzzled and slightly hurt by Mike's obvious determination to keep her separate from his family. Despite her happiness in his return she couldn't pretend that all was well. The chasm that yawned between their minds, hardly noticeable when he'd been on the run, was very obvious now, and their mutual passion could make only a temporary bridge.

"What have we got to decide?'' she asked.

"Labor. You need some. I've arranged for a couple of workers to come and see you tomorrow. If you don't take to them, just send them away and I'll find some more. The decision is yours.''

Kirsty thanked him and suppressed her private opinion that any labor he could pick up at this time in the season was unlikely to be worth having. But she had a pleasant surprise when Fred and Frank turned up next day, two wiry brothers mounted on ponies. They came from the other side of Dartmoor and had lost their farm when they could no longer afford to run it. Working for the most notorious woman in the neighborhood didn't bother them. All they cared for was the land and the chance to stay on Dartmoor. When Kirsty broached the subject of wages they informed her that they had settled "all that'' with Mr. Stallard, who would be paying them. Kirsty suspected that Mike was paying over the odds, but she was too relieved to have knowledgeable help to make an issue of it. They started at once, and by the end of the first day she knew she could safely leave matters to them. They tended Everdene with loving, expert hands, giving her time to concentrate on her pregnancy. After a week she was treating them like favorite uncles, but she never quite sorted out which was Fred and which was Frank.

Mike insisted on paying for the reconnection of the telephone, and Kirsty let him, since it was clear he would be spending a lot of time on it for his work. "I'll have to return to London now and then," he told her, "and now we can keep in touch."

"Mike, I don't understand. How long are you planning to stay?"

He looked at her squarely. "Are you prepared to marry me and live with me in *my* home?"

She shook her head.

"Are you prepared to marry me at all?"

"I don't know," she said slowly. "Can't we put that off for a while?"

"Looks like we'll have to. Let's take it a day at a time and see how we go."

Kirsty agreed with this. It might not be very farsighted, but she was so much happier now than she had ever thought to be that she was almost afraid to make any positive decisions, for fear her good luck should vanish.

After a few days Mike disappeared to London, returning soon with a computer and a fax machine. These necessitated more telephone lines, which were not immediately forthcoming. Mike promptly called someone named Harry. The lines were installed next day.

"How do you get everyone jumping like that?" Kirsty asked the following afternoon. They were taking a leisurely stroll, accompanied by Tarn.

"It's easy if you know the right people," Mike said with a shrug. "Also I own a lot of shares in the phone company—at least, New World Properties does."

"New World Properties," she said, savoring the words.

"It has a fine ring about it, doesn't it?" he asked. "I wanted something that sounded visionary, because that's what I'm doing."

"But what exactly does the firm do? Just build?"

"*Just* build?" he echoed scandalized. "There's no *just* about it. Putting up new buildings is the most creative thing in the world."

"That depends on how you feel about modern architecture," Kirsty replied firmly. "Personally, I can do without most of it."

"I'm surprised you've ever seen any."

"Dad and I visited a big city once," she said. "We both hated it. There was no room to breathe. The people had tight, hard faces, and they avoided each other's eyes. It was like being among zombies. And the noise was unspeakable."

"You get used to it," Mike observed. "And then the quiet troubles you just as much. I was kept awake last night by a twig against my window. It was only a soft tap, but it was driving me mad. I had to get up and snap it off."

They had climbed up to the tor that rose at the back of the house. Huge rocks rose in menacing tribute to some ancient god, and all around them the countryside was in a riot of spring, with a gentle beauty that made the winter terrors hard to imagine. Kirsty let the silence fall, hoping that the loveliness would affect Mike, too. To her satisfaction she saw that he was looking around him with real attention. She smiled and said, "What do you think of it now?"

"I was thinking how many houses I could build on all this space," he said, and her mood vanished abruptly.

"Even you'll never manage that," she said. "Dartmoor is a national park, specially protected."

"Protected from me, you mean?" he asked wryly.

"From people *like* you," she agreed.

He sighed with impatience. "For *developer*, read *monster*. I get a little tired of being regarded as a cross between Vlad Dracol and Attila the Hun. Some of us actually benefit the community, but you never hear that side of it. It only takes one troublemaker determined to hold up progress by clinging to a tumbledown shack that he'd be better off without, and everyone forgets the jobs a development can bring. It's always the awkward cuss who's the hero, never the developer."

"Good," Kirsty declared belligerently. "Down with progress! Long live the awkward cuss!"

"Thank you," he said grimly.

"Why should the developer be a hero? He gets all that money."

"He gets a damn sight less when he's been held up for months and had to pay a dozen lawyers to get his plans through countless unnecessary enquiries."

"Who says they're unnecessary? People who are going to lose their homes to a developer are entitled to a say."

"They're unnecessary because I always win in the end," Mike said with reckless candor. "And if I'm the developer they get other homes that are at least as good, with proper amenities, so they've lost nothing, have they?"

"Except their friends and neighbors," Kirsty said quietly.

"Yes, well, friends and neighbors can be a mixed blessing. You should know that. I'm sorry," he added quickly, putting an arm about her shoulders, "I didn't mean to be hurtful, but you of all people shouldn't be sentimental on that score. I'm up against sentimentality every day of the week."

"And you've no time for it, have you?"

"Not much. It does too much damage and no good. Of course people's feelings matter but—well—"

"Not if they hold up the march of progress?" she asked, surveying him.

He was warming to his subject and missed the edgy note in her voice. "That's right," he agreed.

"But I expect you've got ways of dealing with that, haven't you, Mike? Tell me, just how do you convince an awkward cuss that his home isn't worth holding up a few extra jobs?"

"You don't. You convince the local council, and they put a compulsory purchase order on the property," Mike said bluntly, annoyance making his speech unguarded. "There are ways around opposition."

"And one way is wearing people down like the Chinese water torture," Kirsty said bitterly.

"What do you mean?" Something in her voice told him she wasn't talking generally anymore.

Kirsty pulled a letter from her pocket. It came from F. Colley & Son and had arrived that morning. She'd refused the firm's last offer as firmly as she knew how, but they were still hassling her, evidently hoping to tire her out. "These people must be soul mates of yours," she said in disgust.

As Mike glanced over the letter she went on, "They've been bothering me for the past year. Dartmoor is covered in tourists in summer. They've usually read *The Hound of the Baskervilles,* and want to see where 'it really happened.' I make a little extra money by serving teas in the garden. Last year I served a group of men who were interested in the house.

"They started saying what a wonderful site for a hotel. With the planning restrictions, virtually the only way you can set up a hotel on Dartmoor is to convert an existing building. They wanted to turn the barn into a restaurant, with plastic cows and wax milkmaids, 'to capture the spirit of old Dartmoor,' as one of them put it. I just laughed, but I've had no peace from them since. Mike?" She touched his arm. "Mike?"

He seemed to shake himself out of a trance. "Sorry, I was just thinking."

"You look struck all of a sudden. Do you know these people? They've got a London address."

"Yes, I've heard of them. I shouldn't worry about them. If they've been writing to you for a year without doing anything further it means they've nothing up their sleeve. Forget them."

"If you were them, how would you get me out?"

He grinned. "Well, the first thing I'd do is hide your shotgun. Let's go home."

As summer advanced, the moor filled up with tourists. They were mostly pleasant people whose only desire was to share the beauty and peace that Kirsty enjoyed every day. She knew this and tried to be tolerant, but their numbers destroyed the very peace they sought, and she longed for them to go.

As her pregnancy went on she found that a calm had settled over her. A question mark lay over her future, but she was contented with the baby she carried and her man, and other problems reached her only distantly. Mike worried about leaving her alone during his trips to London and tried to find a woman to live in to help with the housework, but without luck. On one memorable occasion he even brought down his own housekeeper. She entered into instant hostility with Tarn and departed after two days, muttering, "primitive," and "what do they think I am?"

Mike stayed a week, then began to pack again. "I'm not looking forward to going home," he told Kirsty as he brought his bag down into the kitchen. "She's going to bend my ear about her sufferings with 'that hound,' and I'll probably have to double her wages."

"Tarn suffered, too," Kirsty said indignantly. "She tried to keep him out of the house, and when he presented her with a peace offering she screamed and called him a revolting animal."

"In view of the fact that the peace offering was a rat, you can hardly blame her," Mike pointed out with some feeling.

"Tarn's the best ratter for miles. It was a great honor. If she can't appreciate that, we're better off without her. And what you thought you were up to, bringing a town woman here when—"

She broke off to look out of the window at the yard, from where she'd heard a noise. A car was approaching slowly, making heavy weather of the soft ground in a way that reminded her of Mike's first vehicle. It slithered to a stop and a well-dressed man got out and began to walk about, looking around him with distaste. A second man left the car but stayed by it, apparently unwilling to venture any farther. When he finally moved he halted after the first step and cautiously examined the sole of his shoe. Kirsty watched, torn between indigna- tion and amusement.

But her amusement faded when they opened the door to the henhouse and looked inside. It was a brief visit as a riotous clucking drove them out again to find Kirsty awaiting them. "What do you mean by poking around?" she demanded.

"Are you Mrs. Trennon?" one of them asked.

"I'll ask the questions. What are you doing here?"

"Our business is with Mrs. Trennon, not her labor- ers," he said truculently. "Tell her we're from F. Colley & Son."

Kirsty's face became grim. "Mrs. Trennon isn't here," she said coldly. "And she wouldn't want to see you if she was. So you can just go."

"I don't think so. I think we'll wait . . ."

"We'll see," she said grimly and turned back to the house. Mike looked on in alarm as she got out the shot- gun. "Must you respond to every situation with that thing?" he asked. "There *are* other ways."

"Not for vermin," she said firmly. "I've got two men from Colley's out there and I'm fed up with being pes- tered by those people."

"Let me see if I can get rid of them first," he said. "If I don't manage it you can come out with both barrels blasting. Agreed?"

"All right. But I'm not feeling patient."

"Do me a favor. Stay well out of sight."

She compromised, watching him through the win- dow, but staying well back. She couldn't hear, but she saw Mike approach the two men and say something. Watching him, Kirsty realized that he had an air of natural authority that was unmistakable. The men spoke only a few words before getting back into the car and driving away.

"You see?" he said cheerfully on his return. "And you were going to waste good shot on them."

"Ah, but think how I'd have enjoyed it," she said wistfully. "Mike, I'm at my wit's end with those people. They just don't know how to take no for an answer."

"They won't bother you again. Take my word for it."

"But what did you do?"

He hesitated. "I just reminded them that they're little fish swimming in a sea full of big sharks," he said at last. "They got the message." He kissed her. "I have to go now. I'll be back as soon as I can."

It was only after he'd gone that Kirsty realized he'd spoken of his London base as "home." For most of the time they'd been together they'd stayed in harmony, but some little slip like that would remind her of the reality. As always when he went away she wondered if he would come back. As she lay alone at night she would brood, thinking perhaps she should have accepted his offer of marriage. But by day she saw again that it was impossible. Mike had never said he loved her, although he seemed fond of her, and she couldn't rid herself of the conviction that his possessive instinct was behind the offer. He wanted the child she was carrying, and he was doing what he felt was the right thing. But she didn't want to be married out of pity or gratitude. The disaster of her first marriage was too much of a warning.

Mike was in London for two weeks, longer than he had intended. When he finally managed to clear his desk, he got into his car and drove through the night, reaching Dartmoor in the early dawn. He was traveling slowly now, trying not to fall asleep at the wheel. Halfway across the moor he stopped and scrambled down a bank to a stream he could see glittering in the sunlight. After splashing cold water on his face he felt better. His spirit was battered after a day spent having fierce arguments with his senior staff, and now he yielded to a temptation to linger. The sheep, which wandered the moor freely, were grazing contentedly on the far bank, indifferent to the noisy turbulence of his other life, indifferent to him. There was something pleasant in the thought. He grinned at his own fancies and made a mental note to tell Kirsty.

The thought of her made his grin become a tender smile. Often she made him uneasy. She was like Dartmoor itself, wild and primitive, qualities that complicated life. He was more used to the order of straight lines and precise angles. In his view nature was there to be tamed by man, and not only did Kirsty not share that opinion, but since he'd known her she'd never yielded an inch—over anything, he suddenly realized. Beneath her soft, mysterious beauty she was made of the granite on which the moor itself rested, and which gave it its timeless quality. He could neither tame her, make any impression on her nor get her out of his blood. He could only come back to her.

When he returned to the car, he saw he was no longer alone. A man was leaning against the hood, watching Mike's approach, a sullen look on his face. With him was a boy of about sixteen. He bore a brotherly resemblance to the other, but in contrast to the older man's oxlike appearance, his face was finer, with a wild rebellious look.

"Can I do something for you?" Mike asked.

"P'raps. P'raps not," the man said insolently. "I wanted to get a good look at you."

"I don't believe we've met before."

"Folks are talking about you. We all know who *you* are."

"Which is more than I can say about you," Mike said in a hard voice. "What's your name?"

"Abe Mullery." He indicated the boy with a jerk of his head. "My brother David. Our brother was Peter Mullery, him what she killed."

Mike's eyes grew cold. "If you mean Mrs. Trennon—"

Abe spat. "Mrs. Trennon! That's a laugh. She weren't no proper wife to Jack Trennon. She was bad luck to him and bad luck to my brother. She's bad luck to any man who crosses her path."

Young David spoke for the first time. "She's evil—a witch—they used to burn witches."

"You're too young for that kind of hatred," Mike told him seriously.

"I know what's right. It ain't right that she should get away with what she did."

"She didn't do anything."

"You don't know," the boy screamed. "She's fooling you like she fooled Peter and she fooled Jack, and they're both dead."

"He thought the world of Peter," Abe explained with a nod in his brother's direction. "We all did, and to us nothing's bad enough for the woman who killed him. So I came to warn you, friendly-like, get out of here for good. Leave her to us."

"Get off my car and out of my way," Mike said in a voice whose calmness didn't hide its dangerous edge.

"It's a nice car," Abe observed, not moving. "Shame if anything were to happen to it—or you."

"Nothing's going to happen to me," Mike said steadily. "But if you don't beat it you'll be very sorry."

Abe laughed. "You gonna make me sorry, are you? You, with your rich man's hands that never did a day's work. Talk. That's all you're good for. How you gonna make me sorry, eh?"

"Like this," Mike said. The next moment Abe was sitting in the dust, spitting out a tooth.

"Don't judge by appearance," Mike advised him. "I spent years on a building site and it's made me tougher than you'll ever be. A year in jail was a great help, too. And you, youngster, don't let them poison you with their hatred of an innocent woman. Live your own life."

But from David's hard, defiant gaze he knew his advice had fallen on stony ground. The boy helped his brother up, but his eyes stayed fixed on Mike. "They used to burn witches," he repeated. "But not now."

Mike turned away, appalled. As he drove home he reflected on Abe's threats, should he ever leave Kirsty. But that wasn't going to happen. Sooner or later she'd see reason and come to live with him in London. It was just a question of waiting. His spirits began to rise. He felt as if something had been settled, as though by the mere act of defending Kirsty he'd made her his own.

She was waiting for him in the yard, having seen him coming from a distance. When their first embrace was over she exclaimed, "Your shirt's torn. What have you been doing?"

He looked at where the sleeve had ripped away at the shoulder. "This shirt wasn't made for fighting in," he observed cheerfully.

"Fighting?"

In his euphoria he missed her note of alarm. "Not fighting exactly, more like scuffling. I only hit him once, but he'll think twice before he gives me any more trouble."

"Mike—who was it?"

"Abe Mullery. He and young David were there, talking a lot of nonsense about your being a witch. Abe doesn't like my being here to protect you, but I saw him off." He put his arms around her. "You're mine now, woman," he said in an exaggerated caveman voice. "Ancient tribal law—man who fights for woman claims her." He kissed her briefly. "They're right, though. You *are* a witch. You cast a spell over a man and make him want to do anything to make you his."

He tightened his arms to give her a fuller kiss, but for once she was unresponsive, even trying to evade him. He drew back and looked at her, puzzled, and saw that her eyes were full of horror. Too late he cursed his own tactlessness.

"Do *anything?*" she whispered.

"Kirsty, I'm sorry, it was a joke. I didn't mean—hell, I don't know what I did mean."

"But you enjoyed fighting for me, didn't you?" she accused him.

"I enjoy a good fight. I always have. It has nothing to do with you."

"Let me go, Mike," she said, beginning to struggle in his arms.

"I'd rather not. Can't we kiss and make up?"

"We've nothing to make up about. We haven't quarreled. It's just that—I need to be alone for a moment."

"So that you can brood about a careless remark and tell yourself that's how *they* died? They didn't. Their deaths had nothing to do with you."

"You don't know that. Nor do I. And I never will. As long as I live I'm never really going to know how guilty I am."

"You're not guilty about anything. You can't help being beautiful and desirable. It's a gift, my darling..."

"It isn't," she cried, "it's a curse, and I'll carry it all my life. Please, Mike, let me go."

"Kirsty—"

"Let me go."

Startled by her shriek he dropped his arms and stood back quickly. "I'm sorry."

"I'm sorry, too. I guess I just do harm by being myself. Mike, why don't you go away from me while you're still safe?" Without waiting for an answer she turned and ran into the house and up the stairs.

"Oh, dear God," he murmured in despair.

Chapter Eight

Spring passed into summer. The colors of Dartmoor exploded in glorious profusion, and Kirsty increasingly left the jobs of the farm to Fred and Frank, while she concentrated on serving tea to tourists. The swelling of her body seemed to make little difference to her agility, but a calm had descended on her. She knew that all was well with her baby, and therefore all was well with her. If Mike asked her how she was she would chuckle and say, "Splendidly bovine, thank you." But she didn't say bovine disparagingly as a town woman might have done. Rather it was an expression of her contented unity with everything about her.

After his encounter with Abe and David, Mike insisted that either Fred or Frank should sleep in the house if he had to be away. But his trips to London became fewer. He told himself it was because Kirsty needed him, but if he was totally honest he knew the noise of the place was beginning to get him down. Days spent haggling with people who never said exactly what they meant left him thinking longingly of Kirsty's habit of saying what she thought the moment she thought it. Even the suits that Tarn regularly ruined seemed a small price to pay for an honest welcome. But he learned his lesson and started doing the last lap of the journey in jeans.

He found Kirsty with the pigs one afternoon, not feeding them, but happily scratching the ears of Cora, who had recently received a visit from the boar. "We're being motherly together," Kirsty told him. "We're due at roughly the same time."

"You're not going to have seven, are you?" he asked nervously, and she chuckled in delight.

"At one time you could never have made a joke like that," she recalled.

"At one time I didn't have much to joke about. Now I have everything, and I owe it all to you." He was pulling her back against him with his arms crossed in front of her, nuzzling her neck. "Two months," he murmured. "It's an age. Why can't you have it tomorrow?"

"Perhaps I will," she said serenely. "I was a seven-month baby."

"Then there's something we ought to talk about," he said firmly.

"You and your fancy plans for putting me into a plush private hospital!" she said with a face of disgust. "All right, go ahead if it'll make you happy."

"You mean that? I can book you into the Bellingham Maternity Clinic?"

"It means, you rotten fraud, that I know you already *have* booked me in. They wrote to me, not realizing that

I didn't know a thing about it. Oh Mike, your face! You look so guilty!''

"You're not mad at me?"

She kissed him. "I forgive you."

"Actually, there's something else we ought to discuss," he ventured. Now, surely was the moment to ask her again to become his wife, while she was in an amenable mood. While he was choosing his words with care they heard someone calling from outside. Mike sighed and gave up the attempt for today.

"I know that voice," Kirsty said. She went out into the yard, and a moment later Mike heard her exclaim, "So *there* you are!" sounding equally amused and exasperated.

Then a man answered, "Well, now, don't I always show up like a bad penny? And don't you always forgive me my transgressions?"

Something about the man's voice filled Mike with dread. He couldn't exactly place it, yet it had a dreadful familiarity. He looked out and stiffened with shock and distaste at the sight of Caleb with his arm around Kirsty's shoulder. She was smiling as she said, "I shouldn't forgive you for leaving me in the lurch."

"Darlin', it broke my heart, but if I'd stayed around I'd have been in deep trouble and no use to you."

"Don't tell me. The less I know about your peccadillos the better," she said, laughing. She looked up and saw Mike framed in the doorway, watching them both with a grim expression. Caleb started back in mock terror at the sight.

"I'm harmless, I swear it," he vowed. "Lord, but you're a man with a terrible punch. I felt it for a week afterward."

"Pity it didn't keep you away," Mike retorted grimly. "What the hell are you thinking of to show your face back here?"

"Mike," Kirsty intervened quickly, "it's all right. Caleb apologized to me about that—"

"It wouldn't have happened if I hadn't been drunk," Caleb confirmed cheerily.

"He swore it wouldn't happen again, and it hasn't," Kirsty said. "I couldn't have managed without him after you went—him *and* Jenna. They're a couple," she added, trying to dispel the dark frown that was fixed on Mike's face. "They've been working for me together."

"I haven't noticed them around."

"Ah, well, I had to sort of make a quick exit," Caleb said. "But it's all put straight now. I came back to see if Kirsty needed my help—"

"She doesn't," Mike said shortly.

"Hey," Kirsty said, indignant at this high-handedness.

Mike turned to her. "Are you going to take his side—against me?" he asked in a low voice. "After what happened?"

Caleb drifted a few feet away, just far enough to give the other two the illusion of privacy, but not quite out of earshot.

"Mike, Caleb is family," Kirsty said firmly. "He's Jack's cousin. He stood by me when I needed it, and I won't turn against him just because he blotted his copy book once. That's not how families behave."

"But I'm your family now," he said furiously. "At least, I ought to be. If you weren't so stubborn we'd be married by this time."

"And then you think you'd have the right to order my friends away? Think again."

"Well, you have some very funny friends," he grated. "When are you going to see sense and marry me?"

She sighed ironically. "What a loverlike speech, Mike! How tender! How sensitively phrased! How do I ever manage to resist you?"

Out of the corner of his eye Mike could see Caleb grinning. He swore under his breath, furious at Kirsty's defense of a man he regarded as a ruffian. He turned sharply and went into the house, hoping she would follow but not daring to demand it in case he antagonized her. To his relief she came in a few moments later.

"How can you stand up for him?" he grated.

"I don't know. He's a scoundrel, but he has a kind heart, and he's come to my rescue a dozen times."

"He also pawed you about."

"Mike, please try to understand. Men have been trying to do that ever since I was fifteen. I don't like it, but I can't change it. Now I simply divide them into the ones who turn nasty when I reject them and the ones who say sorry and back off. Caleb said sorry." She looked at him significantly. "And he didn't ask too many questions about your presence here that night. He might have made things very difficult."

He turned away and took a deep breath. "I see what the problem is," he said. "You've got used to thinking of yourself as a woman alone, who *has* to compromise with brutes like that because you need their help. I understand that, and I don't blame you—"

"Thank you," she said ironically.

"But you're not alone anymore. You've got me now. You don't need Caleb. I can take care of him and all your other problems."

"Caleb's not a problem. He's my friend."

"Why do you keep on saying that when you know it makes me angry?" he snapped.

Her own temper kindled. "Did someone pass a law making it illegal to say things that make you angry? Strange that I didn't hear of it. Or is it that your employees keep quiet until you've laid down the official line, and you expect everyone else to do the same? Including your wife, if you had one. How lucky that I'm still a free woman and can speak my own mind about my own friends in my own home."

He glowered. "There's obviously nothing further to say."

"I wish I believed that, but I'm dreadfully afraid that you're going to keep on until you 'wear down the opposition' in your own delightful phrase."

"Why must you take everything I say the wrong way?"

"Because I'm never sure what the right way is. You're always so certain that you know best."

"But I—oh, to hell with it!" he said savagely and walked out. In another moment he was in his car and heading away from Everdene.

He was maddened at the sense of having been worsted in what should have been a simple, logical argument. He was used to winning arguments, but not with Kirsty, who seemed to live by a set of rules that were unknown to him and which he could only dimly perceive. Whenever he thought he'd finally understood how she saw the world everything seemed to shift, and he was back where he'd started.

He remembered the days following his escape, when the moor had been covered in snow and damp fog, so that he could see only a few feet and seemed stranded in a lunar landscape. Shapes loomed at him without warn-

ing and the ground fell away under his feet. Life with
Kirsty had taught him that Dartmoor wasn't just a place,
but a state of mind, where strangers could become dis-
orientated. If only he could get her away from here, to
what he still thought of as civilization. Then, surely,
everything would be all right. After driving for half an
hour he turned back. He felt calmer now.

But his calm was shattered by the sight of Caleb sitting on the grass. Caleb rose when he saw the car and
deliberately went to stand in the middle of the road.
Mike braked sharply.

"You only just did that in time," Caleb observed with
a silent laugh. "How you would have loved to just drive
on over me. But then, our Kirsty wouldn't have liked you
so well."

Mike's gorge rose at that casual "our Kirsty," but he
kept his temper and said evenly, "If you don't get out of
my way I'll put it to the test."

"What a violent man you are!" Caleb said softly.
"That's a mistake. Kirsty hates violence, having seen so
much of it. If you understood her as well as I do, you'd
know that." He grinned at the sight of Mike's knuck-
les, white at the effort at control. "You're ungrateful,
too," he chided. "If I'd been to the police with what I
saw that night, you'd be back in prison now. But I held
my tongue. You should thank me for that, not try to
blacken me."

"Don't try to fool me," Mike said coldly. "You had
no idea who I was, or you'd have given me away at the
first chance."

Caleb shrugged. "I knew all right. And I'd have
handed you in if it was just a question of you. But I
didn't want to bring the police down on my sweet Kirsty. Besides, I got my price."

"What the hell do you mean by that?" Mike demanded thickly.

"I think you know." He smiled abstractedly, as if recalling a pleasurable experience. "Kirsty was *very* grateful, and Kirsty's gratitude is—shall we say—like no other woman's?"

A red mist swam in front of Mike's eyes. He was lost in it, possessed by a storm of such violent feeling that he was sure he'd leapt onto Caleb and throttled him. Then the mist cleared and he found that, incredibly, he was still sitting at the wheel, and Caleb was still standing there, regarding him with an amused expression.

Mike looked at him as he might have looked at a filthy thing that had just crawled out of the ground. He was sick with loathing. Caleb was saying that Kirsty had slept with him to buy his silence—and done so within a few hours of lying in Mike's arms.

"You're lying," he managed to say. "Kirsty wouldn't—"

"Kirsty was very determined to protect you," Caleb interrupted. "*Very* determined. It's the truth all right. So it's a moot point which of us fathered that little bundle she's carrying. But I don't blame her for choosing you. You can give her more than a poor traveling man."

"My God, to think she calls you her friend!" Mike breathed. "And you serve her a dirty trick like this. Did you really think I could be turned against her by the likes of you? I can spot lies when I hear them. I'm warning you for the last time, get out of here and don't come near Everdene again."

Caleb gave his silent laugh again and stepped away. "I was going, anyway," he said. "But I'll be back. When you're tired of playing the country squire, you'll leave Dartmoor, and then Kirsty will need me again. Folk around here hate her even more now you've arrived to make her life easy. They think she's getting away with it, you see, and they won't stand for that. When you've gone they'll close in on her, and I'll be there to take care of her and claim what's mine. I can wait. I've waited this long, and a little longer won't bother me.''

He stepped smartly away from the car as Mike started the engine. Mike didn't favor him with another look, but drove on toward Everdene. His face was calm and his hands on the wheel were steady. But within a mile of his destination he swung the car abruptly aside and headed out into open country. He drove without stopping, anywhere, and when he finally halted he had no idea where he was.

He discovered he was actually shaking with the storm of feeling Caleb's words had created in him. The Gypsy's dark, mobile face swam before his eyes, smiling monstrously while he spilled poison.

It wasn't true. It couldn't be true. The candid, beautiful face that glowed on the pillow in the morning couldn't be a mask for deceit, because if it was, then nothing was worth living for.

Voices shouted together in his brain. *She's bad luck to any man who crosses her path— She's fooling you like she fooled Peter and she fooled Jack— I got my price— She's evil—a witch—like no other woman—*

He slammed his hand on the steering wheel and the riot shut off abruptly, leaving an echoing silence behind. He was making a fuss about nothing. All he had to do was go home and tell her what Caleb had said. She would deny it and reassure him, and that would be that.

There were a thousand ways to phrase the question. ''Caleb says you're passing his child off as mine. You don't mind if I ask, do you?''

Or— "You'll never believe what happened, Kirsty. You're supposed to have slept with that piece of scum soon after I left. Isn't that a laugh? You won't mind just denying it?"

Cold, ironical rage, directed at himself, rose in him as more possibilities came into his head. "Of course I don't believe it, whatever made you think that? I just thought I'd ask..."

Or he could just come right out and say "I haven't forgotten that you sheltered me and risked your own safety to save my life—but would you mind confirming that you're not a lying, treacherous trollop? And now that I've shown you that for all my fine words I'm no better than all the other louts who've poisoned your life with their easy, smug judgments, I'll pack my bags and leave to save you the trouble of throwing me out."

That one would bring the house down.

Mike groaned and dropped his head onto his hands on the wheel. After a while he became aware of an awesome quiet about him. He got out of the car and realized that he'd driven up onto one of the high granite tors that were dotted about Dartmoor. The ground fell away below him, gray and purple in the evening light. He had never felt so alone in his life.

The granite had stood here for millions of years. Prehistoric men and women had used it to build burial sites and primitive homes, some of which still endured. Its permanence seemed to mock his torment.

As he sat down on a rock his hand brushed something soft and delicate. Looking down he found a clump of wildflowers, growing in the rock's crevice, seemingly content to put forth their beauty in this barren home. Kirsty had told him that such mysteries were to be found everywhere on Dartmoor.

His first encounter with the moor had been harsh and bitter, but he'd discovered a flower of such beauty that he'd reached out yearning hands to her and made her his own. Or so he'd thought. In fact she'd eluded his attempts to pin her down in the contract of marriage. Now he found she was more elusive than he'd dreamed. What he thought he knew about her might be no more than shadow. What he'd feared might be the truth.

He'd never asked himself if he loved Kirsty, but he knew now that she was vital to him, and if she could not be trusted, then nothing and nobody could. But trust was suddenly complicated. Believing in someone meant not only trusting their actions, but also their motives. It could mean thinking well of them even if they were driven to do what seemed wrong.

She had protected him in any way she could. If that meant sleeping with Caleb, had he the right to blame her—for anything? She'd saved his life, his sanity and his future. How much more was a man entitled to ask?

He struggled to recall her ever saying that the child was his, but couldn't. He'd taken it for granted as soon as he saw her, and she hadn't denied it, but perhaps she didn't know and had merely been swept along by his decisiveness. The thought paths divided and subdivided in his exhausted brain until he felt he would go mad from the howling chaos in there.

Then he heard a snap. It was the faintest sound but it silenced the inner uproar and brought him back to reality. He was sitting on a high tor in the gathering darkness, and there in his hand was the flower that his fingers had uprooted from its rocky home. The beautiful head lolled brokenly.

In the same moment he seemed to hear a woman's anguished voice crying in the wind, "He should have trusted me."

He got slowly to his feet and made his way back to the car. He drove down slowly in the darkness, and it was another hour before he reached Everdene. The lights were on and he could see Kirsty standing in the yard, looking out anxiously over the moor.

"I was afraid you'd got lost," she said.

"I nearly did, but I found my way home at last." He kissed her. "Let's get into the warmth."

"There was something you wanted us to discuss just before Caleb arrived," she reminded him. "What was it?"

Now was the moment to ask her to marry him, as he had been going to do earlier that day, and in doing so, prove that Caleb's slanders had no power to touch him.

After a moment he said, "Nothing—that is, I don't remember. It can't have been very important."

He hated himself, but he couldn't help it.

Kirsty didn't have a seven-month baby, which, as she pointed out to Mike, was useful, because it would have gotten in the way of the harvest.

When the time for the reaping came, Mike found himself divided. A bad harvest might help in his campaign to lure Kirsty to London. But a bad harvest would break her heart, and that he couldn't bear. Cursing his own folly he bought a new combine harvester, the latest, the best, and left her no choice but to accept it. She argued, but not for long, and he had the satisfaction of knowing he'd pleased her.

They harvested a bumper crop, and the look on her face was worth a million to him. But then he escorted her to the harvest festival service in the church, and the chill hostility on her neighbors' faces made her ask to leave early and sit in silence all the way home.

"Kirsty, let's leave here," he begged. "Come away with me, and forget them."

She didn't answer, and a few moments later he touched her face and found it wet.

Their life together wasn't perfect. Both were quick-tempered and stubborn, and they squabbled, made up and squabbled again. Caleb's wild accusations were ignored, forgotten. Mike was very firm about that. But sometimes, for no reason, he would grow quiet and troubled and prefer to be by himself. What Kirsty read into these moods he didn't know, but she would become a little tetchy at the same time. Then he would remove himself to prevent an argument turning into a row. When he returned he would find that she'd gone to be with the animals, as though only they could calm her.

Sometimes he told himself that it was time he said goodbye. But he never said it. The sight of her face could always move him so deeply that he wondered if he could ever leave her. She needed him. She might be too proud to acknowledge it, but he knew, and that knowledge had to be his comfort.

One evening, as the summer was turning to autumn, he left the house in exasperation and drove off to put a distance between them. After a few miles he stopped the car and got out. Dusk was falling, and the last of the tourists had gone. All around him he could see the moor stretching in its ripe beauty. Now it had a gentle, inviting quality, and with no one else in sight he had a strange sensation, as if the loveliness of the landscape were for him alone. He chided himself for being fanciful, but the thought persisted, and he decided he would tell her about it when he returned. It would please her.

A few drops of rain landed on his arm. Looking up he found that the sky had changed as if a mask had covered it. Now, over the lovely features lay a threatening gloom. All about him the wind was rising, rustling the long grass. The rain began to fall faster, great heavy drops that threatened to soak him.

Suddenly, inexplicably, he was afraid. He shouldn't have left Kirsty alone. He tried to tell himself to be sensible. The baby wasn't due for another month. But it didn't help. He was consumed with a driving need to get back to her, because of—what? He couldn't tell, but his fear was growing.

In ten minutes he reached the farm and hurried inside, calling her name. The silence told him that she wasn't there. She'd spoken of checking the flock, and when he ran back into the yard he saw that the tractor was gone.

It was all right. If he only waited patiently she would return in a few minutes, laughing at his fears. He was saying all this to himself as he got back into the car and headed for the uplands.

The wind had risen almost to a gale as he arrived, making the trees stretch and bounce madly against the lowering sky. He saw the tractor first, standing abandoned at the edge of the field, but there was no sign of her, or of the dog. His cry of "Kirsty," was snatched away into the rain.

But a moment later he heard a bark, and Tarn appeared in the doorway to the sheep hut. He didn't race toward Mike as he would normally have done, and suddenly this seemed ominous. Kirsty was sitting on the floor with her back against a wall, gasping frantically.

When she saw him she cried, "Mike," in a voice full of gladness that went to his heart.

"Darling," he said, using the term for the first time without knowing, "what happened?"

"The baby's—coming. I was all right and then— started suddenly."

"That's impossible," he said, sounding firmer than he felt. "It's not due. It's only eight months."

Incredibly she managed a cheeky grin and gasped, "Can't . . . count yet . . ." The words ended on a groan. Her face was taut with pain and her breathing was coming harder.

"I'm getting you to hospital," he said grimly.

But she gripped his sleeve. "No . . . time . . . few minutes."

"But I don't know what to do," he said, appalled.

Again her face showed a gleam of mischief as she patted her stomach. "Don't worry. We do."

She seized his hand again as another contraction caught her. Instinctively he put his free arm about her shoulders, drawing her back against him, and it seemed to be the right thing to do, because she gave a sigh of contentment. Then he had the feeling she'd forgotten him, her whole attention concentrated on the baby who was fighting to be born into these unfriendly surroundings. Only her hand, squeezing his, seeking comfort and bestowing it, told him that he was still part of her consciousness.

Outside he could hear the rain lashing madly against the side of the hut, and through the open door he saw clouds being driven across the sky. If only, he thought, he could have got her to the safety of a hospital, where babies ought to be born. But he realized that she didn't share his anxiety. This wild, inhospitable place was home to her, a place where she never felt threatened or afraid. For a moment he allowed himself to be comforted by her calmness. She knew what she was doing, so it must be all right. But immediately he was filled with fear lest something should go wrong. She could die up here with only his useless, ignorant self to care for her. She might be dying this minute, and he didn't know what to do.

"Mike . . . Mike . . ."

"Yes, darling . . . what's happening?"

"It's coming . . . quickly . . ."

He laid her back and moved to where he could help the baby in the final moments. Kirsty's breathing grew faster, and suddenly a cry broke from her, different from any sound she'd made before. It was a cry partly of pain, but mostly of triumph as she summoned the energy for the final push, and the child emerged into the world, straight into its father's hands. At once it began to cry in thin, protesting sobs.

"What is it?" Kirsty asked, gasping.

"A boy."

She held out eager arms. He tore off his jacket, wrapped it around the little scrap and gave him gently to his mother. Kirsty looked down tenderly at her son, and Mike saw a light on her face that made him hold his breath. After a moment she looked up and gave him a smile that seemed to reach out and draw him into the magic circle. An absurd happiness possessed him. He wanted to run out into the rain and shout to the blazing heavens that they could do their worst because his son was born and nothing else mattered. But he didn't. Instead he said prosaically, "Now I'm going to get you to the clinic," and let his gentle touch on her cheek say the rest.

He half led, half carried her the few yards to the car, and eased her into the back seat. His heart was in his mouth as he began to ease the car down the slope to where there was a track. At every bump he tensed and glanced quickly over his shoulder, but Kirsty said easily, "Don't worry. We're fine back here." He found himself repeating silently, "We're fine...*we're* fine...we, both of us." Two people where an hour ago there had been only one.

It was a miracle, and he'd been there, been part of it. He was a pioneer, the first man ever to make such a discovery. There had been fathers before, but none of them could have experienced the miracle as he had. The others only thought they knew.

Kirsty's voice, drowsy and content, reached him from the back. "Did you realize you're grinning like the cat that swallowed the cream?"

"I'm not," he said, self-conscious.

"You are. I can see you in the mirror." She reached forward and laid a hand on his shoulder. "You know now, don't you?"

And he answered quietly, "Yes, I know." He'd been wondering how to tell her of the secret he'd discovered, but of course, she'd been there before him, waiting for him to catch up. He wondered now how he could have been such a fool, and the happiness swamped him again, making him want to tell all the world that he was a fool, and it was wonderful.

In half an hour they reached the hospital. He'd used the car phone to alert the staff, and when they arrived Kirsty and the baby were pounced upon by starched nurses who whisked them away into white-walled, disinfected regions where he wasn't allowed to follow.

This was what he'd wanted, but now he found he didn't like it. Relief at seeing Kirsty in capable hands was succeeded by a feeling of anticlimax and discontent. What did these efficient strangers with their machines know about seeing a child born?

A nurse appeared, pen in hand. "I'd like to take some details about your wife, please," she said.

"She isn't my wife," he said abruptly. "My name is Mike Stallard."

"Are you any relation?"

For a fraction of a second Caleb's jeering grin seemed to hang in front of Mike's eyes. Then he was banished. "Yes," Mike said firmly. "I'm the baby's father."

Chapter Nine

Kirsty had hated the idea of the expensive private clinic, but in the time following Rob's birth she was grateful to Mike for insisting. She'd been unprepared for the flood of adoration that had swamped her the first time she held her baby in her arms. Now, free of other responsibilities, she could float on that blissful tide, with nothing to do but enjoy her baby.

He slept in a cot beside her bed, and when he awoke in the night she was on hand to assuage his hunger. He drew his life from her now as much as he had in the months he'd spent inside her, and there was nothing sweeter than the feel of his tiny mouth sucking the milk that flowed freely for him. The nurse had offered her a bottle if she was unable or unwilling to breast feed, but Kirsty was a woman of the earth and one who had only recently discovered the depths of her physical nature. To embrace her lover or suckle his child were, to her, part of a single act of love.

When the first pain had caught her while she was alone on the uplands, she'd been alarmed. But now that it was all over and her baby safe, she wouldn't have had things any other way. To give birth with only Mike beside her had been an experience that words couldn't describe. She only knew that she had felt closer to him at that moment than ever before. Even their fevered lovemaking paled beside the sense of total union she'd experienced as they helped their son into the world together.

Now she needed to know if he'd felt the same. She was almost sure that he had. There'd been a look in his eyes she'd never seen before. But she wouldn't be sure she'd read him right until she saw him again, and she waited for his first visit with a pounding heart. Many times she pictured the door opening, the sight of Mike's face— would it be grave or smiling?

In the event, it was neither. She was dozing when he arrived and awoke to find him sitting there, leaning over the crib, studying the baby with a look of awe on his face that mirrored the one she'd seen there at the moment of birth. A deep, blissful contentment pervaded her. Then Mike glanced up and saw her, and the next moment they were in each other's arms.

"Are you all right?" was his first question.

"I'm fine, and so happy. Mike, tell me you're happy, too."

"Do you really need to ask me that?"

She shook her head.

"I was just getting to know him," Mike said. "He's so . . . perfect."

They were the words that a million fathers had spoken, but they sounded newly minted coming from this one man.

"What did your parents say when you told them?" she asked eagerly. "Will they be coming to see him soon?" Instead of answering, Mike got up and went to look out of the window. Kirsty waited, unable to believe what his silence suggested. "Mike, you *have* called them?"

"No," he said, his eyes fixed on a tree outside.

"But—they're your parents. This is their grandchild—their first one, isn't he?"

"Yes, he's their first grandchild," he said quietly. He turned back to her, and she was shocked at how drawn his face suddenly looked. "Kirsty, please don't press me on this."

She put out a hand to him. "Mike, what's wrong?"

He shrugged. "It's really very simple. They don't like me, haven't done since I grew up. If it comes to that, I don't blame them."

His tone was light but beneath it she could hear his pain like a cry, and it seemed to shiver through her. Once before she'd empathized with his suffering, when Con had gone abroad and it seemed that Mike's hope had gone with him. In that moment she'd thought she'd known what love was, but now she realized that had only been love's infancy. The bonds that united them now were stronger and more lasting. "You don't really think that," she said gently. "I don't believe they dislike you. They're your mother and father. Look." She brushed tender fingers over Rob's cheek. "Could you ever dislike him?"

He shook his head. "But that's different."

"Not to them. All our lives we'll remember how our son looked at this moment, and what we feel for him in thirty years will have grown out of what we feel now. It's like that with them. They still love you. Believe me, Mike."

He hesitated. Part of him wanted to believe, but another part shied away. "They may love me," he said slowly, "but they don't *like* me. They're appalled by how I turned out, but I couldn't have been any different. They seem to think that modern progress is an invention of the devil, and life ought to go on in the old way forever. Sometimes you remind me of them. Look at the fights we've had just because I wanted to modernize Everdene, and you want to keep it preserved in aspic."

"That's not true," Kirsty said quickly. "It's just that some old ways are worth preserving."

"You sound like my mother, only she'd have said *all* the old ways should be saved."

"I wonder if she would, or if you've just misread her." Kirsty smiled and touched his cheek in an echo of the way she'd caressed her child a moment ago. "You do tend to get a bit paranoid if people don't agree with you," she said, her tenderness taking the sting out of the words.

"Kirsty, you don't understand. They're—" it was hard to say the word but he forced himself "—*ashamed* of me. I used to see it in their eyes when I went home, as though it was a crime to be successful. I don't understand why, but that was how they saw it. I wanted to buy them a house in a better area, but they weren't interested."

"Perhaps they'd been happy where they were."

"How could they be? They were as poor as church mice."

"Oh, Mike," she said helplessly. "Oh, Mike."

"It's a fight to give them anything. They didn't want to take money from me, so in the end I just paid it directly into their bank account. It's there if they want it, but they probably feel they'd be contaminated if they touch it. I've tried to share my success with them, but they don't want it."

"Perhaps they want what your success has taken away," Kirsty suggested.

He stared. "Such as what?"

"You. Maybe they want their son—not a tycoon trying to move them away from their friends, but a son who loves them."

"But of course I love them," he exclaimed. "I've always tried to do my best for them, make them proud of me, but they just turned away. They didn't even want to come to my wedding."

Kirsty was torn by pity. Behind the words was another story that Mike didn't know he was telling, but which stood out clearly to her. She could see the simple couple with their solid, old-fashioned values, proud of their son, but scared of him, too, and saddened by his lack of understanding. And she could also see the boy who still lived beneath Mike's bullish manner, a boy who was bitterly hurt at his parents' seeming rejection.

"When I was put on trial they thought I was guilty," Mike went on. "They'd always known I'd come to a bad end, and their worst fears had been fulfilled."

"They actually said that?" Kirsty demanded, aghast.

"They didn't have to," he said firmly.

"Mike, I think you've read them all wrong, just as they've read you wrong. Give them a chance. Tell them they've got a grandson."

"All right. When I get home."

She glanced significantly at the phone by her bed. "What's wrong with now?"

He looked at her for a long moment, then picked up the phone and dialed swiftly, as if he was trying to finish before he changed his mind. Kirsty could hear the ringing sound on the other end, then a click and a man's voice. Mike said, "Dad," and there was a silence before the man spoke again.

Kirsty sat tense, listening. Mike was awkward and unhappy and it had the effect of making him sound belligerent. She couldn't make out what his father was saying, but she could hear the silences, and a certain unyielding quality in the old man's attitude came through clearly.

He's afraid of Mike, she thought, *just as, in a different way, Mike is afraid. And they're both getting defensive. If only I could get them together. But they're bound to come and see the baby.*

"I rang to tell you—that I've got a son," Mike was saying. "He was born yesterday. We're going to call him Rob." There was a murmur from the other end, then Mike said awkwardly, "I'm not married. Why should that matter? I just thought you'd like to know about the baby. That was all—that's right—tell Mom. Goodbye." He set down the receiver and sat staring at it.

"The very first thing he said was, 'We didn't know you were married,'" he told Kirsty. "The first thing. Not 'That's wonderful,' or anything like that. Just a moan."

"I think they were just hurt because they thought you'd got married without telling them," Kirsty soothed him.

"It was a disaster. I knew it would be. I shouldn't have listened to you."

"Mike, they're old. They need time to get over the shock. The last year's been rough on them, too. Think what it must have done to them, seeing you in prison."

"They never did."

"They *never* visited you?"

"My father came once. I refused to see him. I feel bad about that now, but at the time I felt so humiliated I simply couldn't face it. He obviously hasn't forgiven me for that."

"His pride is uncomfortably like yours, when you think of it," Kirsty observed.

Mike looked at her for a moment, colored and said nothing. Kirsty didn't make the mistake of speaking again. Mike wasn't comfortable delving into his own feelings, and today he'd told her a great deal about himself, much of it painful. She was content to let time do its work.

That night, as Kirsty held her child against her, she thought about her own family, in which there had been love to spare and everyone had shown their feelings freely. It had left her with the strength to endure what came after. How different it had been for Mike, who'd felt so alienated from his parents that he'd shut them out of his pain. Now it seemed that a gulf also separated them from his joy.

"But we're going to change all that," she whispered to Rob. "You need grandparents, and I can't give you any. But just be patient. I'm working on the problem."

Mike collected her a few days later. On the journey home he hinted at a surprise awaiting her, but wouldn't divulge details. "You wait," he kept saying, evidently enjoying himself.

As the car stopped in the yard a middle-aged woman with a strong, kindly face, came to stand in the door of the house. She came over and quietly took the baby to make it easier for Kirsty to get out.

"This is Mabel," Mike said. "She's your surprise. She'll take care of Rob."

Before she could stop herself Kirsty burst out, "But he's my baby. I want to look after him. I'm sorry—" she turned quickly to Mabel. "I didn't mean to be rude but—"

"Look," Mike said, taking her shoulders and turning her slightly. "Look all around you. You have two babies, and Everdene is the other one. Do you think I haven't learned by now? Well, a mother shouldn't have favorites. Everdene is still going to need your care as well."

Kirsty looked at him, taken aback by this new perceptiveness. Mabel broke in on her thoughts, handing Rob back to her, saying, "You'll be wanting to show him his home," in a voice that had a faint trace of Scottish accent.

Kirsty began to relax. Mabel's shrewdness in returning the child to her instead of carrying him in herself had struck just the right note. Holding Rob closely she stepped into the house to find the kettle singing on the stove and everywhere spotless and welcoming. Mabel made her sit down while she made the tea. As she set out cups and saucers she told Kirsty about herself. Her list of previous employers was impressive, and Mike's confirming nods informed Kirsty that he'd checked out every reference.

"You might find this a little dull after some of the exciting places you've worked," she ventured, feeling slightly overwhelmed.

"I was born on a farm," Mabel answered placidly. "They said no one for miles could match me for milking. Are you nursing the child yourself?"

She added the last question quite naturally, as though it had grown out of the previous remark, which, to a farm woman, it did. Kirsty replied equally naturally, "Yes, I want to as much as possible," and felt that Mabel was a kindred spirit. She relaxed some more.

Later that night, as he watched her suckle the child, Mike said gently, "So despite my overbearing ways, I do sometimes get it right?"

She touched his cheek in a gentle caress, feeling more perfectly united with him than ever before. If he had asked her to be his wife at that moment she would have said yes with all her heart. Instead he said, "I've never seen so many flowers except in a flower shop. Where do they all come from?"

"The red roses are from you, as you well know," she said with a smile. "The wild flowers are from Fred and Frank. And the chrysanthemums are from Caleb. Don't look like that. I know you don't like him, but it was a nice thought."

"Was there a message with them?"

"Yes, it's there."

Mike picked up the scrawled card and read the hateful words, " 'Here's to the family's newest member.' " There was a silence, before he asked in a strained voice, "What does he mean by that?"

"Mean by what?"

"Family. Our baby is no part of his family—*is he?*"

"Gypsies are very family minded," Kirsty said serenely. "Jack was Caleb's cousin, so I'm his cousin, too, so little Rob is a member of Caleb's family. It makes perfect sense to them—and to us, too, doesn't it, precious?'' she enquired of the baby, who was regarding her solemnly. ''You want all the relatives you can get.''

''I disagree,'' Mike said coldly.

''Mike, please. The Gypsies will be gone soon. Don't let's have a row about it.''

''Very well,'' he said quietly, ''we won't have a row about it. We won't need to discuss it at all. My work will take me away for a while.''

''You're going back to London?'' she asked, looking up quickly. ''You didn't mention it before. In fact you definitely said you could be here for quite a while.''

''I was wrong. It's time I returned.''

''Will you be away long?''

''I don't know. Does it matter?''

''I shall miss you. But then, I've got *you*, haven't I?'' Kirsty asked, returning her attention to the baby. ''We can keep each other company.''

Mike watched the two of them for a long moment. If she'd asked him to stay he'd have changed his plans at once, but mother and child were totally wrapped up in each other, as if they existed in a separate world, and he had the feeling she'd forgotten him. After a while he left the room.

With Mike away Kirsty soon discovered that it was Mabel who made life possible. Mabel was a tower of strength and equal to every crisis. She could keep Rob totally safe and happy, leaving Kirsty free to care for the farm with an easy mind, but she was free from jealousy, and when Kirsty was driven home by the ache of missing her baby, Mabel would lay him in her arms at once.

She possessed her own little car, in which she made trips to the village, where she soon became aware of the talk about her employer. She was a gregarious soul with a love of gossip, but she also liked to judge for herself. She'd decided in Kirsty's favor on the first day, and nothing she heard against her altered that by a fraction. When Kirsty said longingly that she wished she could keep Rob with her while she was working, it was Mabel who got out her needle, tore up some old clothes and fashioned a sling in which the child could snuggle safely on his mother's back. After that, Kirsty kept him with her always, unless she had to go far from the house, and then she handed him over reluctantly.

She discovered that she felt Mike's absence differently from before. She looked forward to his return, but there was no ache of loneliness, because he had left part of himself behind. Her new love absorbed her in total joy. To hold Mike's son against her, to fancy she saw her lover in the child's face, this was happiness. It was more. It was complete fulfillment.

She returned one afternoon to find Caleb holding the baby, while Mabel regarded him with a doting smile that made it clear Caleb's charm had worked overtime. Jenna leaned against the wall, a jealous, sulphurous presence. "We'll all be leaving soon," he said, referring to the Gypsy families who were camped on the moor. "I came to ask you to bring Rob to visit us one evening. The grandmother would like to meet him."

"I'd love to, but I can't bring Rob out onto the moor at night. It's freezing."

"Wrap him up well."

"No," Kirsty said firmly. "Bring the grandmother here."

"Right. Fine. Tomorrow night." He handed Rob back to Mabel, planted a kiss on Kirsty's cheek and put his arm around Jenna's shoulders. "We'll see you then."

"We'd better start cooking for a hundred," Kirsty said with a laugh when they'd gone. "He'll bring more than the grandmother."

"Now there's a funny thing," Mabel mused. "You both say 'the grandmother' instead of 'his grandmother.'"

"She's everyone's grandmother," Kirsty explained. "Heaven knows whom she's really related to. Probably not Caleb. She's a sort of wise woman, and the Gypsies don't feel a baby's had a good start in life unless he's had her blessing."

As if to prove how well she knew him, Caleb returned the following night with the grandmother, three aunts, four uncles and any number of cousins. They all crowded into the kitchen, exclaimed over the baby and downed the fruit punch Kirsty had prepared. She was glad to have them. Mike had been gone a month, there was still no news of his return, and it was so long since she'd been to a party.

Fred and Frank dropped in and promptly started flirting with the most attractive women there, who received their advances with cheerful acceptance, to the disgust of their menfolk. An argument might have broken out, but someone produced a fiddle, and the next moment everyone was dancing with everyone else.

Kirsty took part in a couple of dances, then went to sit beside the grandmother on the settle. The old woman might have been any age up to a hundred, but her eyes were still sharp, and she held the baby firmly on her lap. Little Rob lay sleeping, oblivious of his surroundings, but one tiny star hand clutched a small twiglet, symbol of nature's blessing. The grandmother had given it to him, and now she was chuckling at his tenacity in holding on to it. "He's one of us, no doubt of that," she said.

"Yes, he belongs here," Kirsty said seriously. "I'm going to teach him to love Dartmoor and protect it."

"Right, but I meant more than that, didn't I?" the old woman asked, peering at her with gleaming eyes.

"Did you?" Kirsty frowned, not sure she'd heard the grandmother properly against the noise of the fiddle. "What did you mean?"

"Oh, you're a sly one. We'll say no more. All that can wait until later, eh?"

Kirsty was about to ask what she meant when she became aware that the noise was dying. The dance had stopped and everyone was staring in the same direction. Looking up, Kirsty saw Mike standing in the doorway, his face tight with anger. She rose to greet him with a glad smile, but it died at the sight of the look he turned on her. It was almost one of hatred. "My friends came to celebrate our son's birth," she told him.

"So I see. It's a little late for him to be up, isn't it?" Mike responded coldly.

"He was just going back to bed." Kirsty turned to take Rob from the grandmother, but the old woman no longer had him. Caleb had stepped in and lifted the child, holding him strongly in both arms. He was smiling at Mike in a way Kirsty didn't understand, but she understood that Mike was on the verge of breaking out into violence. She swiftly took Rob and gave him to Mabel, who turned to go upstairs. But Mike stopped her. "What's that filthy thing in his hand?" he demanded.

"It's a Gypsy blessing," Kirsty explained quickly. "It means he'll grow up at one with nature. On Dartmoor it's a sign of good luck."

Mike's face was very pale as he tore the twig from his son's grasp, crushed it and threw it on the floor. "That's one kind of luck he can do without," he muttered.

A quiet fell on the little crowd. They exchanged nervous glances like people who'd witnessed a desecration. Slowly they began to edge toward the door, until there was only Caleb left. His face still bore a cold, catlike smile as he approached Mike and paused. "That was a very silly thing you did," he said softly.

"Get out of my house," Mike told him in a deadly voice.

Caleb shrugged and went to the door. Before leaving he blew a kiss at Kirsty.

When they were alone she eyed Mike frostily. "I know you're tired after a long drive, but was that really necessary?" she demanded.

He turned on her like a man drawing a sword. "*Tired?* Do you really think this is about tiredness?"

"I don't know what else it's about."

"Perhaps it's about me, and what a fool I've been— how I've believed in you and never asked any questions, even when they were burning in my brain so that I nearly went mad. Perhaps the time has come to ask them."

"What questions?" she cried. "I don't know what you're talking about?"

"Don't you, Kirsty? Was I really not supposed to get suspicious about the way you favor that lout although you know how I feel about him? When a woman defends a man that stubbornly there's usually a reason."

"I've told you the reason," she said hotly.

"I know the reason you've told me, and I know the reason *he's* told me, and they're not the same reason."

"The reason *he's*—? Caleb has told you—what? I don't understand what any of this is about. When did you talk to Caleb?"

"The day he came back and we quarreled about him. I drove off, but when I returned he was waiting for me." Mike had a sensation that the room had grown very hot as he came closer to the thing he'd sworn not to say. "Do you know what he told me? About our baby?"

"I've no idea," Kirsty whispered.

At the last moment, too late to draw back, he saw that she was speaking the truth. He had a blinding vision of her clear, candid face, a face that he was about to strike with words that would kill whatever love she had for him. He shuddered and stepped back from her. "It doesn't matter," he said.

"Of course it matters. Mike, what did Caleb say to you about Rob?"

"I said it doesn't matter," he shouted. "I never believed it, anyway."

Into Kirsty's mind came the grandmother's cunning face, inviting her into a conspiracy. "He's one of us, no doubt of that . . . you're a sly one."

She flinched from the memory. It was monstrous, impossible. She heard her own voice say, "If you never believed it there's no harm in telling me."

"Please, Kirsty. It was just the shock of coming home to find—let's leave it."

"I can't leave it now, and you know I can't. *What did he tell you?*"

In total despair Mike said, "He said you'd slept with him to keep him quiet about me, and there was no way of knowing which of us fathered Rob."

He waited for her outburst, but there was nothing but total, terrible silence. Her face was gray, as though she'd died while she listened to him, and he knew he should have done anything rather than repeat those words. It was too late now. He'd murdered something that was irreplaceable. But like a fool he blundered on, trying to make it right. "I told him to get the hell out and not to come back here with his lies," he said desperately.

She didn't seem to have heard him. "And this happened the day Caleb returned?" she said slowly, as if trying to take it in. "But that was two months ago. All this time you've been thinking—?"

"I told you I didn't believe it," he said, interrupting her quickly.

"You never told me what he'd said," she breathed, "never gave me a chance to defend myself."

"How could I? It would have sounded like an accusation."

"An accusation?" She gave a bitter laugh. "What a fine sentiment! I'd rather have an honest accusation than the kind of unspoken doubt that's been in your mind. To me that's a kind of treachery. You believed the worst when you came through that door tonight. Don't deny it."

"I hated the way you've always defended Caleb against me, as if you had a tenderness for him."

"I did. As a good friend, but that was all. And that friendship is over if he's been lying about me. But I can hardly believe it—Caleb—"

But even as she said the words a thousand small ominous memories came together in her head. She'd always known he was an unscrupulous rascal to others, but she'd persisted in believing him kind and well meaning toward herself, because she'd desperately needed to believe in someone. She recalled the sudden flare of lust in his eyes, his amiability toward Mike when

Mike had beaten him. Would any man be that amiable—or would he plan a subtle revenge against that man and the woman who'd rejected him? And the grandmother's insistence that Rob was one of them. Caleb had lied to her, too.

"I'll never forgive Caleb for this," she said in a hard voice. "I never slept with him, Mike. It was a pack of lies to get back at both of us. And if he hadn't overreached himself tonight, I think he'd have succeeded."

"I didn't believe him."

But from the way Kirsty looked at him he knew she despised his protests for the feeble things they were. He might not have believed Caleb, but he hadn't entirely disbelieved him, either.

"All this time," she murmured, "I thought we were growing close at last, but I never knew you at all, did I? Any more than you knew me. I might have slept with him to protect you, Mike. I'd have done *anything* to protect you. But I would never have deceived you about it."

"I knew that," he said desperately.

She shook her head. She seemed to be in a dream. "No you didn't. You ought to have done, but you didn't."

He didn't know what to say. While he watched, she turned and went upstairs, and he heard her footsteps vanishing down the corridor.

He was shaking. Suddenly the room was filled with ghosts. Kirsty's own spirit seemed to be there still, her eyes filled with disillusion. But behind her stood his father and mother, who'd rejected him because—he took a shuddering breath as his mind finally made the leap— because they felt he'd rejected them. That was what Kirsty had tried to tell him, but in his blind stubborn-

—

ness he hadn't wanted to see it. Now it was happening again. And it was almost too late.

He climbed the stairs very slowly. He was afraid of what the next few minutes would bring. His whole life might hang on them. He could see no light under her bedroom door, and when he tried the handle he feared to find it locked, but it gave at his touch.

Kirsty was sitting on the bed facing the window, her back to him. Her tiny bedside lamp cast a little dim light, but apart from that the room was in shadows. She looked up as he approached, and the sadness in her face made him drop to his knees beside her and put his arms around her waist. After a moment he felt her stroking his hair. Relief that she didn't turn away from him made him tighten his hold. "I never meant to tell you," he said huskily.

"Better that than have it hanging over us," she said quietly.

"But you must understand—"

"I do," she interrupted him. "Don't say any more. I was too hard on you. Look." She showed him the paper she'd been holding in her hand. It was Rob's birth certificate, with his own name on it as the father. "You told them that, didn't you?"

"Of course I did," he said eagerly. "In my heart I always knew you'd never deceive me. I should have clung to that, but I don't find it easy to trust people."

"And I was too trusting," she sighed. The next moment her voice had hardened. "Caleb never sets foot here again. As far as I'm concerned, he no longer exists."

He had no doubt that she meant it literally. Beneath her soft beauty, Kirsty had a quality that was as unyielding as granite. A chill went through his heart at the thought of how totally she could reject someone—perhaps himself, one day. That mustn't happen.

He looked up into her face, pulling her forward until her long, magical hair fell over him. "Kirsty, let's get married at once," he pleaded. "I need you. You and Rob give a center to my life, and without it I'll grow worse. You can stop that."

But she shook her head slowly, making the tresses dance against his face so that tremors went through him. "We're not ready to be married, Mike. Sometimes I think we never will be."

"But I want you," he said stubbornly. "And I want my son."

They were the wrong words, the acquisitive words he'd used so often that now he knew no others. He tried again. "I need you, Kirsty. And you need me—more than ever now you know you can't rely on Caleb."

"Mike, I can't marry you just to get a bodyguard."

"And what about Everdene? How will you fight off the predators without me?"

There was a catch in her voice. "I don't know. I only know that we don't belong in the same world."

"You're wrong," he said. "There's one world where we both belong."

He drew down her head until their lips met. The touch made shocks of electricity go through him and through her also. He sensed her instant response and knew this was one place where she couldn't deny him. "Our world," he said against her lips, "that we made ourselves—a world where no one else belongs."

She murmured, "Yes," against his lips, and took his face between her hands, kissing him tenderly yet with desire. It was so long since their last lovemaking, but now her young, strong body had recovered from its trial, and was ready for passion. He could feel it in the soft caresses of her mouth, in the vibrancy of her warm flesh and in the hot, musky perfume that made his head spin.

But she forced herself to draw back. He could feel the effort it cost her. "Mike, perhaps we shouldn't do this. It will only make it more difficult."

"Difficult to do what? To leave each other?"

"Perhaps. If we have to."

"Then I'm going to make it difficult," he said in a purposeful voice. "I'm going to make it as hard as I can for you to leave me."

As he spoke he reached across and switched out the bedside light. His fingers were working on the buttons of her shirt. He had them open in a moment, slipping his hands inside to touch her bare breasts. She gasped at the pleasure she'd missed for so long. She had meant to be strong, meant to insist that they had too little in common and their passion was not enough. But as she felt the old desire begin to stream through her body everything else fell away. At this moment the desire that only Mike could bring alive was the only thing that mattered. Her breasts were burning from his touch.

She felt his lips enclose one proud, peaked nipple and forks of fire went through her. Moving blindly she slid her fingers into his hair, holding him against her while his lips and tongue teased her to madness and she arched back in ecstasy. He knew now how she liked to be loved, and he was a master of the slow, languorous movements that pleased her. It was hard to believe that only a few months had passed since they'd first discovered their passion in this very room. It was another world and they were different people.

But one thing hadn't changed. Their bodies were tuned to each other with an instinctive harmony that nothing—not absence, hardship or outright hostility—could turn to discord.

Her gasps turned to groans as he continued the purposeful movements of his tongue, circling the nipple with gentle strength, then moving his tongue across with a rasping movement that nearly sent her out of her mind. He drew back and looked at her bare breasts in the moonlight that came through the window. "You're so beautiful," he murmured, laying his face against them. The flesh was warm beneath his cheek, and he could hear her heart beating strongly and slowly, beating with the passion he had inspired. The thought inflamed him and he began to remove her remaining clothes. She helped him, then pulled his buttons open and ran her hands over his chest in sensuous invitation.

As he lay down beside her and began to run his hands over her body Kirsty had a sudden wild sense of freedom. Every lovemaking before this had been overshadowed, either by fear or by caution during her pregnancy. Now there were no constraints, just the two of them and what they felt for each other. Primitive passion swept through her like the wind sweeping across the moor—timeless, elemental, created out of nothing and hurtling to a mysterious destination. The tenderness that usually infused her feelings for Mike vanished to be replaced by the raw, lusty need of female for male, Eve for Adam, earth for fire. Her caresses grew more intimate and demanding as she claimed him for her own. She wanted every part of him, but first she would savor the delight to come.

With loving hands she traced his frame, enjoying the long, muscular thighs with their hint of steel, the taut buttocks and lean strong hips. Every inch of his firm body thrilled her. He was watching her out of half-closed eyes, not familiar with this mood, for in the past he had taken the lead. But the experience of giving birth had taken her where even he could not join her, and now she was beyond him, a teacher where she had been a pupil. Her movements had a controlled erotic aggression that was as exciting as it was strange.

Kirsty sensed his tension. He wasn't sure whether to oppose her or go with her. His mind said one thing and his senses another. Her exploring hand found his manhood, enclosed it in long, clever fingers and squeezed gently. The deepening of his breathing told her the battle was going her way.

She began to tease him in ways that once she couldn't have dreamed of, ways she didn't know she knew. After the first shock of surprise he surrendered to her. He couldn't help himself. Her enchanting seduction was a revelation to him, but an even greater revelation was what he was discovering about himself. An elemental spirit seemed to have entered him, stripping away the calculating outer skin he'd assumed and forcing him to rediscover the intense, emotional man that nature had created him. For years he'd hidden behind protective barriers, but Kirsty had always found ways to force him out from behind them. That was why part of him feared her—and why she was utterly necessary to him.

When her teasing became too much he moved over her, feeling her legs part in welcome. He found his home in her, kissing her with fierce tenderness, rejoicing at the feel of her soft thighs tightening around his loins. Candid and open in her daily life, she was no less so in her passion. As her sexual confidence had grown so had her frankness, and now she was voracious in her craving for him. There was nowhere to hide from her, had he wished to. But there was nothing he wanted less. He met frankness with frankness, driving into her with a vigor he'd feared to use before, and she uttered little cries of delight that spurred him on.

When he sensed their moment coming he slowed the pace, prolonging the pleasure and murmuring into her ear, "Tell me you'll never leave me."

."Never," she gasped mindlessly.

"You must always be mine. Promise."

Through her gasps he just detected the word "Promise..." She began to writhe, urging him on, looking up beseechingly into his face. He smiled and obeyed her unspoken plea. He'd been tired when he arrived an hour ago, but he was tired no longer. The night stretched ahead invitingly, a night when he would make her his own again and again until they were both exhausted. He moved faster, driving the pleasure to exquisite heights, renouncing the caution that had kept him safe and abandoning himself only to her. He had his reward in the convulsions that shook her and the light in her eyes as they looked up into his at the final moment.

They rested for only a little. She was ready for him again almost at once, as eager as he to prolong the night. She was a healthy young animal, brimming with energy to take him on and win. Once he stopped for breath and her laughing voice reached him. "Tired?"

"Don't think it for a moment," he said, returning to the fray.

It was dawn by the time they called it a draw and lay, worn out in each other's arms. He slept first. Kirsty watched the first light break over the moor and thought of the things she had learned that night; things about Mike, but mostly about herself. It had ended well. What had begun in gloom had ended in a merry spirit, yet now that her body's clamorous demands were satiated, for the moment at least, she had to return to reality and the fact that so many things hadn't changed.

Their worlds might prove impossible to bridge. Looking into the future she saw the time coming when they might have no choice but to say goodbye. But even as she saw it her arms tightened about him, and her heart cried, "Not yet."

Chapter Ten

The following day Kirsty went, grim-faced, to that part of the moor where she knew the Gypsies camped, but they were gone. They must have left at first light, for there was no trace of them. Satisfied for the moment, she returned home. Briefly she considered telling Mabel that Caleb was barred from the house, but decided against it. For all her good qualities Mabel was a gossip, and Kirsty didn't want this story all over the moor. He was gone. Let it end there. She never mentioned her journey to anyone.

Christmas was drawing near again, and she looked back on her last two Christmases, marveling at how different this one would be. She had her baby and her man, and things were almost perfect.

But one thing prevented their being completely perfect, and she had her reminder one day when she was doing some shopping in the village and found herself confronting Mrs. Mullery in the street. The older woman looked at her without the old hatred, but with a weary melancholy. "I heard you had a baby," she said.

"Yes, a little boy," Kirsty said eagerly, wondering if this might be the start of a reconciliation.

But Mrs. Mullery only looked at her for a long moment. "Now you know," she said quietly. "Now you know."

She passed on without another word, leaving Kirsty shocked and pale. The words had gone straight to her heart. It was true. She'd discovered the all-enveloping love for a child that was like no other love in the world. The mere thought of anything happening to Rob was like a pain crazing through her. Since his birth she'd understood what Peter Mullery's mother suffered every moment. She got home as quickly as she could, seized Rob up from his cot and smothered him with kisses, praying fiercely for his safety. A deep instinct told her that the old business wasn't over yet. Something about it was still unresolved, and she was possessed by a terrible fear that the wheel would turn full circle and some harm come to her son.

She prepared for Christmas by baking an old-fashioned cake, the way her grandmother had taught her. It took a long time and needed much stirring, and as she stirred and threw in nuts and fruit and stirred some more, she talked to Rob who lay in his crib in the kitchen, watching her, wide-eyed.

"Your first Christmas is a big milestone," she told him. "Your first tree, your first presents. You'll have to give the cake and turkey a miss because they're too rich for you right now, but perhaps next year—just a morsel—"

She'd stopped work to lean over him, smiling into his face until he smiled back, and she broke into a laugh of delight and tickled his tummy. That made him laugh, too, and they crowed together.

She didn't know why she stopped. She hadn't seen or heard the other presence in the kitchen, but something made her look up to find herself being watched by a young woman who stood just inside the door. Kirsty rose to her feet, feeling apprehension grip her heart. For she knew this glamorous, glossy, mink-clad fantasy creature, who looked as if she'd stepped from the pages of a fashion magazine. But she hadn't. She'd stepped from a photograph that a man had carried with him, and she bore a name that he had murmured in his sleep. She'd come for Mike, as she was always bound to come. In her heart Kirsty had known it.

The apparition smiled languidly. "Forgive me for coming in without knocking. My name is Lois Denver."

Her voice was husky and vibrant, and suddenly Kirsty was horribly aware of her old jeans and sweater. When she found her voice it was to say "I thought it was Lois Severham."

Lois smiled. "It was once, but that's all over now. Do you mind if I sit down?"

Kirsty pulled herself together and remembered her manners. "I'm Kirsty Trennon," she said, pulling out a chair and taking Lois's coat.

Lois turned glowing eyes on her and said graciously, "I've heard *all* about you—Mike's savior. I'm so happy to meet you at last and thank you on behalf of Mike's friends. You're quite a heroine among us, I promise you."

Kirsty turned quickly away to hang up the coat and so was able to conceal her disgust at being thanked in this proprietary way by the woman who'd forgotten Mike when it suited her. "You don't have to thank me," she said, when she'd regained her calm. "Mike has done that."

"I'm sure he has," Lois purred silkily. "He's a man with a strong sense of his duty. Sometimes it's almost too strong. He gets a little . . . carried away."

"Can a man have too strong a sense of duty?" Kirsty asked coolly.

"Perhaps not, but it can be awkward if people start— shall we say—reading too much into it?"

"I'm sure you needn't worry about that," Kirsty replied. "I think Mike is very good at making his meaning plain. I've never found any trouble in understanding him."

Lois smiled like a sleek cat. "Good," she purred. "Then everything's fine." She looked around her. "I can't tell you how much I've looked forward to seeing your home. It's just as Mike described it to me, *and* your dear little baby." She descended on Rob, leaning over him with cooing noises, while he stared up at her, unblinking. "What a *sweet* little chap. I can see why Mike can't tear himself away from him."

Kirsty preserved her cool appearance, but it disturbed her to learn that Mike had talked her over with this woman, had even discussed their baby. There was no reason why he shouldn't, but something in her heart felt it as a betrayal.

Kirsty had grown up among blunt people who spoke their thoughts, and though wise, she lacked the sophistication that would have warned her that Lois might be improvising. A skilled dissembler, who'd known nothing of the baby, might have recovered quickly from the surprise and spoken just as Lois did.

She couldn't see herself through Lois's eyes, and because her beauty was of a different, more basic kind than this glossy creature's, she undervalued it. She saw only her old work clothes and missed the significance of her large dark eyes and curved lips. Nor did she know of the glow of sexual fulfillment radiating from her skin that needed no makeup to give it bloom. But it was immediately apparent to another woman, and Lois's eyes narrowed every time they alighted on Kirsty.

"I'm afraid you've missed Mike," Kirsty said, pouring tea. "He went to London yesterday to tie up some ends with the firm before Christmas." She added, with a touch of forgivable malice, "I'd have thought you'd have known that."

"I did," Lois said quickly. "I'm not here to see Mike. I—we—that is, it seemed better to spend Christmas apart. Things are so—unsettled at the moment."

"You mean you're still married?" Kirsty asked sweetly.

"Technically, yes, but not for long. My husband was going to contest the divorce, but he's changed his mind, and it'll soon be through. Until it is—" she gave an elegant shrug. "We both have ends to tie up. I'm spending Christmas with some friends in Cornwall. I had to pass through Dartmoor, so I thought I'd look in and meet the woman who saved his life. I also—" a look that might have been intended as shyness passed across the perfect features "—I also wondered if you'd give him this." She took out a sealed envelope and offered it to Kirsty. The envelope was redolent of herself—dainty, fragrant, elegant. Kirsty took it with distaste. "You will see that he gets it, won't you?" Lois pleaded.

"I'll give it to him," Kirsty agreed in a voice that had no expression.

"Thank you. Then I'll be going now." She rose and swirled the mink around her shoulders. "I've found out what I wanted to know."

Kirsty stood silent, refusing to dignify this with an answer. Lois smiled at her sweetly, "And you won't forget the letter, will you?" she said softly. "It contains things that are ... very important."

"I've given you my word and I'll keep it," Kirsty said in a hard voice.

"Then we understand each other. I must kiss your dear little boy before I go."

But Kirsty moved too quickly for her, placing herself in front of Rob and seeming to take root in the ground. "Better not," she said pleasantly. "He isn't used to strangers."

"And you're afraid I'll give him germs from the big bad world?" Lois teased. "Well, perhaps you're right. It's a very bad world out there and a very cozy idyll in here. I don't blame you for wanting to preserve it, but all idylls meet reality in the end, don't they? Goodbye."

Kirsty watched Lois's sleek, expensive car maneuver delicately out of the yard, but all she was conscious of was the letter in her hand. The stiff lavender-colored paper seemed to burn her hand, and the perfume disgusted her. She stared at it, longing for X-ray eyes that could see inside to the words that would be "very important" to Mike—and Lois.

In a few short minutes the glossy creature had earned Kirsty's thorough contempt, but she had also succeeded in frightening her. She was right. Their life here at Everdene was an idyll, and idylls didn't last. The real world was always waiting, and Mike's real world was different from hers. They both knew it, and it came between them.

She reminded herself that he wanted to marry her and take her into his world. But he'd asked for the wrong reasons. He wanted Rob, and he needed Kirsty herself as a kind of lifeline. He'd admitted it. Now she found herself wondering how often he saw this woman during his trips to London, and what he had said and done to make Lois so confident that he would be interested in her divorce?

He called her that night. After their usual greetings Kirsty said, "A friend of yours called here today."

"A friend? Who?"

"Lois Severham—or Lois Denver as she now prefers to be called." There was a long silence from the other end of the line. "Mike?"

"I'm still here. I'm sorry Lois bothered you. What did she say?" He sounded uneasy.

"She said her divorce will soon be through. And she gave me a letter for you. I'll keep it safe until you get here. You won't be coming until Christmas Eve, I think you said?"

"I may make it a bit earlier. I don't want to drive on Christmas Eve. I'll let you know."

He arrived the following afternoon. He explained this by saying work was tailing off before Christmas, and Kirsty didn't voice her suspicions that he wanted to read Lois's letter without delay.

She refused to watch as he glanced over the pages. She didn't want to find herself studying his face for reactions. She only turned when she heard him give a grunt, followed by the sound of papers being folded away. "How did she come to be in this direction?" he asked.

"She said she's spending Christmas with friends in Cornwall."

"I didn't know she had any."

"I don't suppose she has," Kirsty said coolly. "She really came to make trouble."

"And she made it, didn't she?" he asked, eyeing her.

"I don't know. Just how much trouble *can* she make, Mike? Perhaps you should tell me."

"None if we don't let her. I haven't taken up where I left off with Lois, if that's what you're thinking."

"But you do see her in London?"

"I can't help it. Hugh put a lot of shares in her name, then gave her a desk and a title, which she still has. The legal position is complicated. I can hardly get ruthless with her when she's had such a bad time. But it's over between us, Kirsty. There's only you. Please believe me."

She gave herself a little shake. "Of course I believe you."

He drew her toward him. "It's nice to think you might be jealous."

"Nonsense, of course I'm not jealous," she said firmly.

"All right, if you say so."

She kissed him. "We're going to have the best Christmas ever."

"Of course we are. Are there any other letters for me?"

"Some arrived in the post. They're over there."

She saw him riffle through the collection quickly in a way that suggested he was looking for something special, but whatever it was he didn't find it, because his face fell. "Any telephone messages?" he asked.

"No. Are you expecting something?"

"Not especially. I just wondered." It was said with something like a sigh.

For the rest of the evening Kirsty noticed a sense of constraint in Mike's manner, which she tried not to attribute to Lois. At bedtime he went upstairs first, but when Kirsty followed he wasn't in their room. Guided by instinct she went to the nursery and found Mike sitting by his son's cradle, his hand on the coverlet, one finger enclosed by a tiny hand. "He's got a grip like a prize-fighter," he whispered as she came closer.

"He's got builder's hands," she said, knowing this would please him. It did indeed bring a smile to his face, but only briefly, and she was left again with the sense of something troubling him.

"Mike," she said when they were lying together in bed, "is there something you want to tell me?"

He was silent for a long time before saying, "I wrote to my parents."

"Good," she exclaimed, surprised. "I'm glad."

"It was the kind of letter you'd have wanted me to write, trying to get closer to them, telling them all about Rob. But they haven't replied."

"It's Christmas—the post is always delayed—"

"I wrote ten days ago. They'd have answered by now if they were going to. I gave them this address. I just have to accept it. They want nothing more to do with me."

"Mike, that can't be true. They're your mother and father. They love you."

"I think they did once. But somehow I threw it away. I'm beginning to see that."

She could have wept for Mike, discovering wisdom only to find it was too late. But her heart refused to accept that his parents' love had died. She was a mother now, and she, too, had learned new wisdom. She put her arms around him and held him tightly, trying to comfort him. At last she had the satisfaction of feeling him drop off to sleep with his head on her breast, but she lay awake far into the night, her heart aching for him.

In the last few days before Christmas he showed a determined cheerfulness that hurt her more than anything. He even pointed out the fair that was scheduled for Christmas Eve on the edge of the moor, and more to please him than herself, Kirsty agreed to go.

It was a fine traditional fair, with toffee apples, fortune tellers and stalls. Mike seemed in high spirits, winning at the coconut shy and claiming a huge teddy bear for Rob. They went through the hall of mirrors, laughing at their own distortions, and he bought Kirsty a candy floss. But it was all hollow and they both knew it.

At last Kirsty sniffed the air and said, "It's going to snow soon."

"Then let's get back as soon as possible. I have too many memories of snow in this place to get sentimental about a white Christmas."

On the journey home the first flakes began to fall, and they were both glad when the lights of Everdene came into view. As soon as they arrived they saw an unfamiliar car in the yard, and Mabel came running out in a state of agitation. "Thank God you're back," she said, and there was a note in her voice that made Kirsty's heart grow cold with fear.

"What's happened to Rob?" she cried.

"He's all right—at least, he seems all right, but she won't put him down."

"*She?* Who's she?" Mike demanded.

But Kirsty didn't have to ask. Lois had come back to reclaim Mike, and that meant taking his child as well.

Anger lent her strength. She got out swiftly and ran into the house, ready to seize her baby from the enemy.

But in the doorway she stopped. The woman holding little Rob was nothing like Lois. She was old, with gray hair and a sharp, lined face, out of which peered two bright blue eyes. She was sitting down with the baby on her lap, while behind her an elderly man leaned over her shoulder. They both looked up as Kirsty appeared, and the man straightened up. As he did so Kirsty got a better look at his face, with its thick eyebrows forming an almost straight line, and she knew who this was.

"You're—Mike's father," she said uncertainly. "And you must be his mother." Suddenly a flood of emotion washed over her. "Oh, I'm so glad you came."

She went forward, her hands outstretched. The enveloping warmth of her welcome brought smiles to their faces, and the old man came toward her, placing his hands in hers. "It'll mean the world to Mike," she said, delighted.

The old people exchanged swift glances and the man said awkwardly, "Maybe."

Before she could speak there was a step behind them and Mike appeared in the doorway. He drew his breath sharply at the sight that met him. Kirsty fixed her eyes on his face, willing him not to suppress his feelings for fear of pain, as she guessed he'd often done before.

For what seemed a long time nobody moved. Then the old man went forward and held out a hand. "Hello, son."

Mike started to put out his own hand in return, but at the last moment a gasp escaped him. A shudder shook his great frame, and the next moment the frail old man was enveloped in a bear hug. Mrs. Stallard sat watching the two men out of eyes that were bright with tears. Then she glanced in Kirsty's direction, and a look of understanding passed between the two women.

She took little Rob from his grandmother, who rose to her feet. "We got your letter, son," she said, sounding a little uncertain. "We couldn't think how to answer it, so—"

Then she was in her son's arms, her tiny frame dwarfed by his large body. His head went down so that Kirsty couldn't see his face, but she was sure she saw his shoulders shake. She uttered a silent prayer of thanks that things had come right for Mike at last.

When the first emotional moments were over nobody seemed to know what to say next. Mrs. Stallard stood back and considered her son, finally saying, "You look better."

"Better than at the trial?" he asked wryly.

"No, I meant before that. You look sort of—real." She uttered the last word with an air of discovery, and to Kirsty's pleasure Mike nodded as if he'd understood.

"I wish you'd told us you were coming," he said. "Then we could have been here for you."

"We didn't decide until the last minute, did we, Martha?"

His wife nodded. "We weren't sure if it was the right thing and whether we could manage the drive. It's such a long way and we only passed our tests recently."

"Your tests?" Mike echoed. "You've learned to drive at your—" Unaccustomed tact made him stop.

"At our age," his mother finished. "And we bought ourselves a nice little car. It's made all the difference."

"But—I wanted to buy you a car years ago, and you wouldn't even think of driving."

"We do lots of things now we wouldn't think of then," his father said. "Your mother's been ill and—"

he took his wife's hand in a revealing gesture "—and for a while the doctors didn't think she'd make it. When she pulled through we decided to make the most of what we have left."

Mike looked stunned. "Mom ill? When did this happen? Why didn't I know?"

His father said gently, "It was while you were in jail. I wanted to tell you about it that time I visited, but—" he broke off and shrugged.

"And I wouldn't see you?" Mike said, very pale. "Dear God!"

Martha touched his arm. "But it was you that saved me," she said, smiling. "All that money you'd sent us, we still had it."

"It bought your mother the best treatment there was," the old man said. He added tentatively, "We always wanted to tell you, but we didn't know how."

Mike stood in silence, digesting the implications of this. "But you wouldn't touch it," he said at last. "You wanted nothing to do with me or my money."

"It was you who wanted nothing to do with us," Martha told him.

He burst out, "How can you say that? You know it's not true."

"Mike," Kirsty said in a voice of gentle warning. He stopped and looked at her, and she smiled. "Give it a chance."

Her smile seemed to calm him. He took a deep breath and said, "We must talk later. There's so much to say— I don't know where to start."

Kirsty touched Mabel's arm and they went upstairs with Rob, leaving the other three alone together. Her heart was singing with happiness for him. She prolonged bedtime as much as possible, and when she came down again George and Martha were alone. "Mike's gone to collect our things from the inn in the village," Martha explained. "He says we must stay here. You don't mind, do you? I know it's your home."

"I'd have been angry with him if he hadn't," Kirsty said warmly.

Martha took her hand. "Come and talk to us. Mike says you took him in when he escaped."

She told the story and they listened, exchanging glances and smiles. By the time she'd finished she could hear Mike returning, and in getting a room ready and his parents installed, there was no time for more talk.

To Kirsty's surprise she had a companion when she did her early-morning chores next day. Martha, well wrapped up, found her way into the barn. "I never could sleep late in the morning," she explained.

"Should you be out?" Kirsty asked, worried.

"I'm perfectly well now, and fit enough to do a day's work. You look as if you could do with some help. Does that boy of mine leave you to do all this alone?"

"No, he's hired some help for me," Kirsty said, laughing. "But I've given Fred and Frank Christmas off. I like to care for the pigs myself, especially since Cora had another litter. She's got the most luxurious pen in the business." She added significantly, "How's that for a bit of property development with all the modern conveniences?"

"Are you telling me my son made this?" Martha asked, half-amused, half-incredulous.

"His best workmanship," Kirsty confirmed.

Martha shook her head in wonder. "I can't get over how much he's changed now he's with you. I don't know him anymore. Or rather—I know him again. He'd become like those buildings he put up, remote and impersonal. All the best of him seemed buried in concrete. But now—I could almost believe that the terrible things that happened to him were worth it since they brought him here, to you.''

She seemed to regard everything as settled, and Kirsty colored a little and said, ''Mike has his life in London, and I have mine here.''

''But the two of you will get together soon, I'm sure,'' Martha said hopefully.

''I don't know. We're very different. We're happy as we are, but if one of us tried to fit in too closely with the other, I think we might end up by splitting up.''

''You don't really trust him, do you?'' Martha said shrewdly.

''Let's say, I'm not quite sure of him.''

''It was because of you that he wrote that letter.''

''But I didn't know anything about it until afterward.''

Martha nodded. ''But it was still because of you that he wrote it,'' she said. She put her hands into Kirsty's. ''Thank you for giving my son back to me.''

She went away without waiting for an answer, and when Kirsty returned to the house she found her at the stove, cooking breakfast. ''Can you manage?'' Kirsty asked. ''It's a bit of an awkward stove.''

''It's rather like the one I had when we were first married,'' Martha said calmly. ''Do you remember, George?''

Her husband grinned and nodded, and Kirsty had a sudden impression of their marriage, beset by hardship but with the love always shining through. Mike was watching his parents, as though intent on missing nothing. He didn't speak, not even to point out that he could have bought his mother the latest and the best, if only she would have let him.

At breakfast Martha sat with Rob in her arms. "I can't get enough of him," she said blissfully. "My, but he's like you at that age."

"Is he?" Mike asked, looking into the baby's face.

"Not in his appearance, but in his ways. Look at how he's reaching out already. You did that. I remember your little hands always stretched out eagerly to people and things, as though you wanted to have your whole life there and then." She hesitated, then met her son's eyes. "Perhaps we weren't very understanding."

Mike didn't answer, but Kirsty had a feeling that his throat had tightened.

After breakfast it was George's turn to hold his grandson, while Martha insisted on cooking the lunch, as well. "I'll help you," Mike offered.

"Oh, heavens!" Kirsty's exclamation was soft, but they all heard it and laughed.

"You've tried his cooking then?" Martha asked with a twinkle.

"Actually it's very unkind of me to make fun of Mike's cooking. I was glad enough of it when he was on the run. He had to stay indoors for safety, and he looked after me wonderfully. He makes beds better than I do."

"Tarn appreciates my cooking if you don't," Mike said to hide the fact that he was coloring.

After lunch Martha begged permission to put Rob down for his nap. Mike went upstairs with her, and when he came down he found Kirsty shrugging on the sheepskin jacket that had been his gift to her. "Where are you going?" he asked. "Surely all the chores have been done?"

"I haven't fed the ponies yet."

"Surely that can wait until tomorrow?"

"I should have gone yesterday. I can't leave it another day. They're fighting for their lives at this time of year."

"Then let Frank or Fred go."

"I've given them the day off. Besides, the ponies don't know Frank or Fred. They'll expect me."

"That's the craziest thing I've ever heard."

"Well, you know I'm crazy," she said, winding a scarf about her neck. "I'm not going to change now."

Faced with unanswerable logic he tried another tack. "My parents are here. It's not very polite to them."

"They won't mind anything as long as they've got Rob to play with. Besides, they'll understand better than you do."

"Just the same—"

"I'll only be an hour, Mike."

He was about to protest further when he saw that his mother was standing beside them. "If they need you, you go, my dear," she said to Kirsty, who smiled and went at once.

"Mom—"

"As for you, son, you're a fool. If you weren't, you'd go with her."

"Right." Mike grabbed his jacket and raced into the yard just in time to leap up into the cab beside Kirsty.

"You don't have to come," she said.

He grinned. "Yes I do. My mother says so."

The snow was drifting down with deceptive gentleness, large flakes that fell softly, relentlessly into a white world. Kirsty drove the tractor with care, leaving deep tire marks that showed how deep the snow had already fallen.

At last they saw the ponies, huddled together in stoic endurance, their shaggy coats poor shelter from the cold. Mike jumped down from the cab and helped Kirsty unload the hay from the trailer. He worked hard, but it was her they came to, as though instinctively knowing their true friend. When all the hay was unloaded he was ready to go, but Kirsty perched on the wagon, one foot propped casually against one of the huge tractor wheels, and rummaged in her jacket pocket for lumps of sugar which she fed, laughing, to her friends. "It's their Christmas, too," she said defiantly when she saw his face.

"Yes," he said, resigned.

Some people would have found the snow-covered scenery magical, but for Mike it merely recalled last year when he'd nearly died in a Dartmoor winter.

But he wasn't dead. She had saved him. Wherever she was there was life and warmth and true beauty. All things came to her, loved her and were renewed by her. Her face was alight with love as she fondled the blunt heads that nuzzled her, and he realized that she wore the same tender expression as when she held her child or looked at himself. He had one moment of sudden insight, when he understood that to her there was no difference. It was life she embraced wholeheartedly, whether that life was a man, a child, an animal or the fertile land. Only the grand emotions found a place in her heart. She could love or hate, but she could not be mean or trivial. Even her hostile neighbors had instinctively understood the grandness of her nature. That was why they feared her.

Impulsively he went to her and took her face between his hands, kissing her again and again. "You're wonderful!'' he said. She laughed and kissed him back through the falling snow, and they clung together.

But suddenly he was afraid. For a moment he'd been on the verge of promising to give up everything but her, and be only what she wanted. It was a good instinct, because he knew that what she wanted would always be true and worthwhile, but he wasn't ready to yield to it, because it cast doubt on everything he regarded as his achievements. It cast doubt on him. So he held back, despising himself, but unable to do anything else.

The old people stayed for a week, and when Mike returned to London they left with him. After staying one night with him in town they set off home. Mike was still worried at the thought of his mother doing a long spell behind the wheel of their small second-hand car, but he knew better now than to say anything.

"I never thought to see you with a woman like Kirsty,'' she told Mike when they said goodbye, ''a *real* woman, not a shallow painted piece like that other one. You became a hard man, but as long as you can love a woman like that, you'll never be lost.''

"But she doesn't love me, Mom.''

She smiled. ''I guess you're even more of a fool than I thought.''

There was a lot to do in the office, but somehow he couldn't settle into it. The bustle and noise of a successful firm, which had always meant so much to him, now sounded like meaningless clatter. He acquired a tract of open land he'd been after for some time, plus an unofficial promise from the local council that the protests of conservationists would be ignored.

"Badgers, indeed!'' exclaimed the tinny voice from the other end of the phone. "Fancy them thinking we'd hold up an industrial estate to protect badgers.''

"Well, I suppose badgers have to live somewhere," Mike said absently and was recalled to himself by a gasp from the other end.

"That was *you* that, wasn't it, old boy? Been over-indulging in the festive spirit, have you?"

"Probably," he said hastily. "Thanks for the tip-off."

He put the phone down, but even then there was no peace, for Lois swept in, full of stories of the expensive gifts she'd received, the men she'd flirted with, the clothes she'd worn. Mike listened with half an ear to this tale of glitzy self-indulgence. His inner eye saw only white fields and the laughing face of a young woman sitting on a tractor in the driving snow, feeding sugar lumps to the ponies.

Chapter Eleven

Kirsty was in a strange place. It looked like the moor, but mysteriously changed. Everything was either larger or smaller than she remembered, and the sky was red and threatening. She was oppressed by a sense of something terrible about to happen, something she couldn't avoid. Tarn was there with her, the hair standing up on his back in terror at the doom that was coming upon them. He began to bark madly, but the sound seemed to come from a long way off. It went on and on....

At last she managed to tear herself out of the nightmare and awoke to find herself in her own bed with Mike sleeping beside her. Then she realized that she could still hear Tarn barking in the distance, a frantic, insistent sound that went on and on, exactly as in the dream. She glanced at the window and froze. Through the pane she could see the flame-red of her dream.

"Mike, wake up," she cried, shaking him urgently. *"For God's sake, wake up."*

He grunted. He'd only just arrived back at Everdene after an exhausting drive, and it was an effort to wake. By the time he managed it, Kirsty had leapt out of bed and run to the window. As soon as she opened it she felt the heat in her face. The barn was on fire, sending flicking flames up into the night sky, and the wind was driving them in the direction of the house. Horror swept through her as she thought of her little son sleeping directly in the path of an inferno. Barefoot, she tore out of the room toward Mabel's room.

Rob was lying peacefully asleep in his cot. Kirsty wrenched the bed clothes off Mabel, who awoke, looking startled. "There's a fire. Get Rob out and take him to Fred and Frank's cottage," she said. "Tell them we need them."

Mabel grunted and got out of bed. While she dressed, Kirsty wrapped Rob in blankets against the night air. He half awoke and made a small hiccuping sound, and she pressed him to her in a passion of love and dread. "He'll be fine with me," Mabel said firmly. "You can get back to your 'other baby' now."

"Bless you," Kirsty told her fervently and dashed back to her room to fling on some clothes. She found Mike downstairs a few moments later, on the phone. "I've called the fire brigade," he said when he'd finished. "They're on their way, but it'll take a few minutes."

"There are animals in that barn," Kirsty cried. "We've got to get them out."

Tarn was still barking madly outside the barn door, and from inside they could hear the pigs squealing. Two of them had recently farrowed, and it seemed to Kirsty's heightened awareness that the cries of the mothers as danger crept closer to their young had a special agonized note.

Mike opened the barn door cautiously, for fear of a draft that would fan the flames. Inside, the roof was burning fiercely. So far the floor and walls were untouched, but a brand could fall onto the hay at any moment, making the place an inferno.

Kirsty hauled open the gates to the sties and began seizing up piglets. "Just take them out," she cried. "The mothers will follow."

They made several journeys into the yard to dump piglets down next to Tarn. As Kirsty had said, the mothers hurried to keep close to their young. Only Etta remained. She had no babies to give her a direction, and she seemed frozen with terror, cowering back and refusing all attempts to coax her out.

"Right, there's nothing else for it," Mike grunted. Taking a deep breath he bent down, closed both arms around the sow's massive body and staggered out with her into the yard. Etta fought him every inch of the way, thrashing her huge bulk around so that it was all he could do to stay on his feet. It was like carrying a mountain, but he managed it at last and deposited her with the others.

The sows worried their piglets, pushing them with their snouts, making little satisfied noises. But Mike noticed that Cora still seemed distressed, passing anxiously from piglet to piglet.

Nonsense, he thought. Country life had addled his brains and made him fanciful. How could anybody, even a mother, know if there was one missing? But even as his mind reproved him, he was heading back for the barn.

"*Mike,*" Kirsty shrieked. "What are you doing? That barn's going up at any moment."

"Haven't you noticed we're one short?" he yelled back and strode in before he could think about it too much.

You're mad, he told himself as he dived back into the pen. *Stark, staring, raving mad.*

He discovered he knew enough to head for the right place—the rail that ran along the bottom of the farrowing pens to give the piglets an escape from their mother's bulk. Feeling in the dim light, his ears alerted for the sound of the roof beginning to go, he managed to locate a small, shivering body and hook his fingers around it.

Kirsty appeared in the doorway, crying frantically, "Mike, where are you?"

"Get back," he yelled. "I'm coming." He raced for the door just as a burning brand fell from the roof within inches of his ear, and landed in a pile of straw. The next moment he was sprawling on the cobbles outside, breathing in the blessed cool air, and the barn was an inferno.

"Oh, God," Kirsty cried.

But Mike's sharp ears had caught the sound of a bell. A few seconds later a fire engine had swept into the yard, men were jumping down, running about, pulling out hoses. There was a hiss as the water hit the flaming barn.

Fred and Frank had arrived and were taking charge of the animals, shepherding them out of the yard and well away from the fire. "Have you seen Mabel?" Kirsty asked anxiously.

"At the cottage," Fred said briefly. "Baby's fine."

No one spoke for a few minutes as they watched the firemen do battle. Kirsty clenched her hands as she saw the flames reaching yearning fingers toward the house as though inspired by a malignant spirit that wouldn't relinquish its object. But the firemen kept on persistently, doggedly hurling water over the barn until at last the fingers fell back and died away. At last the hoses were turned off, and only the blackened shell of the barn was left.

"You were lucky," the fire chief said. "If you hadn't noticed it when you did it would have spread out of control. Who spotted it?"

"He did," Mike said, scratching Tarn's ear.

"Any idea how it started? Someone been careless with cigarettes?"

"Nobody here smokes," Kirsty insisted.

Firemen had been clambering among the ruins, examining timber with the aid of powerful flashlights. One of them emerged and said, "We'll need a better look when it's light, but offhand I'd say it started in the roof."

"But how could it?" Kirsty asked, puzzled.

The chief looked closely at Kirsty. He was a local man and knew her story. "There are folk around here who'd like to drive you away. How far would they go, do you think?"

"Not this far, surely?" she exclaimed, aghast.

"Maybe. But think about it. We'll be going now."

As they drove to the cottage to collect Mabel, Kirsty's thoughts were in turmoil. "He's imagining things, isn't he, Mike?" she begged. "Who would do such a wicked thing?"

"David Mullery," Mike said briefly. "He said you were a witch, and he thinks witches should be burned."

"But he's only a boy. That's just wild adolescent talk. And why do it now and not a year ago?"

"A year ago you were bankrupt and suffering. Now you've got me and the baby and enough money to protect Everdene. They're more hostile to you than ever now."

"Enough to—?" She drew a sharp breath as a wave of hate swept over her. She had endured whatever treatment had been meted out to herself, but now the life of her child had been threatened, and she was possessed by the oldest, most basic instinct in the world, the instinct of a mother to shield her young. It was savage and primitive, and it knew no mercy.

On the journey home she held her baby close to her breast, and her face was harder than it had ever been.

During breakfast next morning the phone rang. Mike answered, and after a terse conversation he told Kirsty, "We're wanted at the police station. They've got a witness who says he saw David Mullery near Everdene last night."

"Good," Kirsty said in a tight voice. Since the fire, she had a sensation of being another person, without pity and capable of bitter vengeance. It was as though a filter had slid between her eyes and the world, hardening the edges, turning everything to black and white. She was glad. Now she would have the cruel strength to do whatever was necessary to put her enemy behind bars.

As soon as they entered the police station they saw Ned Wilson, a local farmer and one of Kirsty's harshest critics. But for all his hostility he was a just man, and he was the witness against David.

"I was about a quarter of a mile from Everdene when he passed me, running for his life," he told Kirsty. "I thought nothing of it, until I heard that one of your barns had been set on fire."

"The one nearest the house," Kirsty confirmed in a harsh voice that made Mike look at her.

Ned grunted. "From what I hear that young lad has been free with his tongue recently, the burning of witches being his favorite subject. And everyone knows how the Mullerys feel about you. He'll probably get put away for a long time."

"*No.*"

None of them had known that Mrs. Mullery was standing there, but her shriek of agony made them all turn. Her hair, normally pinned severely back, hung in wisps about her face, and her eyes were dreadful. "It's a lie," she said. "He didn't do anything."

"I saw him there," Ned pointed out.

"You saw him on the moor. You didn't see him do anything," Mrs. Mullery repeated desperately. She turned on Kirsty. "You can't say he did. It ain't a crime to be on the moor at night."

"My son could have died," Kirsty said coldly. "If your son was responsible for that—"

"He wasn't, he wasn't. He don't know anything about it." Mrs. Mullery began to gabble. "I told that sergeant—it wasn't my David—it couldn't have been—but he don't believe me—I can't make him believe me—oh, God, they'll lock him away and he's only a boy—oh, God, oh, God, please—please—" She burst out in a babble of incoherent crying.

Kirsty watched her with a heart of stone. What did this woman matter, what did David Mullery matter, beside the baby that might have died? She thought of her son, of holding him against her breast, feeling his head heavy against her, the sweetness of his little hand in hers, and she was invaded by pain at the thought that she might have lost him. How could any woman recover from such a loss?

As though the question had touched a trigger, the crazy filters that had been before her eyes seemed to shift and dissolve. The light altered, grew softer, gentler, yet with a new glow in which she saw things as never before. Mrs. Mullery was no longer an enemy, but a mother whose son had died and who would never recover from his loss. Despite that, she'd defended Kirsty when the pregnancy had become known. Kirsty had thought she was defending their common womanhood. Now she saw that it was their common motherhood that had counted. As it must count now, if the feud was not to darken future generations.

The desk sergeant appeared and spoke to Kirsty. "Young David was arrested this morning," he said. "The formal charges are being drawn up now. Now, madam, that won't help." This last was addressed to Mrs. Mullery, who'd collapsed onto a chair, sobbing hopelessly.

"What are you charging him with, sergeant?" Kirsty asked.

"Arson. Plenty of people heard him say you deserved to be burned."

"But surely that piece of wild boy's talk isn't enough?" she said in a tone of mild surprise.

"It is with a witness who puts him in the vicinity."

Kirsty took a breath and said clearly, "But David never came near Everdene."

There was a small sensation. Ned looked up and said sharply, "I saw him."

"You may have seen him running away from the general direction, but I was out walking myself last night. I saw David near the farm, and I also saw him turn and leave while he was still two hundred yards away. There was a bright moon. It was definitely him."

Ned stared. The sergeant was looking at Kirsty through narrowed eyes but she was only aware of Mrs. Mullery, watching her with disbelief. "Also," she went on firmly, "I've been thinking about it, and I may have started the fire myself. I was up in the hay loft earlier in the evening, looking for my torch, which I'd left there. I lit a match to find it. I blew it out, but it must still have been hot. It probably lay there, warming the hay until a fire broke out."

"Of all the unlikely stories—" Ned muttered.

He was right. It was wildly unlikely, and the sergeant's face showed that he knew it. He went to fetch a higher ranking officer, who beckoned Kirsty into the depths of the station. Mike insisted on going with her, defying all attempts by the officer to dislodge him, and stood behind Kirsty with his hand on her shoulder. From time to time she touched his fingers with her own, but her courage was up, and she faced the hostile questions calmly, refusing to budge from her statement.

"I don't believe a word of it," the officer said at last, angrily. "But if you're determined to clear this young hooligan there's nothing I can do. Get out, the lot of you."

Mrs. Mullery was still waiting in reception, her expression a mixture of hope and despair that lightened to disbelieving joy as David was brought out and released. He looked chastened and scared.

The sergeant flung one final remark at Kirsty. "I hope you know what you're doing. You'll bear a heavy burden if he kills someone next time."

"There won't be a next time," Kirsty said, her eyes on Mrs. Mullery.

She thought she saw Mrs. Mullery give a brief nod, but it was hard to be sure as the older woman scuttled out of the station, clinging onto her son.

Outside Ned confronted Kirsty. "You know that boy started the fire as well as I do. What's going on?"

"I just want there to be an end to it," Kirsty said desperately.

Ned shrugged and began to walk away. But he turned long enough to say, "There'll never be an end to it. Feuds live a long time in this place."

Mike took Kirsty's arm and guided her to the car. He'd watched the incredible scene in the police station in silence, astounded, but knowing he mustn't interfere. He brooded on it all the way home, and then he said, "Was there one word of truth in what you said?"

"Not one," she replied simply. "I never saw David. I never went up into the loft, and I never throw matches around."

"That's what I thought. I couldn't believe my eyes. One minute you were all for vengeance, and the next— you seemed to forget that our son was threatened."

She turned a haggard face to him. "I didn't forget, Mike. But Rob is safe. He's alive. Her son is dead. Peter will never come back. He's *dead*. Now I know what she feels every minute of every day." She raised her hands to hide her streaming face as he put his arms around her. "I killed her son— I don't know how, but I killed him— I'm guilty and I shall always be guilty—oh, Mike—Mike—what am I going to do?"

He held her close, soothing and comforting her as best he could. But he had no answer for her.

Now Kirsty found herself driven by a consuming need to be alone with Rob. She left it to Frank and Fred to make new arrangements for the animals and gave Mabel the day off. Mike melted into the background, as though he understood that she needed peace to forge a new closeness with their child. But she was always conscious of him in the house, part of her love for the baby, as the baby was part of her love for him.

For hours Kirsty sat in the kitchen, bathed in the warmth from the stove, her baby in her arms. Her thoughts were all of Mrs. Mullery, and her heart ached for her. She remembered how the older woman had stood before her in the street, saying, "You know now," with a weary melancholy that seemed to go deeper even than hatred.

So lost was she in memory that when she looked up and saw Mrs. Mullery watching her, she thought she was imagining things. Then her vision cleared, and she realized that the real woman was standing there, in her kitchen.

"I knocked but I don't think you heard me," Mrs. Mullery said, speaking more tentatively than Kirsty had ever heard her before. "The door was on the latch, so I came in."

Kirsty looked at her. "I've been expecting you," she said, discovering that it was true as she said the words.

"Aye. There are things to be said . . ."

Kirsty rose. "Sit down. I'll make us some tea." She adjusted Rob on her arm.

"May I—may I hold your little boy?" But she drew back as soon as she'd spoken. "No, I've no right. Forget I spoke."

"Take him," Kirsty said simply. She lowered Rob gently into Mrs. Mullery's arms. The older woman received him with a look of astonishment. "He's a bonny little lad," she said.

"Yes, and he's all the world to me. You said I'd know, and now I do. I don't blame you for hating me."

"You hated my David for that fire, but you let him go. Why did you do that?"

"You know why. You knew at the time."

"For me?"

"Yes."

"Although it's me that turned folk against you?" Mrs. Mullery said with a kind of dogged persistence, as though she would get the words out come what may.

"I want the hating to stop," Kirsty said passionately. "Nothing can bring Peter back, but I swear to you I never meant him any harm. If I led him on I did it innocently."

The pause went on so long that Kirsty was sure nothing had really changed and she was about to be rejected again. But then Mrs. Mullery said, as though the words were wrenched from her with pincers, "You never led him on."

"You believe that?" Kirsty breathed. "You really believe me at last?"

"I know it. I've known it these last three weeks."

"Three weeks? I don't understand."

"I went through Peter's things. I couldn't bear to do it before. I packed them away and wouldn't touch them. Three weeks ago I opened the trunk and I—I found his diary."

"Did he—mention me?"

"It was all about you, not just then, but going right back. He was mad for you, but he didn't let anyone suspect, just filled his diary with you, saying such things..."

"What kind of things?"

"Like poetry. I didn't understand half of it. It was like he didn't want reality, just dreams. Then—well, you'll

find it all there." She nodded at her bag which she'd set
on the floor. "I brought it for you to see."

Kirsty looked into the bag and took out the diary. It
was a large book with one day per page, and each page
was covered in writing. "Read what it says for Decem-
ber third," Mrs. Mullery told her.

Kirsty found the page and began to read. As his
mother had said, Peter had a poetic streak, and his visions of Kirsty had been wildly romantic and dream-
like.

"For two years I have adored my lady from a distance," he wrote.

"Two years?" Kirsty echoed. "Since he was sixteen?
I never knew."

"None of us knew. He was a secretive lad. Read on."

She has been my Belle Dame Sans Merci, and I have
been content. But a man can't live forever on
dreams. Now I want her to notice me. This year,
when I go home for the Christmas vacation, I shall
ask her to give me work. Then I shall be near her,
and we will talk, and maybe I will dare to tell my
lady that I love her.

Dazed, Kirsty turned the pages, discovering all the
incidents that she remembered, but now projected
through the filter of Peter's lovesick boyish imagination.

We talk about art and poetry. No one has ever spoken to her of these things before. She is friendly to
me, but no more. She's loyal to her husband although he's unkind to her. That makes her even
more perfect.

Later Peter had written:

I'm sure she must see me looking at her, read the love in my eyes. But her manner doesn't change. She seems to be made of ice. Her indifference inflames me. She's like the cruel ladies of the old romances, who scorned their cavaliers until they had performed brave deeds. If only I could do some brave deed for her.

A little later on:

Jack fired me today. I'm forbidden to go near her, but perhaps she'll send for me.

Then:

It's been three days and no word from her. I can't stand it. I must tell her how I feel....

Later the same day there was another entry:

I waited for her in the barn and tried to kiss her. But she was angry. She pushed me away and said she couldn't love anyone. There was something about the way she said it—as though she was terribly unhappy. Jack came in and threatened me, but what do I care? I know now she'll never turn to me. She's determined to be faithful to that coarse brute. Kirsty, my unattainable love...I would gladly die for you....

"The poor boy," Kirsty murmured. "Poor foolish, innocent boy."

"You were innocent, too," Mrs. Mullery said in a bleak voice. "You never led him on. What happened weren't your fault."

Kirsty looked at her, hardly daring to hope. "You really mean that?"

"I mean it. I didn't want to believe it. When I first read that diary I couldn't accept that you weren't guilty. I never told anyone what I'd found. But in my heart I knew the truth." She clenched her hands. "I should have told David, and then maybe he wouldn't have done such a wicked thing."

Kirsty set a cup of strong tea beside her and took back Rob. "I don't think you should blame yourself for David," she said slowly. "Telling him probably wouldn't have made any difference. He's sixteen. He listens to his feelings, not his head."

Mrs. Mullery raised her head and looked at Kirsty. "You're more generous to me than I was to you," she said. "In my heart I think I always knew you weren't the bad woman I painted you. But when Peter died—" she stopped and her eyes filled with tears.

"I know," Kirsty said gently.

Mrs. Mullery took back the diary. "I'll tell everyone," she promised. "They'll all know you weren't to blame."

When she departed a few minutes later, Kirsty went to the door and stood watching the dumpy, determined figure pedaling away across the moor on her bicycle. She could hardly take in what had happened.

She turned back into the room to find Mike there, watching her. "You heard?" she asked.

"Yes, I was eavesdropping shamelessly. I'm so glad that it's all over."

"It'll never be quite over until I know how Peter died. But oh, Mike, I feel as if a dreadful weight has been lifted from me." She put Rob into his cot and went into the arms Mike opened for her, leaning against him contentedly. "This is so nice and peaceful," she said.

For a long moment they stayed without speaking, enjoying each other's warmth. Then a thought that had been hovering on the edge of Kirsty's consciousness for several hours finally made it to the surface. "What on earth made you go back into the barn?" she asked. "It was madness."

"Cora was missing one of her piglets," he explained. He kissed her and added in a teasing voice, "Fancy you not noticing."

"Fancy you noticing," she said in wonder. "Just fancy that."

A couple of days later, Mike said, "I have to go to London and I may be away for a few weeks."

Her heart sank at the thought of being without him, but she said cheerfully, "Yes, New World Properties has had to manage without you a lot recently. I'm surprised you could spare the time."

She had the feeling that he was on the verge of saying something, but he obviously changed his mind. "I shall have plenty to do," she went on. "The place will be swarming with insurance assessors soon, and the barn has to be rebuilt as soon as possible."

He looked up quickly. "There's no hurry, surely? You've got the pigs under cover."

"Yes, but I don't want that eyesore standing there like that. Besides, it isn't safe."

"Fine. Pull it down, but don't rebuild it for the moment. Wait until I come back."

"Why?" she demanded, baffled.

He seemed to search for an answer. "So that we can discuss it," he said at last, lamely.

"Discuss a pig barn? Are we going to have negotiations at boardroom level? Shall I get Etta in to appraise the situation and put her trotter mark on an application in triplicate?"

"Better get Cora," he observed with a grin. "She owes me a favor after that piglet."

But although he entered into the joke, his manner was abstracted, and Kirsty could tell his mind was elsewhere, probably in London with his work. It was obvious that his old life was calling to him, and he was responding.

Suddenly it seemed ominous that he was leaving for an indefinite time. She tried to push the thought aside, but it continued to trouble her while Mike was doing his packing. It didn't escape her that he was taking more of his things than usual.

He kissed her heartily when he left and promised to call her when he arrived. Kirsty got on with her work, refusing to notice that she felt lonelier than ever before, when he'd gone away. But the feeling pressed in on her. It was only a short time since she'd been rejoicing at the change that seemed to have come over Mike, as though the man she'd first loved had been given back to her. Now she was full of apprehension as she sensed that they were coming to a crossroads. Very soon something would happen—*must* happen—to settle things one way or another.

By now she knew how long the drive to London took, and when she could expect him to call. But the usual time passed with no sign from him. She waited one hour, two, three. At last she could stand it no longer and dialed the number of his apartment. It took a long time for him to answer, and when he did he sounded irritable. "I was worried about you," she said. "I thought you might have had an accident."

"No, nothing like that," he said hastily. "I'm sorry, I should have called you, but I got swamped as soon as I arrived. I'm going to be up all night working."

"In that case I won't keep you," she said quietly. "Good night, Mike."

She put down the receiver and sat staring at the phone. There had been some noise going on in the apartment behind Mike, and although she'd tried not to eavesdrop she couldn't blot out the distinctive, husky voice of Lois. It was the voice she heard in her nightmares.

After a while she forced herself to get up and climb the stairs wearily to bed.

In the next few days she discovered a change in her life. People who had gone out of their way to give her the cold shoulder, now went out of their way to smile. Mrs. Mullery had done her work well. Yet Kirsty could still sense a faint reserve behind the smiles. She was acquitted of leading Peter on, but he was still dead, and Jack was still blamed.

Mike called her twice, but their conversations were forced. Kirsty couldn't forget the echo of Lois's voice in his apartment late at night, and he always seemed in a hurry. She had the sensation of hanging suspended in limbo.

But limbo was abruptly shattered one afternoon. Needing to be alone, she'd escaped the house and gone for a walk, taking only Tarn. About half a mile from the house she came upon two men she'd never seen before. They were so intent on what they were doing that they didn't notice her, and she had time to study them. One had an instrument that looked like a camera tripod, except that what was on top was no camera. The other was making copious notes. She approached them. "I don't think I know you," she observed pleasantly.

The younger of the two men gave her a bored glance. "Don't s'pose you do," he responded, going back to his notes.

"I only mention it because you're on my land."

"Are we?" This time he didn't even look up.

"And I'd like to know what you're doing here."

"Keep your hair on," the young man said insolently. "We're only doing a survey."

"*A survey?* On my land? Without my permission. Just who do you think you are?"

"Look, lady, don't get uptight with me. I'm just doing my job. I was told to make a survey of this land."

"By F. Colley & Son, I presume?"

"In a manner of speaking. If you don't like it, take it up with head office."

"Right," she said grimly. "I will."

A few minutes later Mabel was startled to see Kirsty come into the farmhouse like whirlwind and make straight for the phone. Mabel listened in alarm as Kirsty summoned a taxi to take her to Plymouth railway station, but before she could ask any questions Kirsty had vanished upstairs, reappearing several minutes later with an overnight bag. "I'm going to London," she said.

"You look as if you've seen the devil!" Mabel exclaimed.

"Not yet I haven't, but I'm going to confront him, and when I do he'll wish he'd never taken me on. Where on earth *is* the wretched thing?" She was rummaging in a drawer as she spoke.

"Where's what?" Mabel asked, dodging papers that went flying as Kirsty tossed them out.

"The last letter that Colley sent me. I need it for the address. They've been trying to force me to sell Everdene, and now they've actually had the nerve to survey my land, although I've told them a hundred times that I'm not selling. Will you call the station and check the trains to London?"

Mabel complied, and by the time Kirsty had found the letter she was armed with the information that there was a train in an hour. "But it's a terribly long journey," she warned. "More than four hours, and it'll be midnight before you arrive. Wouldn't it be better to wait for Mike to come back, and let him deal with it?"

"Mike 'dealt with it' last time," Kirsty observed dryly. "He swore I wouldn't be troubled again, but here they are, trampling over Everdene. There's the taxi. I'm off now." She stopped and gave Rob a passionate hug. "Wish your Mommy good luck, darling."

In half an hour she was in Plymouth, which was as far afield as she'd ever been in her life. Most towns made her uneasy, but this town was on the coast, and the empty vastness of the sea pleased her because it reminded her of the moor.

But now she had no attention for the sights. She was on deadly earnest business. She told the driver to head for the railway station in such a grim voice that he stared at her.

The train was packed. She reached London tired, hungry and stiff from sitting still too long in a cramped position. As Mabel had predicted, it was midnight. The newsstands and food kiosks were closed, and the night life of the station was getting under way. People with nowhere else to sleep were settling down on benches, the cleaners were out, and members of the Salvation Army were wandering the platforms. One of them approached Kirsty. "Is someone meeting you?" she asked pleasantly.

"No. I was just wondering what to do."

"Let's have a cup of tea and talk. I'm Sergeant Ann Mully."

She produced a drink from the Army's van and said, "You're older than they usually are."

"They?"

"The youngsters who run away from home, thinking the streets of London are paved with gold. They're easy prey for the pimps and dealers, who pick them off at the stations. We try to get in first."

"I've just come to see someone," she said. "I'm going home tomorrow."

"Good. In the meantime, we have a hostel nearby, if you like."

"Thank you," Kirsty said gratefully.

She traveled to the hostel in a van, accompanied by several youngsters who were no more than children. She shuddered, thinking of the fate Ann Mully had outlined and feeling as if she'd come from a clean world to a dirty one. Later that night she fell asleep in the hostel bed, thinking of the wind on the moor, of nuzzled greetings from shaggy ponies, of Rob nestling sweetly against her neck and of Mike. But instead of tender memories of him she could only remember the self-conscious way he'd told her not to rebuild the barn, and her dreams were haunted by Lois's voice.

Before she left next morning she showed Ann the address and received directions. "Go into the subway station just along the road," she said. "Get out at Oxford Circus."

Kirsty made her way to the station and found herself descending an escalator deep into the earth. There seemed to be hundreds of people, all going down with her, down and down, until she was sure they would all end up in hell.

She was even more sure of it when she found herself in the first subway station she had ever seen, a narrow tube of a place that made her feel as if she was being crushed. The next moment the train came screaming out of the tunnel with a clanking din of such awfulness that she was sure the noise would pull her apart.

How did anyone ever live in a city, she wondered as she got into the train and clung to a strap while she was swept through black tunnels. It was like a living nightmare. But it was Mike's world.

Finally, with relief, she emerged once more into the air. A newspaper seller on the corner directed her, and she set off determinedly for her goal. It turned out to be a huge functional building of incredible ugliness that made her shudder. Kirsty pushed open the big glass doors and found herself in a large echoing hall, whose only occupant was a man in uniform sitting behind a desk.

"Have I come to the right place for F. Colley & Son?" she asked him.

"That's right. What name is it?"

"Mrs. Kirsty Trennon."

"And you're here to see—?"

"The managing director."

"Is he expecting you?"

"No, but he's going to see me."

"I doubt that. He's a busy man—"

"And I'm a busy woman, but I've come all the way from Dartmoor to tell him what'll happen to him if he doesn't stop persecuting me."

"Perhaps you'd care to sit down, madam?" the man said smoothly, picking up a telephone.

At that moment the lift arrived, and the doors opened to allow two people out. "Don't bother," Kirsty said.

Ignoring his shout of, "Hey, come here!" she made a dash for the lift, pressed hard on the first button she found and managed to get the doors shut before she could be intercepted. The next moment the lift was carrying her up. She had no idea where the managing director would be, but the top floor was a good place to start, so she headed there.

After six floors the lift stopped and she emerged to find a female receptionist standing in readiness. "You can't just barge in on the managing director without an appointment," she said frostily.

But she'd miscalculated. Her words showed Kirsty that the uniformed man had called her, which meant this was the right floor. "Can't I just!" Kirsty exclaimed, her eyes glinting. "You just see if I can't."

The receptionist promptly made her second mistake, trying to block one of the three corridors that led off from the lift. "Thank you," Kirsty said. "I was wondering which way to go." With a swift movement she slipped her arm about the receptionist's waist, as if preparing to waltz, swung her in a hundred and eighty degree turn, released her and was gone before the woman could do more than splutter with indignation.

She began to run, anxious to get to her destination before reinforcements could arrive. She could see a separate area at the end of the corridor, with its own plate-glass windows, and its own two receptionists rising, ready to do battle.

"Don't stop me," Kirsty warned them as she whirled through the glass doors. "Don't even think of trying."

Perhaps it was the glint in her eyes that made them fall back. An oak door confronted her. She approached it unmolested and threw it open. Then she stopped, frozen to stillness by the most complete shock of her life.

There was Lois, standing directly in front of a tall window, smiling up at a man, her hand caressing his cheek while her body pressed seductively against his.

And the man was Mike.

Chapter Twelve

In that tense, shattering moment, while they all three stood there like figures on a frieze, Kirsty realized that she had always known this: not the details, but the fact that Mike gave her only a small part of himself and concealed the rest. The moment had always been inevitable.

Lois was the first to recover, and her light, rippling laugh broke the silence. "How delightful," she said. "But you should have let us know you were coming. I don't think Mike was quite prepared for the—er—surprise. Were you, darling?"

Mike was very pale, but he spoke composedly. "Please be good enough to leave us, Lois."

Before doing so Lois touched his arm in a proprietary way, brushing off an imaginary speck. The drama was wasted on Kirsty whose heart had frozen, so that she was able to tell herself she no longer loved Mike Stallard or cared what he did, as long as he left Everdene alone.

Having made her gesture, Lois swayed gracefully across the room to pass Kirsty in the doorway, turning as she did so. A less distracted man might have noticed how exquisite she looked next to Kirsty's functional clothes and weary, strained face. But Mike kept his eyes on Kirsty, and the minute they were alone he came across the floor to her, hands outstretched. "Darling, what's wrong? What's happened to bring you here like this? Why didn't you call me?"

"I didn't know you were here," she said, evading him and walking deeper into the office. "I came looking for F. Colley & Son. I had no idea they were you."

"I didn't know myself at first. World Properties took them over while I was in jail."

"Oh, you can do better than that," she challenged, turning to face him. "You recognized the name the first time I mentioned it. You went very quiet. I didn't think about that at the time, but now I see why."

"I recognized the name, yes," he agreed. "There'd been some talk of buying them out before I was arrested, but when I took over the firm again there were a million things that needed my attention before I could check what we'd acquired. When you showed me that letter I realized I didn't know whether I owned them or not. I checked it out, found that I did and ordered them to leave you alone."

"And of course they just happened to disobey you," she said caustically. "Who do you think you're talking to, Mike? The village idiot?"

"Kirsty, I swear I'm telling you the truth. I thought the matter was settled until they arrived that day. I got rid of them by telling them who I was and making it clear it wasn't to happen again."

"Did you? Is that really what you said, Mike?"

He paled. "Are you calling me a liar?"

"I don't know what to call you. All I know is that you very conveniently persuaded me to stay in the house, so I never heard what you said to those men."

"That was because I didn't want you to know I had any connection with Colley. I knew it would make you think even worse of me than you already did. But does it matter? I got them off your back."

"Unfortunately you didn't," she said cuttingly. "Colley have put a team of surveyors on my land now." Mike swore under his breath, but she ignored him and carried on. "That's why I'm here. I came to see the head of the firm. And it was you all the time." Her voice broke on the last word as the full extent of her disillusion washed over her. Mike came toward her but she backed away. "Don't try to touch me, Mike. Let's have a little honesty between us at last."

"Kirsty, I swear I knew nothing about a survey."

"Of course you didn't," she cried sarcastically. "And it's just coincidence that you told me not to rebuild the barn. You and Colley have got plans for that site, haven't you?"

"I've got plans, yes, but not the kind you think. Kirsty, you have to believe me."

"No I don't, Mike. I don't have to believe you, or trust you, or—or love you. I did once, but that's in the past. You've been deceiving me for months, not just about this, but with Lois."

"What you interrupted just now was a goodbye—"

She gave a cruel laugh. "Some goodbye."

He colored. "Unfortunately, Lois is hard to persuade. She won't believe I'm not coming back to her."

"Don't tell me. I'm not interested. I should have listened to her when she came to Everdene, but like a fool I listened to you."

"Do you really think I was carrying on with Lois when I asked you to marry me?" he demanded.

"I think you wanted your son. How long would we have lasted once you'd established your claim? A nice quick divorce with the judge awarding custody to you because you could give Rob money and luxury and a brand new mother waiting in the wings. What could I offer him in comparison? Trees and clouds and horizons, spring dawns and animals that press against you so that you can feel their warmth. *Life.* But how much would a judge think that counted against solid bricks and mortar? What do you know about life?"

"I know now," he said. "I want these things for him, too."

"Oh come on, Mike. At least be true to your convictions. I know how you'd have reared our son. You'd have given him planning permission on a prime site for his first birthday—plus a few other little toys, like people's hearts to play with. Thank God I learned the truth in time to stop you."

"Kirsty—"

"I'm going now. I'll send your things here. I don't want to see you at Everdene again. You don't belong there."

"It's the only place I belong now," he said quietly. "It's my home."

"Mike, you don't know what a home is. All you know is property. Rob and I will make our home without you."

She saw the sick look that washed over his face, and for a moment she pitied him. Then she remembered how long and systematically he had deceived her, and she hardened her heart. "There's nothing more to say. Goodbye, Mike."

She ran from the office, fearful that he might try to stop her. In seconds she was plunged back into the bedlam of London, but now it was worse, for the city had filled up with people. She hailed a taxi, knowing she couldn't face the subway again. Everything in her was concentrated in one instinct, to get back to Dartmoor where the air was clean and there was honesty and peace. She hated Mike for ever coming there, polluting its freshness with his glib words and his acquisitiveness, but above all with his betrayal.

On the long journey home she sat tense and rigid, fearful that her heart would break in this crowded place, and she would give way to her grief before strangers. By the time the train pulled into Plymouth she was aching all over, and she was exhausted from emotion and lack of food. There was a long wait for a taxi, and then the trip home which seemed to take an age. As soon as she reached the moor she felt herself grow a little calmer as the place exerted its timeless spell. Here she could find the courage to pick up the pieces of her shattered life again. About half a mile from home she paid off the taxi, choosing to walk the rest of the way in the fresh air and let the sunset ease her heart a little.

All through the last few hundred yards she was thinking of little Rob and the feel of holding him against her. Mike's child, a reminder of a man she never wanted to think of again, yet infinitely precious for his own sake. She began to run.

As she turned into the yard she noticed that Mabel's little car wasn't in its usual place. Suddenly her heart began to beat with apprehension. Her hand trembled as she opened the front door. The house seemed ominously silent as she hurried in. She called out, "Mabel, are you there?"

The sound of the front door shutting behind her made her whirl around. Then she drew in a swift breath. Standing there was Caleb.

He looked horribly different. The mask of amiability had fallen from him, and now she could see how cold his eyes really were. "Hello, darlin'," he said, and his mouth stretched in a smile that wasn't a smile. "I dare say you weren't expecting to see me."

"Where's Mabel?" she demanded breathlessly.

"She went shopping."

"And took Rob?"

"No, I told her he'd be safe with me."

"Where is he?" Her voice rose frantically. "Where's my son?"

"All in good time. You and I have some talking to do first."

"Give me my son and get out," she said deliberately.

He laughed, but it wasn't a nice sound. "That's what I've always admired about you darlin'. Your spirit. That's how you'll be when we're in bed together, all fire and fight. I've looked forward to that a long time. I'm a patient man you see. I can enjoy something more for having put it off until the right time. But I reckon the time for patience is past."

She felt sick, but she found the strength to say, "I'd as soon sleep with the devil as with you."

She thought she was on her guard, but Caleb moved with incredible speed to seize her hair and pull her against him. His mouth descended onto hers in a hard, determined kiss. She tried to twist her head away, but his grip on her hair was tight and she couldn't move. She could feel him laughing as he kissed her, and she clenched her teeth to deny his tongue entry. Hate pervaded her. And fear, too. Caleb had a wiry strength that she couldn't overcome.

He drew back but didn't release her. He was still laughing. "That's the stuff. Fight me. We'll have a grand old time." She managed to land a blow that startled him just enough to make him release her. But he came after her, eyes glinting, seized her and threw her so that she landed on the settle. Then he sat beside her, crowding her so that she couldn't get up, and started to talk in a reasonable tone that was more frightening than violent.

"I've never let a woman bother me the way you have, Kirsty. But you're special, always have been. I'd have married you if I'd been the marrying kind. I thought of staking my claim straight after Jack died, but you weren't ready, what with feeling guilty and all. No—" he stopped her as she tried to throw him off. "Don't go. Not when we're just getting friendly." He touched her face, caressing her, while waves of nausea washed over her. Only the thought of her baby kept her going.

"I went away to let you know what it was like coping without me," Caleb said. "I meant to come back and collect in the summer, but I had that little bit 'o trouble with the law. And when I did get back, *he* was around, so I had to rethink my plans."

"So you spun him a lying tale about being Rob's father," she said contemptuously. "How disappointed you must have been when it didn't work."

"Didn't it work? Where is he now then? Not here, is he? When will he be back?"

"Where's my baby?" Kirsty screamed.

"Safe where he won't interrupt us just now. You've kept me waiting too long, and now I'm going to take what belongs to me."

He yanked her close. Revulsion gave Kirsty the strength she'd prayed for, and she managed to land a punch straight in his face. Startled he fell back long enough for her to wriggle free. He came after her but she was ready for him, jerking up her knee at just the right moment. He gave a howl of agony and doubled up, but recovered almost immediately and struck her hard enough to fell her. Her head hit the stone floor, and she lay dazed, watching Caleb through half-closed eyes, with no strength to defend herself further. She was vaguely aware of him slipping a hand into his pocket and coming out with a wicked-looking knife.

"Right," he said coldly and dropped on his knees beside her. The last thing she saw was Caleb looming over her and the knife coming nearer.

In the first moment after Kirsty left him, Mike was too stunned to think clearly. Then he reached out for the phone to call the downstairs reception desk and have her stopped there, but he dropped his hand again. Whatever he did she wouldn't listen to him right now.

Lois slipped into the room, smiling. "I gather she's gone," she said.

"Only for the moment. I'll catch up with her," he vowed. His voice became coldly ironic. "Thank you for that piece of troublemaking, Lois. It was right in your style. But it won't work. I've been telling you for months that it's over and I meant it. I wasn't as ruthless as I should have been because I was trying to be kind. I made the mistake of thinking of you as a victim. But it was awesome the speed with which you dumped Hugh and tried to latch back on to me when the pendulum swung my way again. Almost as awesome as the speed with which you dumped me in similar circumstances."

"You've always hated me for that, haven't you?" she asked in a husky voice, tremulous with something that might have been emotion.

"I did once, but that was a long time ago—when you mattered to me. Then I felt sorry for you, but even that died when I saw the lengths to which you were prepared to go—a letter that contained nothing important, just so that you could visit Kirsty and plant suspicions in her mind, turning up late at my apartment and now this last."

"Darling, I've been acting in your own best interests. I know you so well, you see."

"You've never known me, Lois," he said seriously. "I can't blame you for that because I've never known myself, but thank God I do now."

"Oh, come. You don't seriously expect me to believe that you've been converted to love among the cows?" As she had done earlier that afternoon she swayed toward him and put up a hand to pat his cheek, trying to use her seductiveness to deny his words of rejection. And, also as before, she met only chilly indifference.

"I don't care what you believe, Lois," he told her simply. "I only care what Kirsty thinks." He removed her hand firmly. "I want your desk cleared and you out of this building, for good." Without waiting for her answer he touched an intercom button on his desk. "I'm leaving now," he informed his secretary. "Bring me any letters that need signing."

She entered a moment later, closely followed by a young man in spectacles. He looked worried. "You can't mean to leave now," he protested. "We're meeting that pack of troublemakers any minute."

"Troublemakers?" Mike echoed coldly. "If you mean conservationists, say so."

"I've heard you call them troublemakers."

"Not recently you haven't. You meet them, Richard. You're my assistant, and it's time you got used to running the place."

"But if we're to have any hope of shutting them up it really needs you to negotiate," Richard insisted. "You're the one with the genius for offering apparent concessions that don't mean anything."

Mike looked up form his signing. "I suppose I earned that," he said grimly.

"But it's the first rule of business. You always said—"

"Don't tell me what I always said," Mike snapped. "Listen to what I'm saying now. It may be the first rule of business, but I should hate to think of it being engraved on my tombstone."

"They're here now," his secretary said, glancing into the outer office.

"Fine. Send them in. Good morning, everyone, come right in. This is my assistant, Richard. I'm afraid I have to go now, but just tell him how you want our scheme modified and he'll do it."

Richard gasped. "Modi—"

"Just do whatever they want, Richard." Mike went to the door, but there he stopped. "Who's running Colley's affairs now?"

"We left old man Colley in charge."

"Fire him. Buy him out. Anything. But get rid of him."

On the drive to Dartmoor Mike was almost lighthearted. At Everdene Kirsty wouldn't be able to walk out on him, and once he could make her listen, everything would be all right.

His watch told him that Kirsty had just time to catch the next train to Plymouth. If he drove fast he might even make Everdene before her. He wove expertly in and out of the London traffic, but already his mind was leaping ahead to green fields and windswept moors.

About halfway there he encountered a traffic jam. After sitting, fuming, in a standstill for an hour, he knew he'd never get there first. He stepped on the gas and reached Dartmoor as dusk was falling. He was tired but also exhilarated.

About a mile from Everdene he looked for the lights of the house, but could see none. He began to feel uneasy. Surely she couldn't have left?

His unease deepened as he swung into the yard and saw the front door standing open, although there were no lights on in the house. Suddenly a hideous fear possessed him. His mother had said, "As long as you have Kirsty, there's hope for you." But if he were to lose her...

He ran inside calling, "Kirsty—*Kirsty.*"

A soft moan answered him. Looking down he saw something lying in a heap on the floor. He put on the light and saw Kirsty dragging herself painfully to her feet. "My God!" he exclaimed in horror. He took her in his arms and helped her to the settle. His blood ran cold as he got a better look at her.

Her marvelous hair was gone. Someone had hacked off everything except a couple of inches. "Who did this?" he breathed in a fury.

"Caleb—" she gasped. "He's got Rob. I found him here waiting for me. We've got to go after him."

He helped her up and out to the car. His mind was seething with a thousand questions, but this was no time to ask them. "Where will he be?" he asked tersely as he started the engine.

"I don't know. I'm not sure if he's alone or if they all came back. I can tell you where they usually camp." She gave him directions in a shaking voice. As he drove he risked taking a hand off the wheel to take hers. She returned his squeeze, all anger forgotten. Nothing mattered now but their son.

"What did he do to you?" he managed to ask.

"Not what I was afraid of. He tried, and I fought him. He hacked my hair off just before I passed out, but I think he must have taken fright, then, and run for it. But he's got Rob," she cried out in agony.

After a while they saw distant lights. As they grew closer the Gypsy camp became plain, lit by fires. A group was standing watching their approach.

As the car stopped, Caleb shouldered his way to the front. "I've been expecting you," he announced with a grin.

"I've come for my son," Mike said deliberately.

"You mean *my* son," Caleb corrected him. "You thought you could steal my son as you stole my woman, but I've come back for them."

Looking around frantically, Kirsty saw Jenna standing nearby with Rob in her arms. Two large women tried to bar her way, but she thrust them aside and went up to Jenna. "Give him to me," she ordered.

For a moment she thought Jenna would obey, but a look of fear crossed the young woman's face, and she shook her head. "I daren't," she muttered. "*He* told me not to."

"But you don't have to do what he tells you," Kirsty cried in despair.

"I got to," Jenna declared sullenly. "It's the only way he'll stay with me."

"And you want to stay with a man like that—who abuses you and doesn't care for you?"

"I love him," Jenna said defiantly. "I know he's a wrong'un but I can't help myself." A look of stupid cunning came into her eyes. "One day he'll grow tired of dreaming about you, and then he'll love me."

She tightened her arms around Rob. Kirsty felt as though knives were ripping through her with the need to take her baby, but she didn't dare try it in case there was a fight and he was harmed.

She hurried back to where Mike and Caleb were confronting each other. "If you were one of us, there would a simple way to settle this," Caleb was saying, with his terrible blank smile.

"How would we settle it?" Mike demanded.

"With knives. The true father will win because he'll fight harder for his son," Caleb said. A murmur of agreement went around the crowd.

Mike said calmly, "That sounds reasonable enough. I'll fight you. If I win, you stand back and let me take the child. Agreed?"

"Agreed," Caleb said with a grin. "And when I win you give up all claim to him."

To Kirsty's horror Mike nodded. "Agreed."

"Mike," she whispered.

She wasn't sure he heard her. His eyes never left Caleb. As he stripped off his jacket she glanced at the car, with its telephone that could be used to call the police. But a couple of men were lounging against it, and she knew she'd never get past them.

Caleb held out a knife to Mike. It was a wicked-looking thing with a slightly curved blade that reflected the dancing light from the fires. The two men faced each other, Caleb slight and lithe, Mike heavier and powerful. Kirsty held her breath.

Caleb moved first, launching himself at Mike with lightning speed, his knife aimed with deadly precision. Mike parried the blow and knocked him sideways, but as he fell Caleb shot out a leg and brought Mike down with him. He was fighting dirty, kicking and punching, jabbing his knife near his opponent's eyes, so that Mike was constantly defending himself against foul blows instead of attacking.

Caleb managed to get on top but Mike exerted all his strength and threw him over his head. Caleb was up like lightning, seizing Mike's right arm which was close to him and sinking his teeth into the wrist. Mike's face was contorted with pain as he fought to free himself. Caleb's vicious cheating was doing its work. Mike's fingers slackened on the knife enough for Caleb to wrench it from his grasp. The next moment they were on their feet, and Caleb was holding both knives at Mike's throat.

"That's it," he yelled. "I've won. The child is mine." He turned a wolfish face on Kirsty. "He agreed to it in front of everyone," he cried. "Now I'll take what's mine. My son—*and my woman.*"

His arm snaked out to seize Kirsty. She struggled but he held her tightly. "Mine," he repeated. "If you want your baby you'll stay with me."

"No." The shriek made everyone turn to see Jenna, wild-eyed and bitter. "No," she screamed again. "You can't have her. I won't let you."

"You," Caleb laughed. "Who are you to say what I can and can't do?"

"I can stop you. I can tell them what you told me."

Caleb's face changed, the sneering amusement wiped off as if by a cloth. "Shut up!" he snapped.

Kirsty wriggled free of him and snatched Rob from Jenna with one determined movement. Jenna was too preoccupied to stop her. Everything in her was concentrated on Caleb, and for once there was defiance in her face. "I'll tell them," she screamed, "about how Peter Mullery died."

Caleb tried to laugh. "Everyone knows how he died," he sneered. "Jack Trennon killed him."

"No one killed him," Jenna said desperately. "It was an accident. He fell down that bank because a stone gave way beneath him, and you saw it and kept quiet because you wanted Jack Trennon put in jail.''

"Oh, God!'' Kirsty gasped. "Poor Jack.''

Jenna turned to the crowd gathered around her. "He told me one night when he was too drunk to care what he said. He said he wanted *her*,'' she threw a hand out in Kirsty's direction, "and he let Jack take the blame to get him out of the way. He told me that—*me, that loves him. He's never cared how he hurt me, so now I'll hurt him.''

"Try it,'' Caleb said, sounding shaken. "You'll never dare repeat that story.''

"She won't need to,'' said a voice behind him, and everyone swung around. Caleb uttered a violent oath at the sight of two policemen. The next moment he'd taken to his heels. He might have made it, but for the crowd of Gypsies who blocked his escape. "Get out of my way,'' he raged. "I'm one of you.''

"So was Jack Trennon,'' said a man in the crowd.

Before Caleb had time to argue further, the policemen had taken hold of him and were urging him irresistibly toward their car. Mike followed them. "When you're charging him for concealing evidence,'' he said, "you can add kidnapping. He took my son.''

One of the policemen nodded. "So we gathered, sir. Your nanny called us.''

For the first time Kirsty realized that Mabel was there, too. "How could you go off and leave him with Caleb?'' she demanded.

"But how was I to know—he seemed such a friend of yours? You invited him over that night for the party.''

Kirsty checked herself. Mabel had no idea how that fateful evening had ended. She'd been putting Rob to bed. When Caleb turned up she'd taken his word that it would be all right.

"Thank you, anyway, for calling the police," she said. "Let's get home now."

In the car on the way home she spoke only once. "Did you hear what he said? Peter's death was an accident."

"And the swine knew it all the time and kept it to himself," Mike added. "I hope they put him away and lose the key."

Kirsty stayed silent after that. She sat holding Rob tightly, and when they reached Everdene she wouldn't let him go, insisting on putting him to bed herself. It was an hour before she could bear to leave him with Mabel.

Mike was waiting for her on the landing, trying to read her face as she emerged. The next words they both spoke could decide everything.

But there were no words. She stayed back in the shadows, and his heart was wrenched with love and pity as he saw her head, without the beautiful flowing black locks that had always enchanted him. He opened his arms in silence, and she went straight into them. As they clung together, all need for words passed away.

He drew her into their room and sat on the bed with her in his arms. Kirsty went with him, passive for once, as if the events of the night had drained her. Once she looked up and caught a glimpse of herself in the mirror and looked quickly away. In the past she'd cursed her beauty, seeing it as something that blighted her life, but now it seemed to her that it was all gone, at the very moment when she'd learned to value it. As she'd stood in the flickering fires and heard Caleb propose his monstrous bargain, and Mike agree to it, a thousand fears had risen shrieking at her, and now she must try to voice them, without the magic charm of beauty to help her.

"He won," she said, speaking in a muffled voice against Mike.

"What do you mean?"

"He won. Caleb. He said the winner would be the father, and you agreed. And then he won."

"I only pretended to agree because I had no choice. It was the only chance I could see. If the police hadn't arrived then, I'd have gone straight to them. It didn't mean that I believed Caleb's lies."

He lifted her face to his, overcoming her efforts to hide. "I learned long ago always to believe the best of you Kirsty, because the best is always true. I only wish I'd given you reason to feel the same about me. But I'm not as bad as you think. I haven't been two-timing you with Lois. That's been over a long while. She never cared for me, only for what I could give her. And no man who'd loved you could look at another woman."

"Loved—me?" she said in heartfelt wonder.

"With all my heart and soul. I should have told you long ago, but I was afraid of my love, afraid of all the truths it could make me face. I didn't want to face them. But I finally have. I hadn't meant to tell you like this, but we must start understanding each other. I told you I had plans for that barn, and I have. It's where I'm going to work. My assistant will run the company in London, and I'll head our new conservation unit down here."

"A conservation unit? You?"

"I'm still a builder, but from now on I want to create without destroying. I'll have to go to town sometimes, but not often. That's why I was in London for such a while this time. I was tying up ends before the change."

"But why didn't you tell me?"

"I was saving it as a surprise for you, and then I was going to say it's time you stopped fobbing me off about our wedding and set the date." He searched her face. "Well?"

Her answer wasn't the one he'd expected, but it was the perfect answer. "Mike—make love to me."

He nodded, understanding, overjoyed. Nothing about her had been destroyed. Her beauty was timeless and ageless like spring rain or summer flowers. But he couldn't tell her because she wouldn't believe words. He could only show her in ways that were better than words.

"Come to me, my darling," he whispered.

From the moment she laid her lips on his he knew that this time was going to be as never before. One last barrier had been crossed, and now she no longer feared her own sexual magic. Instead she called it to her aid, glowing in his arms, telling him of her love with every movement, every caress. Outside the moor was ready to burst out with its new spring life, while in their perfect union another renewal was taking place. Earth met fire, heart met heart and love was reborn from love. And all of these are eternal.

* * * * *

COMING NEXT MONTH

#751 HEARTBREAK HANK—Myrna Temte *Cowboy Country*
Principal Emily Franklin was meeting with local bad boy Hank Dawson to discuss his daughter's schoolwork. But when the meetings continued, rumors raged—had the rodeo star lassoed the learned lady?

#752 AMAZING GRACIE—Victoria Pade
Gabe Duran collected antiques; his new neighbor Gracie Canon restored them. Desire for the same collection had them fighting over something old; desire of another kind had them trying something new....

#753 SWISS BLISS—Bevlyn Marshall
Consultant Susan Barnes had jetted to the Alps on business. Brusque Swiss hotel owner Maximillian Kaiser was as corporate as they came... until passion burst in—without an appointment!

#754 THERE AND NOW—Linda Lael Miller *Beyond the Threshold*
When Elisabeth McCartney appeared in 1892, the townspeople called her a witch. Jonathan Fortner called her the love of his life. How could she tell him a lifetime lay between them?

#755 MAN WITHOUT A PAST—Laurie Paige
Sutter Kinnard was determined not to disappoint the woman he'd protected like a sister. But Meredith Lawton's dream of a perfect marriage was a terrifying challenge to a man without a past....

#756 BRIDE ON THE LOOSE—Debbie Macomber
Those Manning Men
Straitlaced secretary Charlotte Weston was mortified! Her teenage daughter had tried to bribe Jason Manning, their laid-back landlord, into asking Charlotte out. He'd honorably refused... and made the dinner date for free...!

AVAILABLE THIS MONTH:

#745 SILENT SAM'S SALVATION
Myrna Temte

#746 DREAMBOAT OF THE WESTERN WORLD
Tracy Sinclair

#747 BEYOND THE NIGHT
Christine Flynn

#748 WHEN SOMEBODY LOVES YOU
Trisha Alexander

#749 OUTCAST WOMAN
Lucy Gordon

#750 ONE PERFECT ROSE
Emilie Richards

Linda Lael Miller

the author of bestselling historical and
contemporary novels,
presents her readers with

two stories linked
by centuries, and by love....

There and Now

The story of Elisabeth McCartney, a woman looking for a love
never to be found in the 1990s. Then, with the mystery of her
Aunt Verity's necklace, she found her true love—Dr. Jonathan
Fortner, a country doctor in nineteenth-century Washington....
There and Now, #754, available in July 1992.

Here and Then

Desperate to find her cousin, Elisabeth, Rue Claridge searched
for her in this century . . . and the last. She found Elisabeth, all
right. And also found U.S. Marshal Farley Haynes—a nineteenth-
century man with a vision for the future....
Here and Then, #762, available in August 1992. SELLM-1

FREE GIFT OFFER

To receive your free gift, send us the specified number of proofs-of-purchase from any specially marked Free Gift Offer Harlequin or Silhouette book with the Free Gift Certificate properly completed, plus a check or money order (do not send cash) to cover postage and handling payable to Harlequin/Silhouette Free Gift Promotion Offer. We will send you the specified gift.

FREE GIFT CERTIFICATE

ITEM	A. GOLD TONE EARRINGS	B. GOLD TONE BRACELET	C. GOLD TONE NECKLACE
# of proofs-of-purchase required	3	6	9
Postage and Handling	$1.75	$2.25	$2.75
Check one	☐	☐	☐

Name: _____

Address: _____

City: _____ State: _____ Zip Code: _____

Mail this certificate, specified number of proofs-of-purchase and a check or money order for postage and handling to: HARLEQUIN/SILHOUETTE FREE GIFT OFFER 1992, P.O. Box 9057, Buffalo, NY 14269-9057. Requests must be received by July 31, 1992.

PLUS—Every time you submit a completed certificate with the correct number of proofs-of-purchase, you are automatically entered in our MILLION DOLLAR SWEEPSTAKES! No purchase or obligation necessary to enter. See below for alternate means of entry and how to obtain complete sweepstakes rules.

✂ SS3U

ONE PROOF-OF-PURCHASE
To collect your fabulous FREE GIFT you must include the necessary FREE GIFT proofs-of-purchase with a properly completed offer certificate.

(See inside back cover for offer details)